BOUQUET OF BAMBOO

by

SARAH STEEL

Published by **CHIMERA**
ISBN 9781780807010

HAMMER AND TONGS

Teddy Carmichael cursed as the slice of fried bread slipped from his leather-gloved fingers. Retrieving it from his lap, he tossed it down onto the spotless white tablecloth and once again attempted to top it with the entrails of a pheasant. His efforts to spread the purplish-brown offal were game, but futile. 'There'll be precious little hunting this season,' he grumbled, 'and the cost of stabling is soaring.'

Seated across the table, Lady Maycott averted her gaze from her husband's useless gloved hand. The sight of Teddy - only a year ago her vigorous lover - now unable to execute even the simplest of civilised tasks filled her with anger; not with pity or compassion, but with an impatient rage. She took a small forkful of white pheasant breast and sank her teeth into its succulence even as her eyes darted back to the gloved hand. Once that same hand firmly cupped and squeezed her naked bosom. Once it spanked her bottom so very harshly. Once it held her cunny so dominantly. A tide of colour crested in her cheeks as, swallowing the meat, she remembered the way it used to be. Flickering her green gaze once more across the highly polished silverware, she watched the gloved hand gripping the fork, spearing the fried bread and guiding it unsteadily to the open mouth above. This time, there was no mistake. Teddy nodded his satisfaction, chewed noisily and continued his one-sided conversation.

'There's talk of the few remaining farriers being pressed into service,' he remarked. 'Just imagine, old girl, not a blacksmith to be had.' He then turned the subject to mechanised warfare and the rumours of tanks replacing the horse.

Lady Maycott closed her eyes. The war was such a bloody nuisance. It had the effrontery to begin on her twentieth birthday. *Give the Kaiser a sound hiding and home for Christmas.* How hollow those boasts sounded now. In the Spring of 1916, Teddy took her in his Rolls to the edge of the rolling chalk downs. There, with the fat tyres slowly sinking into the soft sedge, they listened to the sound of distant gunfire travelling across the Channel. 'Softening up the Hun,' Teddy observed, and later, as the sunset darkened into the violet light of dusk, he took her with his customary brutal tenderness. Facedown, her naked breasts crushed into the sumptuous leather upholstery of the spacious car, he ripped her panties down and bared her buttocks. He tongued her cleft searchingly, and then bit her plump bottom cheeks before harshly spanking their soft round ripeness...

Swallowing another mouthful of pungent game - the cock pheasant had been well hung - Lady Maycott shuddered with pleasure, remembering...

Teddy knelt behind her, so assured, so masterful. Thumbing her spanked cheeks apart, he eased his length into her bottom. Her throat tightened remembering the hot plum of his glans stretching her open. He withdrew slowly, raking the heat of her cleft before bringing his hardness back to her sphincter. She remembered the feel of his pulsing shaft tap tapping at her tight, resisting anal whorl, his hot breath at her neck as her cheeks suddenly clenched and her coy denial enflamed his lust...

'And the French are proving quite useless,' Teddy's voice broke into her reverie, his tone echoing the despair of his Whitehall masters. 'Absolute shambles! But there's some progress in the air war, it seems,' he crowed. 'We're putting up Sopwith Camels for the next offensive. Might prove decisive.'

She closed her eyes and remembered... remembered his ardent vigour that April evening on the downs. Pinned into the leather, her mouth and nipples crushed into the sleek hide, she remained tense and dry despite her excitement, tense and dry and difficult to penetrate. Teddy snarled his frustration, and Lady Maycott's grip on her heavy silver cutlery tightened as she recalled his carnal grunt echoing around the spacious Rolls as he knelt, his hard thighs straddling her soft flanks, in the dark warmth. He teased her anal whorl a little before attempting to prise it open, but even the hot juice from her pussy failed to grease her recalcitrant ring. Cursing softly, he reached back into the darkness and snatched a silver flask from the walnut cabinet. Using his teeth to unscrew the top, he forced the flask's neck down between her buttocks, pouring the trickle of brandy into her sphincter. The alcohol seared, causing her tight hole to pucker in response, and then open somewhat. How she shrieked as the raw spirit burned her sensitive flesh, but lubricated at last, she accepted his thick shaft with smothered squeals. He filled her rectal heat urgently, and she vividly remembered the warmth of his sac as his balls slapped her wet slit with every thrust.

He pumped harder, deeper, faster, filling and stretching her ruthlessly. The springs of the venerable Rolls squeaked as he rocked over her with increasing frenzy, crying out obscenities more suited to the hunting field than the marriage bed. Gripping her blonde mane as fiercely as he would the reins of a bolting hack, he rode her superbly, finally slamming into her with a soft yell as his seed flooded her. Her own cry of raw pleasure drowned out his deep moans as they came together in the darkness of the brandy fumed luxury car...

'Bloody politics!' Teddy ranted, his words muffled by the glass of claret pressed to his greasy lips. 'Anarchists, socialists, bloody Bolsheviks having a field day. We're doomed, old girl, mark my words. When this show's over, our kind won't count for much. We'll be a class without a voice.'

Lady Maycott sharply dismissed his pessimism by tossing down her napkin. She had thought of a bread-and-butter pudding for dessert as an economy measure, but bridling under the constraint of shortages, she had instructed the kitchen to send up an apple charlotte instead. Teddy tucked in with gusto.

After coffee, she intended to ask him to pleasure her. He had returned from Verdun severely wounded, and she had been able to do nothing except watch his tortuous recovery. He still possessed a mouth, however, and she watched his teeth flash now as he spooned apple charlotte unceremoniously between his lips. She watched his teeth, and imagined them at her nipples as he chewed unselfconsciously. She imagined his mouth at her moist pussy, his lips sucking while his teeth nipped and his flickering tongue searched her silky depths.

'Teddy?'

He looked at her, bringing his one remaining gloved hand up to pass his napkin over the custard on his unshaven chin.

'Teddy,' Lady Maycott repeated in a fervent whisper, her green eyes glistening with excitement. 'After coffee, do you think we... we could?'

'Could what, old thing?'

3

'Ride. Ride out with the hounds, like we used to.'

The napkin dropped from his lifeless gloved fingers. 'B-but...' he stammered.

She rose from her chair, palming her thighs and then clasping her hands together over the mound of her pubis. 'It has been ages since you've ridden me, Teddy, and taken the crop to me. You must be aching to get up in the saddle, my dear.'

Across the white tablecloth, the crippled officer trembled impotently in his wheelchair.

Up early the following morning, Lady Maycott gazed out through the lead glass of her bedroom window. Naked, she took a perverse pleasure in the chill of the crisp, frosty dawn. Pressing her firm breasts against the cold pane, she gazed out over the chocolate-brown of the ploughed fields and the faded gold of the November stubble. Good hunting weather. Capital for a keen, hard ride. The crisp going was perfect for the chase.

She sighed. Like his French allied forces, Teddy had been quite useless last night. After coffee, one- handed, he attempted to satisfy her by knuckling her pussy with a limply clenched gloved fist. Utterly useless, no appetite for the sport, and this morning between her clamped thighs her desire still smouldered. At the window she pressed her plump breasts against the cold glass, gently crushing their ripeness and raking her proud nipples into pleasurably painful peaks. Warm juice coated her labial lips as it flowed slowly from her inner heat. *Bugger the war!* The useless gloved fist had merely managed to awake, but not slake, her appetite.

Moving slowly across the carpet, her naked buttocks rippling sensuously, she paused before her full-length cheval looking glass. Her hands rose to her breasts, and savagely palmed their soft warmth. Within the clutch of her whitening knuckles the captive flesh burgeoned. Thumbing her already stiff nipples, she inched her thighs wider apart. In the dull glass her golden maiden fern sparkled and the wet pink slit below winked at her. Closing her eyes tightly, Lady Maycott groaned as her longing wept freely from her smouldering cunny.

To horse! A good gallop was required, she decided. Rummaging feverishly, she snatched out a crisp balconette from her chest of drawers and, facing the cheval glass once more, she dragged the delicate garment up over her belly, and then eased her breasts into the waiting cups, filling their cool void with her bulging warmth. In the cheval she studied the proud swell of her tamed bosom, fingering her nipples as they dimpled the taut silk. With mounting excitement she wriggled into a crisp blouse, buttoning it tightly down from her throat to her belly with slightly fumbling fingertips. Disregarding her cami-knickers and the kiss of their satin cloth at her cleft, she rummaged frantically in the darkness of her wardrobe for her cream jodhpurs. Barely keeping her balance, she flexed her knee and guided her prinked foot into the tightness of the whipcord, relishing the fierce embrace of the stretchy fabric as it sheathed her upper thighs.

Turning, she glanced over her shoulder. In the glass she saw each of her ripe bottom cheeks clearly delineated, cupped, bunched and squeezed within the stretchy jodhpurs. The taut seam bit into her cleft with a soft, sweet pain as it swept up between her thighs to her belly, dividing her outer labia with a fierce pressure and causing her innermost sex lips to juice. Facing the glass again she carefully thumbed the waistband to ease the whipcord away from her sensitive pussy, which kissed the taut stretch farewell, dampening the jodhpurs. Then her fingers flew around to her buttocks to pluck the material away from her aching cleft.

She struggled into the suppleness of knee length leather riding boots, a tight and pleasurably arousing fit. The smell of leather pleasantly filled her nostrils and her eyes sparkled as they gazed directly into their own reflection in the clouded glass. The tang of polished hide haunted her, deliciously stirring her memory and her bowels.

She selected a bottle-green fitted riding jacket, and then patted a velvet bowler hat into place on her head. Snatching up a pair of yellow kid gloves and a riding crop, she paused once more to study the effect in the looking glass.

The pert bowler sat tipsily on her piled-up golden hair. On impulse she plucked it off, and skimmed it across the carpet into a shadowy corner of her bedroom. She dropped the crop and impatiently began forcing her left hand into a tight yellow glove. She lowered her face, biting into the edge of the glove to pull it on, and her wet lips left a dark stain on the bright hide. Stooping, she plucked her crop up off the floor - twenty-two inches of whippy bamboo sheathed in closely stitched leather with a cruel little ox blood loop at the tip.

Swish! Lady Maycott cracked the crop down against her right boot. Teddy's prediction rankled in her proud mind. *So we will count for nothing, eh?* One hundred years ago slipshod grooms or light-fingered pantry men would have felt just such a crop across their bared buttocks.

Swish! The leather lashed down once more, snapping loudly against her boot with a satisfying crack. One hundred years ago servants cringed before the Maycott lash, and they would still be trembling one hundred years hence.

The stables once held fourteen hunters, six hacks for carriage work and assorted ponies, but now there was only a box for Ramilees, her bay gelding, which he shared with the apple harvest. The ripening fruit gently perfumed the darkness, competing with the bittersweet reek of dung.

Lady Maycott tightened his martingale before leading Ramilees out into the brisk autumn air to saddle up. She selected a light shallow Spanish saddle with a stout silver pommel rarely seen in the shires. Mounted, she walked him on with a gentle kick of her heels. As they passed through the gates a startled jay flashed down with a shrill cry from an elm tree, and the flash of colour caused the gelding to shy. She pressed her knees into his sides, and golden sparks flew up from his hooves as Ramilees trod the frosted cobblestones skittishly. She showed him the whip. He calmed down at once, steadied, and then sprang forward into a gentle canter. The surge of the gelding between her tightly jodhpur-clad thighs brought Lady Maycott's pubis up against the pommel, and as the horse quickened its pace her pouting labia pressed hard against the silver knout, kissing it through the wet stretch of her whipcord.

Her mount headed down the rutted lane at a brisk pace, skirting Home Farm before settling down into a steady gallop along the mossy path stretching beneath denuded beech trees. As her pubic mound ground into the hard silver pommel she decided to take the left fork through the spinney. Ramilees responded obediently to the light touch of the crop, cannoning through the undergrowth. The trimmed birches and ash trees greeted her thighs with stinging caresses as she plunged through the dense copse.

She emerged at the far edge of the spinney feeling hot, wet and savagely aroused. Reining the gelding up sharply before the iron fence, she dismounted. Ramilees dropped his head to nibble the turf as Lady Maycott peered through the tree tops at the distant red brick chimney stacks of *Marlton Manor*. Sliding her crop beneath the Spanish saddle, she tested the springy turf with the toe of her mud-flecked boot. At the black iron railings of the boundary fence she erased a rime of silver frost from the length of cold metal with a yellow leather fingertip, and then casually destroyed a spangled cobweb, which shivered and shrivelled at her touch.

Marlton Manor. The Elizabethan red-brick chimney stacks, gaunt and spindling, rose up through the distant encircling trees. Once a bustling county seat - Boxing Day hounds would meet there to mire its manicured lawns - the manor now served as a nursing home requisitioned for the care and cure of wounded officers. Not physically wounded soldiers like Teddy, but dotty ones gaping and staring through wide, unfocused eyes. She grew somewhat melancholy at the thought of those wasted young lives, virile young men who now remained indifferent to the charms of the pretty young VADs nursing them.

Several months ago, in a brief bout of petulant boredom, young Lady Maycott toyed with the idea of offering a supervisory hand at *Marlton Manor*. Disciplining those delicious little uniformed VADs would have proved enjoyable war work; severely reddening their pert little bottoms for the slightest misdemeanour would have given her great pleasure. But with papa sleeping through the war years on the back benches of the Lords, and mama sending white feathers to pacifist poets and artists, their right honourable daughter was obliged to remain in charge of the family seat.

She gazed across the recently harvested barley field. How times had changed. Was Teddy right? Would her class enjoy no privileges after the war? A generation since, her robust and eccentric great aunt personally supervised the harvest home astride her grey mare. Whispered gossip in the servants' hall informed Lady Maycott when she was a girl that any lusty village lad who caught her great aunt's fancy was summoned to the Hall after the harvest supper to wait upon her pleasure. Her great aunt's pleasure... Lady Maycott pressed her whipcord-sheathed thighs together as she conjured up the image of her great aunt being pleasured by a lusty village lad, his darkly-haired chest rasping her quivering pink nipples as, his clenched buttocks pounding and jerking, he rogered her mercilessly, filling her hot cunny with a glutinous squirt of yeoman's seed. Yes, by God, those were the days, the days when her noble line had a voice that carried clear across the county and beyond, a firm voice accustomed to commanding.

Once again astride Ramilees and nestling her wet pubis against the silver pommel, Lady Maycott guided the gelding back through the spinney at a slow trot. Bending, she ducked to avoid the leafless branches reaching to clutch at her hatless golden hair. Breaking free of the dense copse she rose up in the saddle to view the patchwork of arable, autumnal countryside stretching out before her in the early morning sunshine. In the far distance she spied the square Norman tower of Marlton Parva's parish church. The tiny golden cock of the weather vane glinted in the sun. Marlton Parva was nine fields away. Nine stone walls, hedgerows and wooden fences, with the occasional dry ditch, lay between her and the graveyard beneath the golden cock, with crowded, lichen covered tombs. A cracking ride.

Ramilees galloped smoothly, taking fields of ploughed loam and rough pasture equally in his sure stride. Rising up to each hedge, wall and fence, the gelding cleared them all with bold, brave leaps. Pounding her pubis into the pommel, Lady Maycott's pussy was ablaze, but the violent orgasm she hoped for eluded her.

As she slipped down from her mount at the low wall surrounding the graveyard, her jodhpurs showed the spreading seep of her warm juices. She teetered into the chill of the early morning graveyard, lurching as if drunk from stone to stone. Beneath a deep yew she struggled to peel her jodhpurs down. Snatching off the single rope of pearls always gracing her neck, she worked the shining beads with her gloved fingers, forcing them up into her cunny, and then threading the remainder of the rope against her crease and up between her cheeks, securing it in her sphincter.

She shuddered and squirmed as her rectal warmth tightened, her inner muscles gripping the cold pearls. Her left thigh spasmed, causing one of her leather boots to skid out in a sharp arabesque of fleeting ecstasy. Bending over, her swollen breasts straining within the balconette's bondage, she tugged her jodhpurs and eased them carefully up into her cleft, anxious to keep the rope of pearls in place. Patting her pubis, she stumbled out of the graveyard into the lane and mounted Ramilees again, spreading her buttocks with a moan as she straddled the gelding.

The ringing clip clop of his slow pace echoed around her in the frost-sharpened air as she walked him through the village. The rolling lurch of his motion rhythmically forced the pearls deep into her wet cleft, and her plump, tingling cunny lips chewed with a savage hunger at their hard sheen. The slippery beads ravished the warm juice flowing in her crease, causing wave upon rippling wave of pleasure to tighten the muscles of her belly. Deep inside the tight delight of her anus, the pearls stretched her painfully, and fourteen paces down the high street, Lady Maycott climaxed violently.

Minutes later, recovering her poise outside the shuttered windows of the post office, she patted her pocket with a gloved hand and extracted a silver case. Thumbing it open, she plucked out a dark cheroot. She snapped a match down the silver pommel. Ramilees trod nervously at the sudden spurt of orange flame and the stench of sulphur as she lit the cheroot, and exhaled slowly. A curl of smoke unwound, rising up from the glowing tip, and she gazed at it through pleasure-clouded eyes. In the middle distance she saw a darker plume of smoke curling up into the still air from a red brick chimneystack. The village forge. She frowned. The smithy had been deserted for over a year now. Removing the unfinished cheroot from her lips and tossing it away, she squeezed her knees into her mount and urged him on.

The sound of a hammer striking the anvil rang out like muffled evensong bells from a distant church.

Ting, tang! Ting, tang!

Lady Maycott dismounted, deliberately raking her juiced cunny against the supple leather as she slid down from the Spanish saddle. Tethering her gelding securely, she patted Ramilees as he nibbled a clump of sweet dock. Striding out across the wet turf with silent footfalls, she approached the open door of the village forge.

At close quarters the hammer sounded harshly as it rained down upon the anvil. Pausing at an open window, she peered into the blacksmith's domain. All was dark inside except for the fierce heat of the furnace. Her eyes narrowed, focusing until the darkness within became visible and she caught a slight movement... a shape moving before the open furnace... a man. Then she saw him more clearly and realised with a shock that he was naked! Naked and glistening!

No, he was not utterly naked... a leather apron was lashed tightly below his belly and around his hips, the knotted thongs dangling down over the slight swell of his sweating buttocks. Smothering a gasp of pleasure, she steadied herself at the open window and stared inside.

The young farrier was stretching. Sweat gleamed on his muscled arms and shoulders and his naked spine rippled sensuously. He bent down, his right arm reaching for the bellows, and as he pumped the furnace the cleft between his straining cheeks widened. With a soft roar the furnace became an intense glow flooding the darkness with its crimson blaze. Silhouetted against the dancing light, the silhouetted skin of the sweating blacksmith seemed to be etched with gold. Her nipples tightened as a slow ache bloomed in her breasts. Flicking out the tip of her tongue, she wetted her lips, her eyes narrowing as she gazed at the swathe of the leather apron stretched below his belly.

He was naked beneath it. She knew that beneath the apron's dark hide, his superb cock lay coiled and potent. A thick, yeoman's cock. She bit back a moan as she imagined the apron dropping away, revealing a swollen and erect shaft, erect and nodding ponderously, raking its bulbous helmet between her cunny lips and nestling its cruel hardness deep in her moist warmth. She gripped the stone window ledge as her knees betrayed her by buckling. She cursed silently, hungry for the farrier's meat.

Wiping fresh sweat from his eyes, the naked blacksmith grasped his hammer, weighed it judiciously, and then rained it down repeatedly on a molten horseshoe pressed upon the anvil by dark tongs. Red and silver sparks danced and the blazing orange metal dulled to a crimson glow. The flashing hammer beat yellow and gold sparks out of the cooling ore, and as he worked, the smith's leather apron became taut against his thighs. The outline of his cock and balls was unmistakeable and unavoidable to her greedy green eyes.

She drew the tips of her gloved fingers up to her lower lip, dragging the soft flesh down to reveal neat, cruel white teeth. She swallowed as she stared at the bulge beneath his leather apron. Her tongue darted out to lick the leather at her lower lip, thrilling to the tang of the hide. Leather... a feral, brutal taste...

Spreading his thighs wide, the naked, sweating farrier resumed punishing the anvil with his hammer, and watching him, Lady Maycott felt her belly implode with a divine warmth as, deep down inside her, the slippery pearls churned.

The gallop home was as breathtaking as it was breathless. Lady Maycott gulped down choking mouthfuls of the raw November air as Ramilees charged across the fields and ditches. Barely able to see through her tear-filled eyes, she gave the gelding his head, gripping the reins tightly. Squeezing her jodhpur-sheathed thighs into his warmth she crouched low in the saddle, grunting softly as the silver pommel punished her pubis.

Ramilees cantered into the yard, clattering on the cobbles. Panting, she dismounted and unsaddled him. Then, plucking away the wet whipcord from her seething cunny, she staggered indoors. Upstairs in her bedroom she peeled off her boots and riding habit and eased the pearls out with a grimace of mingled pain and pleasure. Then she locked herself in the bathroom and collapsed across the cool linoleum floor. Only her hammering heartbeats were audible in the silent stillness. Stretching out slowly, her legs parted, she tossed her crop and gloves aside and closed her eyes.

Gradually her racing pulse decelerated. Outside in the elms rooks were calling loudly. She *must* have him, have him all to herself, and soon, *bloody* soon. She must have him in the darkness of his forge. With the furnace flaring, bathing the darkness in a golden glow, she would be stripped naked and coupling with the farrier, demanding he pleasure her, ravish her, again and again, until she collapsed in the straw writhing and exhausted.

She drew her thighs together firmly. The crisp wisps of her pubic bush crackled gently, and she shuddered. She squeezed her thighs tightly together, and then slowly inched them apart again. The chill air of the unheated bathroom caressed her wet heat and her pussy tingled in response. Her breasts quivered, her nipples darkening as they peaked, the gloom of the smoke-filled forge filling her fantasies. Her fingers sought and found her breasts, teasing their creamy flesh. She gasped softly as she conjured up the hiss and roar of the pumping bellows, the orange glow of the quickened furnace blazing behind her tightly closed eyes. Her fingertips paused at each nipple, worrying the stubby peaks, and then tweaking and pinching them with savage tenderness.

Lady Maycott felt the power of her rank and privilege surge through her veins and flood her body as potently as lust. She knew exactly what she wanted to do with this strapping young yeoman, all but naked in his supple leather apron. She tucked her knees up against her breasts and lay on her side. The dark opening between her thighs widened as she sighed, imagining the blacksmith kneeling before her, his head bowed submissively; kneeling before her, his eyes clouded in fearful dread as she stood over him, her thighs spread, her gleaming boots astride. She would level the tip of her crop at his chin and force his face upwards a fraction in order to stare dominantly down at him. Then the little loop of leather at the tip of the crop would rake down to torment each of his nipples. She would make him hard, as hard as the iron he hammered at his anvil. Lady Maycott squealed softly as she pictured the leather apron bulging as it betrayed his thickening response, a cock as hard as iron.

Her imagined control over him aroused her fiercely and left her inner thighs glistening. The thought of dominating this mere farrier, of exercising her rank and privilege over him, sharpened her keen sexual arousal. He would be hers absolutely to command and control at her whim. Naked, her crop raised, she would be able to dictate in explicit detail how she wished him to satisfy her desires. She would drag the tip of her cruel crop down across his belly to tap tap the concealed bulge of his erection. Hard meat. And as the crop dominantly addressed the supple leather, the trembling farrier would shut his eyes and groan, terrified to obey her commands to pleasure her, but even more terrified of disobeying her instructions to do so. And

9

she would relish his distress, whipped if he did not ravish her then and there, and with even worse penalties to pay should his deeds ever be discovered. Yes, she longed to have him naked and trembling in her absolute thrall.

She moaned aloud and raked her thumb-tip against her hot cleft. She imagined the farrier quivering as her crop dominated the bulge at his leather apron, and shivered as she heard his groans soften to moans. Then, dragging the tip of her crop up his glistening torso, she would press it firmly into the softness of his sweat-soaked throat. Her domination of him now complete, she and she alone would decide when he could swallow.

She rolled over onto her back and drew her fingertips down to the base of her belly. At her golden bush she plucked up stray strands until her flesh stung. Her soft bottom cheeks, pressed against the cool floor, clenched in response to the brutal punishment of her coils, and her plump outer labia, now sticky and slippery with a creamy rime, peeled apart hungrily. She skimmed the exposed inner lips of her sex with her thumbnail as she pictured herself lowering them against the obedient blacksmith's waiting mouth. In her heated imaginings her thumb-tip became his tongue, a thick yeoman's muscle flickering and probing, and then plunging deep - *hard* and deep. Her spine arched off the linoleum and her buttocks clenched, imagining...

Suck. The innocent word sounded like an obscenity as in her mind she heard herself give the blunt command. *Suck*. She shivered at the sound of her own assured voice, a voice accustomed to being obeyed, as she demanded to be pleasured by the blacksmith's lips and tongue. *Suck*. Obediently he would drag her moist flesh lips into his rough mouth. She quivered as she imagined his lips, and then his tongue, becoming busily subservient. Forcing herself down over his face she would thrill to the feel of his unshaven jowls rasping her exposed flesh. Then, swaying her hips sensuously, she would dominantly roll her cunny across his up-tilted features, smearing them with her warm juices.

Cowering, he would shrink away, no doubt amazed and frightened by her aristocratic excesses and her ruthless dominance. A swipe from her crop, she resolved, would still and steady him instantly, bringing his face back between her parted thighs. Then a second stinging lash would bring his tongue forth into her eager warmth. He would be hers absolutely - utterly hers to control and command.

Out in the elm trees the rooks grew increasingly raucous. Lady Maycott rolled over and crushed her breasts into the hard surface of the bathroom floor. Grinding sinuously against it like a snake sloughing its skin, she kissed the cold linoleum passionately with her nipples, belly and pussy lips. The frenzy of her slow, deliberate gyrations increased as she inched her buttocks up. She gripped them, her fingers dimpling and whitening the plumpness of each peachy mound as she pulled them apart, exposing the shadowy valley between.

A thread of spun sugar flowed down from her smouldering pussy and the warm ache between her buttocks became a delicious discomfort. She rehearsed ordering the blacksmith to kneel against her thighs, his supple apron slapping her proffered bottom. She imagined the fierce presence of his iron-hard rod poised at her tight sphincter, her young bull of a blacksmith erect, and less than an inch away from her feral heat. She could almost hear him gasping in fear and confusion. And in the darkness of the forge, her puckering anal whorl would glint in another sudden

10

golden glare from the furnace. Impatiently she would scream out her command, her passionate cry as ragged as a rook's. Yet still he would deny her, deny her and refuse to use a titled lady in so depraved, so disgusting a manner.

A perverse light shone in Lady Maycott's sea-green eyes as she rolled sensuously from thigh to thigh across the hard linoleum. She paused with her breasts down, and began rubbing her labial lips into the floor's polished sheen with short, sweeping thrusts of her hips, spreading and splaying her plump pubes as they nuzzled the floor, dulling its shine with their wet heat. So, her farrier would prove shy, and stubbornly so, she mused darkly. Well, all the more sport for her. He would prove shy, stubborn and disobedient, but for well-nigh over six hundred years her noble ancestors had dealt with stubborn disobedience. For well-nigh over six hundred years, the Maycott's had held the whip hand.

The whip hand... she masturbated slowly, deliberately approaching her climax as she paced her self pleasuring. She would, she decided, slowly thumbing her erect clitoral bud, administer the riding crop to the disobedient farrier's naked bottom. Yes she would, and the mere thought of the cane's deliciously satisfying hiss, and of the cracking sound it would make followed by his smothered yell, were enough to make her come right then and there.

Sitting up and addressing her cunny determinedly, Lady Maycott slipped into a reverie of pain, pleasure and punishment. She saw herself pushing the disobedient farrier's head down to pin his neck into submission and surrender beneath her polished boot. And as his bare buttocks rose so would her tightly gripped crop, which would come down with a whistling crack. Entering fully into the reverie of her chastisement of the naked blacksmith, she could almost sense the jerk of his whipped cheeks as he writhed beneath her boot. *Swish, crack!* Again her pinioning boot absorbed the spasms of the whipped man. *Swish, crack!* Just as she imagined the crop slicing into his punished buttocks, she nipped her clitoris savagely. *Swish, crack!* Again relishing his humiliation and pain, she ravished her love thorn...

Seven imagined strokes later, Lady Maycott was rolling across the bathroom floor, and her threshing nakedness collided with the cold iron of the bathtub. Brutally brought out of her reverie, she rose to her feet and shuffled awkwardly towards a looking glass. In the mirror her eyes met their reflection as her nipples kissed their hard counterparts. Hugging the oval glass between outstretched arms and shoving her nakedness into the unyielding glass, she ground her wet cunny into her own reflected flesh and climaxed, shrieking loudly as she pictured flicking up the blacksmith's apron to glimpse the smear of his spurted seed creaming the dark hide. She imagined plucking the leather apron up so his spent semen slithered down to glisten on his belly, and trickled down into the forest of his dark pubic hair. Then she would lower her head and take his stiff shaft between her lips...

A second orgasm ravished her mercilessly, her wail of carnal delight escalating into a primal scream of joy and scattering the rooks from the elms outside.

'No claret sales this winter,' Teddy grumbled, wrestling with his buttered crumpet. 'Dashed if I can see the sense of it.'

Lady Maycott nodded absently. She had been aching all day with a hunger no buttered crumpet could ever fill. For Teddy it was all about shortages; the war had become little more than an impertinent inconvenience for him.

'Damn war,' he muttered for the hundredth time, his mouth full and spitting crumbs. 'And they say the Tenby and Grafton Hunt are having to shoot all their horses to feed their pack. Just imagine. Shooting prize chasers to feed the bloody hounds! Next season there'll be no sport for us at all,' he speculated morosely, pawing at the butter knife with his gloved hand. 'And why? Because they'll have shot all the bloody hounds, *that's* why.'

The clock winking in the lengthening shadows whirred softly as it struck five, and the tinkle of Cambridge chimes instantly took Lady Maycott back to the forge, reminding her of a silver hammer raining down on a silver anvil. Beneath the spotless tablecloth and between her tightly squeezed thighs, her cunny grew as hot and slippery as Teddy's buttered crumpet.

The forge reeked of hot iron and sweat. Blinking, Lady Maycott pressed a lavender-drenched kerchief to her nostrils. The powerfully muscled young farrier continued to ply his hammer rhythmically, ignoring her presence completely.

After several of her crisp commands remained unanswered, she stamped her booted foot impatiently. Her face grew hot and angry as she shouted above the din of the anvil.

Unconcerned and unresponsive, the nearly naked blacksmith continued with his work, the soft leather apron stretched across his loins.

Reaching out, she flicked his bare buttock with her riding crop.

The hammer paused in mid stroke above the molten horseshoe below. Slowly, he turned his face towards hers, his eyes flashing fire fiercer than the flames in the furnace.

Lady Maycott, having unbuttoned her riding jacket and blouse to bare her cleavage, stepped forward boldly. Her soft breasts quivered, the cleavage deeply shadowed by the hot coals. But suddenly confronted by the farrier's sweaty torso and stern frown, her arrogant assurance deserted her. She cracked the riding crop down smartly against her leather boot. No time for discretion or decorum now, she chided herself. Now, at last, here in the heat and the darkness, her longed for prize was only three paces away and hers to command.

Her boldness grew brazen. Descended from a distinguished line of adventurers, Lady Maycott stiffened her resolve. Her people fought under the Lionheart, battled alongside Wellington and covered themselves with glory in the Sudan. A mere farrier was not even a skirmish; he was merely a brute conquest on a cold November afternoon.

She swished the crop out across his leather apron, punishing the bulge of his cock, and her nipples thickened when his erection pressed against the hide as though rising to salute her. The silence in the forge was becoming as overwhelming as the heat. She spoke again, spelling out her crude desires. She spoke not of love but of lust, a stern note entering her voice. He remained impassive, goading her into speaking even more plainly and crudely. She used terms she had heard the farmhands utter when coupling the beasts in the fields. The farrier did not even blink, and losing her patience entirely, she raked the tip of the crop up across his belly and chest to his chin.

To her speechless amazement and confusion, he snatched the crop from her and lashed her breasts with it twice. She screamed softly and clutched her whipped

12

bosom, cupping and cradling its punished flesh.

Tossing the crop down he embraced her roughly, his mouth forcing itself down over hers, and she quivered beneath the dominance of his fierce tongue. His hands gripped her savagely, one clutching her left buttock while the other mauled her whipped right breast. His lips smothered her scream. She pounded her clenched fists onto his slick chest, struggling to escape. It was not supposed to be like this, brutal and sudden. She had come to tease and tantalise, to tame and control, to pleasure herself by punishing him, to use her crop on him and caress his whipped buttocks with her pussy. She had come for conquest, but the brute was mastering *her*, forcing her facedown into the filthy straw.

She shrieked, kicking and biting. The reek of his sweat and his leather apron flooded her brain. The knout of his fierce shaft nuzzled her cunny as it dug into the taut stretch of her whipcord. Then she was lying in the dirty straw, her riding jacket and blouse ripped away to expose her pale flesh.

He straddled her, trapping her between his powerful, pinioning thighs. She squirmed as she felt his hot breath at the nape of her neck. He buried his face in her tousled golden locks, snuffing up her delicate lavender perfume before kissing, licking, and then biting her soft shoulders. And all the time his rough hands were peeling down her jodhpurs, a heartbeat at a time, to bare the inviting mounds of her bottom cheeks.

In a final bid for freedom Lady Maycott shrieked, writhing and wriggling in a desperate effort to twist out of his clutches. But his broad palm cracked down across her buttocks, turning her pale and delicate skin a hot crimson. She screamed shrilly, bucking and jerking beneath him. He spanked her again, and again, as she wailed in outrage. Then, her cheeks blazing beneath his relentless hand, she began whimpering and begging him to stop, but all he did was spank her again even more fiercely. She cried out imperiously, commanding him to cease at once, and he ran a lingering forefinger down between her flaming cheeks, dragging it down the sticky velvet of her cleft. She squeezed her buttocks defensively, and he slapped her bottom again even harder with his free hand as he slowly probed the wet heat of her sphincter with his stout finger. Lady Maycott moaned and writhed between his imprisoning thighs, and her gyrating rump seemed to enflame him. Lowering his face down into the soft swell of her soft cheeks he lapped her cleft with his thick tongue, and then lovingly bit into one of her plump mounds.

The prickling straw agitated her breasts and tummy as his firm hand parted her legs, painfully stretching them. The ache at her juicing cunny became a dull pain, and then suddenly he was no longer pinning her down. But before she could push herself up she heard the hammer coming down, and straining to peer over her shoulder, she saw him fixing horseshoes over each of her ankles. They sank through the soft straw into the earthen floor beneath his sure blows, and cursing profanely, she twisted and struggled in vain, her legs arrowed out behind her utterly immobile now. She slumped down, sobbing into the foul straw. She was utterly helpless, her legs pinned down by hoops of iron.

Two more hammered horse shoes pinned her wrists down into the straw-littered earth. Utterly at the farrier's mercy she renewed her shrill cries of protest, and he used the crop on her as she had planned to use it on him. He subjected her to eleven brutal strokes, each blistering swipe forging a red path across her flesh hotter than

13

the dancing flames in the forge.

Her resistance at last broken beneath the cruel lashing, she shivered in her impromptu bondage, sobbing gently into the straw. Then she gasped when he entered her, easily and assuredly, as masterfully as any aristocrat taking a peasant. His rigid length pierced and possessed her brutally and ruthlessly, surging between her whipped cheeks and deep into the tightly muscled warmth of her anus. In total contemptuous silence he rode her as adroitly as she did her gelding. Within minutes he came violently, and then eased out of her sphincter, dragging with him the hot scald of his yeoman's seed.

Four strokes of the crop later he penetrated her buttocks again, rampant and hard and totally dominant. They came together this time, his seed pumping and flooding her stretched heat. His absolute silence added an erotic charge to her orgasm that made her cry out just as she did when the hunt was in full flight.

Meanwhile, in the haystack behind the smithy, a thin and feral tomcat toyed with the mouse between its paws. The trapped mouse, trembling between the menacing paws, squeaked pitifully, but the tomcat remained deaf to its pleading. The tiny mouse darted left and right frantically, zigzagging in an effort to escape. Sheathing its sharp claws, the cat cuffed the mouse back into submissive surrender with its soft paw.

He wiped her roughly clean with his leather apron before abruptly wrapping it around her head. He swathed her face with it, binding her tightly, forcing her protesting mouth into the warm smear that had moments before trickled out of her anus.

Stunned into silence by the enormity of his crude arrogance, subjugated by the confident brutality of his mastery over her, Lady Maycott grew hot and breathless within her leather hood. She squirmed, sensing his brooding presence so close. She felt him removing the horseshoes pinning her wrists and ankles, but before she had time to react he rolled her over onto her back. She felt his proximity as he mounted her, straddling her dominantly. Moments later his hot semen rained down over her in thick spurting jets, splattering audibly upon her leather sheathed face and her exposed throat and chest. He toyed savagely with her breasts after he came, kneading his seed into them.

The silence became unbearable. Finally finding her voice again, she spoke in a husky whisper. Then she gave a halting command, her own voice uncertain and strange to her ears at first, gradually growing sharper, stronger. But he made no response - none at all. She screamed in angry frustration, her shrill cry hauntingly muffled by the humid confines of the leather hood.

Peeling the sticky hide from her face, he loomed over her, inching his broad buttocks up from his ankles and bringing the length of his pulsing erection between her breasts. Sensing his utter contempt for her she clenched her fists in anger, but did not try to push him away as he lifted and squeezed her breasts around his thick cock. Then he swiftly positioned himself on his knees beside her, and clutching a handful of her tumbling blonde mane, turned her head and forced her mouth onto his fleshy spear, silencing her protests with his iron-hard rod.

That evening there was a hard frost, excellent hunting weather. Dinner was excruciatingly dull.

14

'Deuced rum thing, old girl, what?' Teddy mouthed through his Stilton. 'Just fancy.'

Lady Maycott, unusually pale and still trembling slightly, shuddered with suppressed anger. Easing herself gingerly from one whipped buttock to the other, she shuffled her punished flesh surreptitiously. Simmering with rage, her fingers tore viciously at a bread roll. What the hell was the world coming to? Did the Maycott rank and name count for nought? Was her voice no longer to be heard - heard and obeyed?

'Deafened by the guns at the Ypres barrage, they say,' Teddy remarked to his water biscuit.

His wife looked up, and gazed at him uncomprehendingly.

'The new village blacksmith,' he explained.

The bread roll fell from her numb fingers.

'Mustard gas burned out the poor blighter's larynx,' Teddy continued blithely. 'Deaf and mute, I'll grant you, but a farrier, eh? A farrier back in the forge, now there'll be some sport.'

DICING WITH DEBT

The doormen were not known to the police, they *were* the police, a special branch assigned to keep a careful and caring eye on the young bloods who walked into the *Mayfair Club* every night.

A taxi pulled up and a doorman stepped smartly forward to assist the beautiful young brunette as she alighted. The Right Honourable Frederica - Freddie to her Sloane set - skipped up the marble steps and strode confidently through the gold and onyx doors. Before they closed behind her the undercover doorman radioed in her arrival.

The club was buzzing. Under a single spotlight a kohl eyed Armenian, her naked body glistening with baby oil, was kneeling before a stunning blonde, her parted lips inching up to capture the slice of wet melon lodged in the blonde's sex above her.

Ignoring the lubricious cabaret, Freddie paused to count the chips she'd just purchased. It had meant selling her Treasury Bonds, which meant another blazing row with daddy. Rising up on tiptoe she peered over at the gaming tables. The baccarat table seemed busy tonight. Good, baccarat, getting cards to make that magically elusive nine to beat the banker. She clamped her thighs together to try and suppress the warm surge of excitement in her pussy. She thumbed her gaming chips. Nine fat one thousand pound golden discs, a good omen for baccarat. Her labia juiced, parted and smiled, kissing her silk panties in anticipation of the excitement waiting for her at the green baize.

Braying cheers rang out from the throng of young men and women, especially the young women, crowding around the stage, and two of Freddie's chips fell to the Chinese silk carpet as she jumped in surprise. Bending, she scooped them up, and peering in the direction of the loud applause, she glimpsed the Armenian girl busily chewing on the melon while the labial lips of the blonde trapping her between her thighs ground rhythmically into her upturned face. In the harsh blue light bathing the stage, the kneeling girl was hungrily devouring the shuddering blonde's pussy. Freddie tightened her fist over her chips and weaved her way through the crowd. The atmosphere was heavy with the scent of expensive perfumes, and everywhere gold glinted in the shadows.

The silk backed playing cards flew across the baize, falling facedown. Her pulse quickened, her blood singing loudly in her ears. Before her glass of champagne arrived, she dropped six of her nine silver chips while the suave banker at the chemmy table eyed her appreciatively. She was playing wildly tonight, and before her champagne glass was even drained, she lost her entire stake.

Freddie swooped down on a distant cousin who had just finished sharing a slice of the succulent melon with the naked Armenian. The fragrance of the blonde's pussy was still on his lips, causing his cock to bulge. She hit him up for another silver disc and returned in triumph to the green baize, where she deftly strummed the milled edge of her new thousand pound chip against her pubic mound for luck. She lost it instantly in a wild gamble that landed her two cards totalling eight against the nine she needed to beat the bank. Ten thousand down and it wasn't even midnight.

She eyed the smoke filled room like a lioness scanning the plain for her next kill. There was nothing on the horizon, just the usual gang of gold card carrying glitz groupies who graced the social pages of the glossies. What she wanted was hard cash. Her dark eyes narrowed. Wasn't that Rollo attempting to fondle the performing blonde's bare breasts? Rollo, Lady Gresham's youngest son, was thick as clotted cream and twice as rich.

He was thumbing the blonde's cleft and worrying her tight pink sphincter, bringing her up onto her toes.

Freddie walked up to him. 'Wanna wank?' she asked, smiling wickedly, and he grinned back.

Taking him sternly by the elbow, she navigated him across the silk Chinese carpet, through the velvet curtains and into the loo. Bundling him into a cubicle she banged the door shut with her bottom, unzipped his slacks and fished out his thickening cock. Rollo was easy meat, always had been. She first tossed him off five years ago behind a Land Rover on a rough shoot in Norfolk for a fiver and a slice of his game pie.

Grunting, he closed his eyes and surrendered to her expert grip, buckling at the knees and slumping down in the confined space as she squeezed slowly and pumped deliberately.

Slowly, deliberately and with a maddening, teasing rhythm that both delighted and denied. Sweat blinded him as she delayed his ejaculation, and then, with a blurring flurry of fingers around his fisted cock, she brought him ruthlessly to his climax. Groaning, he came violently as she milked him savagely, his loud squirt echoing in the cubicle as she guided his stream of quicksilver down into the toilet bowl. He sank to his knees, moaning softly as she ran her fingers through his hair and forced him to gaze down into the semen clouded water.

'Good boy,' she whispered, snatching up a handful of paper from the roll to clean her sticky fingers whilst adroitly using her free hand to pluck the keys to his red Ferrari out of his jacket pocket. Easy meat.

Baccarat. She drew the car keys up to her lips to kiss them for luck, the feral whiff of Rollo's seed haunting her nostrils. 'It's the red Ferrari,' she declared, reeling off the registration number, and hesitating slightly over the last two digits, a calculated pretence. More convincing.

The banker was willing to be convinced. He obviously liked this wild young thing frequenting his green baize. She imagined he welcomed her as a vampire would welcome a virgin, open-mouthed, his teeth flashing. 'Are you sure?' His open palm weighed the keys to Rollo's red Ferrari above the seamless green baize.

Freddie, getting wet as the tension and thrill tightened the muscles in her belly the way they did before she climaxed, nodded impatiently and ground her pubis against the edge of the table. Through her dress, her labia pouted and kissed the polished fruit wood for luck.

The keys to the red Ferrari clinked gently as they joined the pile of chips.

The cards whispered across the baize. The smooth blade of the ivory paddle reached down and flicked them over. She managed to suppress her groan as she came, but not her moan as the rake scooped in her final bet.

After bumming a bottle of wine from a crowd she had run into earlier in the season, Freddie left the club.

Out on the steps in the chill night air, she hesitated. The doormen seemed to be having some difficulty refereeing a row. A braying young Rollo was hotly disputing ownership of a gleaming red Ferrari with representatives of the club's management, two Maltese heavies. She giggled tipsily as harsh voices filled the Mayfair mews and took one of the doormen by the arm. 'Lend us a tenner,' she said in a slurred voice, and hiccupped adorably.

The man left the fate of the Ferrari in the balance and produced a note. A taxi pulled up at once, and Freddie was guided carefully towards the open door.

'Double or quits,' she challenged, clenching the crisp tenner in one hand and her lucky gold sovereign in the other. 'Heads.'

'Tails,' the doorman replied.

She spun the sovereign, catching it deftly in midair. 'Heads it is! Hard luck,' she commiserated, flashing the obverse face up to his scrutiny.

He smiled and slammed the taxi door closed. As her cab drew away, he radioed in her departure before rejoining the row in front of the Ferrari.

In the back of the cab, the Right Honourable Frederica plucked the silk of her wet panties from her moist sex lips as she smiled fondly down at her lucky sovereign - her double headed sovereign.

'Damn all bloody politicians!' From his gilded Italianate desk, Freddie's father gazed out between the curtains veiling the large square windows. Across the swathe of manicured lawns flanking the Foreign Office, he watched the silver sunlight dancing on the Thames.

It had been a trying morning with that stupid statement in the House about the Balkans. Idiots! Leave such sensitive matters to those privileged patricians who knew exactly which wheels to oil and which palms to grease. Bloody politicians, estate agents in off the peg suits, what could you expect.

Then, interrupting his mid-morning glass of *Amontillado*, had come the discreet call on his scrambled line. Yet again Freddie had been cutting up rough, and she had the temerity to cash her Treasury Bonds despite his stern warnings not to fritter them away. Blasted baccarat. The girl was out of control. And more monkey business involving young Rollo, the idiot Gresham scion, and a Ferrari. No charges, thank God. Freddie really was the bloody limit, he fumed, watching a barge laden with stinking urban waste being escorted down the Thames by hungry gulls. The brat was running wild. He reached out for the scrambled phone.

'And you're sure the dowager can do the trick?'

'Absolutely. She'll straighten your Freddie out. No doubt about it, old boy. Worked wonders for the Welham girl. Got over her compulsion to shag chauffeurs completely. What? Yes, I've got her number here.'

Freddie's father scribbled down the number, and twelve minutes later he caught his daughter on her mobile.

'Hello daddy,' she said brightly. She lied and pretended to be shopping, scouting for a decent winter coat.

He frowned; he could just hear the background running commentary that put her at the dog track. He barked out directions, instructing her to be at the dowager's by one o'clock sharp, warning her on pain of penury not to be late.

Her taxi slowed down, congealing in the jam at Notting Hill Gate caused by another film shoot. She slipped out and walked the remaining couple of blocks to the posh end of Ladbroke Grove, lined with four and five storey white stucco façades as hard and gleaming as slabs of wedding cake. A prettily uniformed maid admitted Freddie into the salon downstairs and withdrew, returning moments later to escort her up two flights of richly carpeted steps, into what seemed to be a spoof version of a Wimpole Street dentist's waiting room.

She surveyed her surroundings warily. Subtle Swedish lighting effects, decent Adam chairs in prim array and all the right magazines to flick through.

The maid disappeared silently. Across the room a pair of double doors remained firmly closed. Behind them, she assumed, was the dowager. She snatched up a glossy and, skimming through it somewhat petulantly, took stock. She knew of the dowager in a vague sort of way. Incredibly ancient but rather good at getting things sorted. Not so much CAB as AAB - Aristo's Advice Bureau. She had cured the Welham girl, the one with the lesbian crush on the children's nanny, or something like that.

Freddie shrugged, supposing she was here to receive some sort of financial guidance, money management skills, crap like that. She wondered if she could touch the old bag for a couple of hundred.

The Adam chair, un-upholstered and testing to the buttocks, grew increasingly uncomfortable. She wriggled and squirmed. The shadow of a memory stole over her as she sat in the still silence of the waiting room. The memory became less vague, and as it took hold, so did her mounting sense of unease. Then she suddenly realised being here waiting for the double doors to open was just like being summoned to see the headmistress at her boarding school. Recognition swept over her, with the lingering smell of lunch - boiled ham hock, parsley sauce and baked potatoes - creeping down the corridors from the refectory to the head's office.

Painful moments, long, agonising minutes of waiting. Then the even more painful encounter with the fierce headmistress.

Like the hard Adam seat of polished wood biting into the softness of her bottom cheeks, memories of waiting at the head's office door stung Freddie painfully. She remembered sitting on an uncomfortable wooden seat after that lunch of ham hock, sitting and shivering in delicious dread as the rest of the lower sixth whooped it up on the netball court. Ducking out of prep or squabbling over lipsticks would have been sharply dealt with by a slipper wielding dorm prefect just before lights out. But on this occasion, Freddie had been caught cuddling a dean's niece, naked, after lights out.

She giggled as she remembered the dreadful row, but then sobered up at once as she recalled squirming on the hard chair. Outside the netball game was warming up. The squealing, coltish girls dashed up and down the asphalt court, their brassier-free breasts bouncing up and down. Leaping to intercept, or even higher to score, their white panties could be briefly glimpsed as they stretched up to shoot.

'Frederica.' The curt tone, the menacing glint of gold-rimmed glasses perched on the bridge of a beaky nose, the brisk invitation - no, the stern instruction - to enter the inner sanctum of the dominant head. Inside the office there followed a long lecture on the unsuitability at boarding school of intense Sapphic attachments. Freddie, blushing and squirming, was made to confess the grim details - hard nipples touching, and tongue play in the warm wet pussy of the dean's niece. The description of her transgression was met by an intense silence as her face blazed red with shame.

'Across the desk,' came the dreaded command, and she vividly recalled the cruel glint of the bamboo cane as it was retrieved from the walnut cabinet, glimpsed from where one of her blushing cheeks was pressed down into the cold leather of the desk she was bent over.

'No, take your hands away. I'll deal with your knickers presently.'

Freddie obediently levelled her hands, palms down, on the leather blotter, shrinking away from the sure and certain touch of strong fingers flipping up the hem of her grey pleated skirt. Those same fingers, gripping firmly, pinched up the elastic waistband of her panties, and then thumbed them down across the swell of her proffered buttocks. Bare-bottomed and trembling, she cringed as the headmistress strode slowly across the room to the window and drew the heavy curtains closed.

The purposeful tread of the almost silent brogues approached the desk again, followed by the thin whistle of the practice stroke as the whippy wood swished down savagely. Then came the gentle, almost playful caress of the cane tap tapping the tensed cheeks it was about to blister.

There was a sinister *swish* followed by a scream, and her breath clouded the leather blotter. Another *swish* was followed by an even shriller scream. Outside, unseen behind the drawn curtains, the drumming of tightly laced pumps sounded across the netball court, harmonising with the squeals of excited, jostling girls. Inside, there was only the vicious whisper of the searing cane followed by even louder cries of pain...

Freddie blinked and sat bolt upright on the Adam chair. The glossy magazine had slipped from her lifeless fingers minutes before. Her mouth was dry, her tongue

19

feeling strangely clumsy. She swallowed and stood up restlessly, peeling her bottom cheeks away from the cruel wood.

The double doors behind which the dowager held court suddenly opened and a young uniformed chauffeur emerged, stumbling slightly. Red-faced, he frantically stuffed his shirt down into his trousers with one hand, clutching his cap and gloves in the other. He shuffled out through the door that had just been opened by the uniformed maid, who ushered in a matron swathed in sable furs, followed by a sullen little domestic.

Freddie stood by uncertainly. She wondered if she should go in to see the dowager without being officially invited, and decided against it.

The maid chivvied the new arrivals in, and closed the double doors firmly behind them again.

Freddie resumed her uncomfortable seat, and watched the trim little maid depart, the door clicking very softly closed behind her.

Seventeen minutes became twenty three. After thirty-two, Freddie closed her eyes. Her bottom became numb again on the unforgiving chair, almost as numb as it had been when she inspected her stripes after her painful visit to the stern headmistress's office. She remembered peering over her shoulder into the looking glass, peering and counting, with timid bravado, the seven, eight, *nine* red welts slowly paling into a raw blue violet across her tender flesh.

Shaking away her memories, she tried to focus on her present circumstances. What had the chauffeur consulted the dowager over? That shirt being stuffed bashfully into his trousers was certainly suggestive. A discreet cure for the clap, perhaps? Surely not. And what of the sulky little domestic in the dowager's lair right now?

She stood up again, feeling increasingly uneasy. The memory of her caning across the desk of the headmistress was unsettling her. Could the little domestic, escorted by the plump fur laden matron, possibly have committed some misdemeanour, a misdemeanour that no doubt merited discipline - discipline and punishment?

Freddie found herself on her knees in front of the double doors. Tense and quivering, she strained to listen through the wood. There was no keyhole to peep through. Her imagination was forced to snap up every scrap of sound and convert it into pictures behind her closed eyes. She imagined she heard the furred matron levelling solemn accusations against her maid, followed by a shrill squeak of denial, and then her nipples thickened as she fantasised catching the thin wail of a protest...

She sat down on her heels, exhaling her pent up breath. Her mind was playing tricks on her. She had heard nothing, no sharp scolding and no murmured contrition. She sighed, disappointed. The dowager was probably being consulted about some minor matter, smoothing out the wrinkles of an expired work permit, perhaps.

Crack!

Freddie froze.

Crack!

Her heart hammered wildly in her chest as she surged to her feet, listening intently.

Another smacking sound was followed by a shrill scream. A bare bottom was apparently being harshly spanked. She held her breath. Surely the sound of the chastisement was too crisp to be a palm landing against soft cheeks. It had to be a paddle. She swore softly beneath her breath and her nipples peaked in their silk cups, the stiff buds straining as they became almost painfully engorged. She cupped her breasts and squeezed them with fierce affection, almost certain she had correctly identified the instrument of punishment the disobedient maid was being soundly chastised with. But she could not be absolutely sure. No, she would not bet on it, not even if the odds against were generous. The red cheeked domestic was now howling too loudly for Freddie to identify the source of her suffering. Seven-to-four it was a hard leather strap crimsoning her buttocks, eleven-to-eight on a paddle—

The fat matron in furs suddenly swept out of the room, propelling the weeping, whipped domestic before her. Freddie barely had time to jump back to avoid the door hitting her as it opened, and then she finally heard her name being called from inside the room. She passed through the double doors and found herself in a dimly lit room with heavy curtains shutting out the afternoon sunshine, just like in the headmistress's study that fateful afternoon, years before.

The dowager was a slight figure, probably in her late fifties. Her silver hair was swept back into a severe chignon, her firm mouth was free of lipstick and her pale green eyes were as sharp as ice. Her hands were beautiful, delicate and exquisitely manicured, resting together as if in silent prayer in the lap of a black velvet dress. Freddie frowned. The woman before her was surely too calm, too unruffled, to have just beaten another woman so mercilessly, and she relaxed, realising it must have been the fur swathed matron who had punished her own maid. Her inner sigh of relief was almost audible, and the green eyes flickered as though observing it. Then one of the fine white hands gestured to a leather chair.

Freddie sat down, smiling and at ease again.

'Your father and I have spoken at length, Frederica.'

The younger woman inclined her head indulgently, thinking it best to humour the old bat.

'I believe I may be able to help you. That is to say, I may be able to help you help yourself.'

Behind the wing back chair occupied by the silver-haired woman, Freddie saw a French seventeenth century glass-panelled cabinet. Normally reserved for priceless pieces of Sevres and Dresden, this cabinet contained a display of curled straps, coiled whips and gleaming canes. Leather cuffs, ankle restraints and what appeared to be black hoods decked the lower shelves. Yet, she reasoned anxiously, this frail woman was surely incapable of plying any of those brutal instruments. Nevertheless, the glass cabinet morbidly fascinated her with its curled, coiled lengths of hide resting passively within, potent with the promise of pain.

'Am I to understand from your silence,' the dowager's crisp tone demanded her attention, 'that you do not agree with me, Frederica? Very well, you give me no choice.' She clapped her hands twice.

Almost at once a blue velvet curtain parted at the far end of the room, admitting two very athletic-looking young women. Freddie shivered, instantly fearful of their sinuous, ominous strength. Dressed alike in tight white vests and bottom hugging white shorts, white ankle socks and white laced pumps, they approached the wing backed chair with unhurried assurance. Flanking their mistress they stood at attention, their buttocks tight and their pumps planted together. Freddie scanned their inscrutable Slavic faces. They were both in their late twenties, she guessed, and both were strawberry blondes, their hair severely cropped around pale faces and seemingly colourless eyes.

'Kristina and Lara,' the dowager introduced each girl with a slight nod in their direction. 'From Estonia.'

Freddie's eyes were torn between the firm outline of Kristina's breasts within the tight white vest, and the other girl's pronounced pubic mound delineated beneath the form-fitting cotton shorts.

Lara turned, her soft footfalls silent upon the carpet as she sauntered over to the cabinet. Lifting the glass lid carefully, she extracted a thick brown leather strap. Unfurling it, she palmed the gleaming hide across her pale thigh.

Freddie swallowed hard, watching her.

'We are going to help you conquer your vicious addiction, Frederica,' the dowager informed her.

'But I don't have—'

'Gambling is a vice,' the dowager said patiently. 'Is it not?'

Freddie lowered her head, avoiding the piercing green gaze.

'Answer me, girl. Look at me and answer my question at once.'

Sulkily knuckling the leather arm of her chair, she remained silent, her head lowered.

'Lara!'

Startled by the dowager's sharp command, Freddie looked up just in time to see the flash of the oiled hide as it whipped down across one of her soft thighs. She squealed in pain and surprise and rubbed at the weal reddening beneath the sheen of her light tan stockings. 'You bitch!' she hissed through clenched teeth. 'My father—'

'Has given me *carte blanche* to cure you of your addiction, Frederica. You are to remain here with me until I am perfectly satisfied you have been cured.'

'No, you're mistaken,' she cried. 'I'm *not* addicted. I enjoy a flutter, but I pay my way, I—'

'Lara.'

The leather strap hissed loudly as it kissed Freddie's thigh again, causing her to fling her head back and scream.

'Pay your way?' The dowager snorted. 'With your allowance and then your capital, and when you've squandered that it's borrowing and worse, I believe.'

'Fuck off!' Freddie struggled to rise as she massaged her ravaged thigh. 'How bloody well dare you—?'

'Sit down and be quiet and,' the dowager spoke in a chilling tone, 'let there be no more foul language, young lady. Kristina and Lara are here to, among other things, improve their English. I simply will not have them picking up bad or improper words.'

Freddie subsided back into the chair as Kristina stepped forward in response to a curt nod from her mistress. Only three paces, but Freddie found the silent movement potent with menace. Both girls were standing over her now, and they were so close she could smell their freshly washed skin. Quivering with suppressed rage she squirmed in the chair, calculating her odds. They were pretty slim, so best to simply play along and agree to anything. A few tears of contrition might please the old biddy. She would play the penitent and be out of there by teatime.

'Put aside any thought of leaving this house until you are cured, girl.' The dowager's penetrating stare read her thoughts. 'It may take days, it may even take weeks.'

Freddie flinched as she saw Lara's hand tighten around the leather strap, and then she felt her heart turn to stone inside her chest. *Days? Weeks? What the hell was going on here?*

'Now,' the dowager continued smoothly, rubbing her palms together slowly as if applying invisible hand lotion, 'I think we had better start again at the beginning. Stand up, girl.'

Capable hands lifted Freddie out of the chair.

'Strip her and prepare her for the question.'

'Look,' she said desperately, 'I'll never play the tables again, I swear, and I'll give up the horses and—'

'Lara, the gag, if you will.'

The strawberry-blonde acknowledged the instruction from her mistress with a polite nod, and Freddie could not believe how quickly the two Estonians stripped her of her clothes before expertly slipping black leather cuffs around her wrists and ankles. A soft lint gag was then thrust between her lips and she was dragged, struggling futilely, over to a wooden trestle. She was bent facedown over the framework and secured firmly to it with the metal rings attached to her leather cuffs. Her naked buttocks offered up helplessly, she finally ceased fighting the inevitable, and the trestle creaked ominously as she slumped over it, crushing her breasts against the uncompromising wood.

'The inveterate gambler lacks order and discipline, Frederica,' the dowager declared sternly, 'and the gambler's appetite increases with each wager in the search for excitement. An addictive vice, but there is a cure. Since you lack discipline, disciplined you must be. And I need answers to my questions, girl. The truth, mind you, or punishment will prompt your tongue. Remember that both Kristina and Lara are simply aching to get busy on your bottom.'

She shivered, clenching her naked buttocks defensively and scrunching up her toes in an agony of expectation. Bare-bottomed and bound facedown, she was utterly helpless before her beautiful tormentors. Twisting her head to one side, she saw the puddle of her shiny nylon stockings lying on the carpet beside her white panties, tossed aside after being ripped off her.

The dowager rose and approached the trestle to whisper instructions to her stern assistants.

Freddie writhed, straining in her bondage in an effort to determine what was about to happen. Her throat tightened as her pulse quickened, and then a sharp, snapping sound made her whole body tense. She could make no sense of it, and stretching in the restraints, she jerked her face up and caught a reflection of herself in an oval mirror. In the silvery glass she also saw the two Slavic girls stretching their hands, fingers splayed, into pale blue rubber gloves.

'Commence,' the dowager muttered, pausing briefly at the side of the trestle to fleetingly caress the dark rift between Freddie's bottom cheeks with one manicured nail. Then a moment later she appeared at the head of the trestle shuffling a pack of cards. 'Inspect her,' she barked.

Rubber fingertips methodically probed Freddie's slightly wet labial lips.

'Nothing there,' Kristina murmured, thumbing Freddie's slit firmly.

'We shall see,' the dowager muttered. 'Hold her down.'

Rubber hands descended fiercely upon Freddie's naked flesh, one over her shoulder, another at the nape of her neck as two more hands rhythmically palmed and smoothed her upturned buttocks. She moaned an outraged protest, but the gag held fast, smothering her cry into a pitiful mewling. Then the cold latex fingers pulled open her bottom cheeks until her yawning cleft ached fiercely.

'Observe,' the dowager instructed, expertly shuffling the deck in her hands. 'You see? Now I cut the pack. A six. Now I shuffle the pack once more. What will the next card I cut be, I wonder? Higher than a six, or lower?'

Rubber fingertips strummed Freddie's anal whorl as she desperately tried to think straight. Somehow she knew her answer would prove vital. Get it wrong and the strawberry-blonde bitches behind her would have lots of fun with her bare bottom. She had to try and think straight. The odds, what were the odds? Fifty-two cards in a pack, ace counts high, so that made twenty and... and... she could not think, she could not calculate. She felt a strangely delicious wave of panic surge up inside her and harden her crushed nipples.

'Higher,' the dowager demanded, 'or lower?'

She closed her eyes. It *had* to be higher... no, it was lower...

'Open your eyes, girl.'

Still trying to calculate the odds she failed to obey the stern command, and a length of hard leather cracked down across her bare bottom, kiss lashing her satin smooth mounds. She spat out the gag and screamed.

'Answer,' the dowager insisted, fingering the edge of the cards.

'Higher!' she sobbed.

The manicured fingers teased out a four of clubs and placed it against her lips. 'Kiss it,' the silver-haired woman whispered.

Freddie's dry lips pressed obediently, submissively, against the cool plastic card.

'Four!' the dowager barked, and instantly Lara swiped the vicious leather strap four times in blistering succession. Shrieking, Freddie struggled to escape the burning strokes of hide across her reddened buttocks.

'Higher,' the dowager demanded softly as she held out a nine, 'or lower?'

Freddie mumbled a response. 'Lower.'

The older woman teased out a ten of spades from the deck. 'Ten strokes,' she ordered.

Perspiring slightly, her damp vest adhering to her round breasts, Lara obediently plied the hide, leaving the English girl's buttocks ablaze.

The dowager forced Freddie to choose twice more, and twice more she lost.

'Bad run of luck,' the austere woman said. 'Another seven strokes, if you please, Lara.'

Afterwards, a sobbing Freddie was made to don a tight rubber mask. It encased her head completely, denying her sight and speech and forcing her to stop crying.

Tiny air holes at each nostril allowed her to breathe, even as the sticky latex wet her hot face with perspiration. That was all she wore as they tied her hands together above her bare bottom, and then attached vicious little peg clips to her nipples. Terrified, and yet also deliciously, disturbingly aroused, she trembled and awaited her fate.

'Bend her over, Kristina. Lara, the cane, please.'

The dowager's commands were executed promptly with one blonde forcing Freddie to bend over while the other swished the supple length of whippy cane in a practice stroke.

'Far flaps,' the dowager stated.

Kristina's fingers picked at the rubber flaps, and a rush of noise bruised Freddie's eardrums, making her gasp.

'I know you can hear me, girl. Kristina, you may also select a cane.'

Freddie shivered as she heard the glass cabinet being opened, followed by the dry rattle of a bamboo cane being plucked out. Kristina returned, and took up her position directly opposite Lara. She sensed them flanking her, but she could not see them.

'Examine her.'

The tips of the canes kissed the swell of her bare buttocks, dimpling her soft cheeks. Expertly, the Slavic beauties worked their canes so the flesh at her crease was opened and exposed.

'Dryish,' Lara announced.

'Excellent. Now we'll see how wet gambling gets the little whore.'

They peeled off her rubber helmet and undid the bonds at her wrists, pulling her upright again. Her legs quivered as the dowager reached out and fingered the peg clips biting into her nipples, first the left and then the right, and she felt a scream building up inside her.

'An even bet for you, girl. Which one will I snatch away first, hmm?'

Perspiration trickled between Freddie's breasts, turning the shadowed curves of her orbs a lovely glistening rose.

'I'm waiting,' the dowager prompted menacingly.

She closed her eyes in despair. 'The left,' she whispered.

'Wrong.'

Her eyes flickered open again in terror. At her nipples she saw the manicured fingernails closing in at each clip, and a sudden snatching movement plucked both pegs away simultaneously, leaving her puckering buds red and ravaged with pain. She screamed.

'Roulette,' the dowager announced placidly. 'Bring your canes with you.'

All through the long afternoon the wheel spun and the ball rattled, clinking as it came to rest. Betting wildly Freddie became engrossed, unaware of how much debt she was amassing. Then she sobered up abruptly and counted her losses, to be paid in cane strokes. She had lost heavily and she panicked, realising her bottom was to be beaten by the blistering bamboo.

'But before we settle your debts, admit it, Frederica,' the dowager urged. 'You enjoyed your game, didn't you?'

She nodded mutely.

'Lara.'

The firm-lipped young woman fingered Freddie's pussy with clinical precision. 'Wet,' she pronounced, holding up a glistening forefinger. Freddie reddened furiously, hating the indignity.

'Exactly as I thought. Time to settle your debts, girl, before you go to bed. Sixteen strokes.'

Kristina and Lara took turns lashing her, their canes swishing down to criss cross the proffered buttocks with crimson lines of torment. The canes clashed above the tortured bottom after the seventh stroke, clattering noisily as their polished lengths collided. Then Lara tossed hers aside and knelt, hugging Freddie's thighs and pressing her face into the captive flesh while Kristina continued to whip her cane down, making Lara scream softly each time the bamboo kissed her cheeks through her tight white shorts. She lapped at Freddie's thigh, tonguing her satin-soft skin as the punishing cane swept down.

Freddie squirmed in her narrow cot. She slept fitfully, lapsing into troubled dreams filled with stern blondes and even sterner punishments. When she woke the sheet beneath her sex was damp with the juices of her nocturnal arousal.

They came for her a little before ten o'clock the next morning. Bundling her into a tepid shower, they soaped and scrubbed her before dragging her out onto the tiled floor of the bathroom to towel her dry.

She fleetingly toyed with the idea of bribing the two slavish blondes, but as the towel fiercely raked the cleft between her cane striped cheeks, she knew it was futile. These stern beauties served the dowager exclusively.

She was dressed in a simple white cotton robe and served a meagre breakfast consisting of an apple, bread and butter and a single cup of weak tea. The tray was then promptly whisked away and she was taken to sit in front of a television with a video player perched on top of it.

'No,' the dowager said briskly as she stepped into the room, 'remove her robe first.' She was dangling a thin leather belt from her left hand, while what appeared to be a rolled up ball of cling-film nestled in the palm of her other hand.

Lara pulled on the belt holding Freddie's robe closed and peeled it away, forcing her to stand up and shrug it off. She blushed with shame to feel so completely owned and controlled. Resentfully, she risked a last bid for dignity by furtively inching her hands down across her belly to protectively cup and cover her pubis.

'Hands up on your head, girl,' the dowager snapped impatiently, and slowly, Freddie obeyed her.

'Dress her in these.'

Kristina took the clear plastic panties from her mistress, and flapping them open gently, she knelt at the English girl's feet. Freddie stepped into the strange underwear obediently, hissing softly as they were smoothed tightly up between her thighs, and clouded over almost at once from the heat of her pussy.

'Now, girl, push them down,' the dowager instructed. 'No, just a fraction.'

Puzzled, Freddie timidly obeyed, pushing the soft plastic down over her hips until her soft bush was exposed and the panties formed a tight, restricting band around her thighs.

Rolling up the leather belt the dowager handed it to Kristina, who kept it tightly coiled while she carefully positioned it at Freddie's vulva, and then suddenly pulled the plastic panties up again to hold it in place.

'We're going to the races, girl. Exciting, hmm? But I want you to try to contain your excitement. I know now how much gaming arouses you. That is the key to your cure. But first, try to contain yourself. I will be watching you very carefully. And as you are visible to me, I shall see if you become wet.'

Freddie, blushing deeply, averted her gaze.

'Wet that belt, girl, and I'll whip you, understand?'

Forced to kneel before the video screen, Freddie watched the replay of a steeplechase. A bunch finish, with the horses fresh and keen, flew past the two-furlong post. Then pause and freeze-frame the horses straining and lunging motionless towards the line with all four feet above the grass.

'Choose,' commanded the dowager, 'and choose wisely. Your odds will be paid out in stripes should you lose.'

Her assistants giggled softly, clearly relishing Freddie's anguish.

The screen flickered, and the horses dashed headlong past the one-furlong mark. Number three looked good, the jockey riding hands and heels, but number five, a length off the pace, was looking even stronger. Then the horses froze once more above the grass.

'Choose!'

Her breasts felt heavy, her tummy muscles fluttered, and down at her hot hive, honey wept freely. The sheer thrill of calling the bet - number three or number five - was propelling her towards an orgasm. Her labia spread apart, riding the coiled hide and silvering it with her wet heat. Number three or number five? It was too delicious trying to decide between them... she was starting to come... 'N-number five,' she groaned.

A manicured nail jabbed down on the control button. The horses drew level, flashed by the winning post, and continued running for another circuit.

Writhing under the belt swiping across her bare bottom, Freddie squealed and pressed her tearstained face up against the screen as, two minutes later, number six flashed by the winning post. Number five trailed in fourth. The belt, wet with her climax, whistled and snapped relentlessly, driving her headlong into another savage orgasm.

'I've spoken with your father, Frederica. You are to remain here until you're completely cured.'

It was Freddie's fifth night in the dowager's Notting Hill lair. 'You shall be cured, my girl, I assure you. It is quite simple. Gaming gives you great pleasure, and so, I have discovered, does being subjected to dominance and discipline. No, do not try and deny it. Therefore, I propose to hand you over to one of my two Slavic beauties. Under the thumb and crop of Kristina, or the heel and the cane of Lara, I think you will be cured once and for all. But which is it to be, I wonder?'

She shivered with delicious dread. Kristina, so cruel with the whippy crop, always happy to flick the little loop of leather up between Freddie's parted thighs to lick her labia with little tongues of fire. Or sweetly vicious Lara, who after several searing strokes of the cane had the disturbing habit of inserting the tip of her quivering weapon between Freddie's striped cheeks, probing the wet pinkness of her tight little anus.

27

Lara or Kristina?

'Full or empty?' The dowager held out both her hands closed into fists. 'Choose.'

Tempted, Freddie succumbed to the wager and tapped the clenched right fist. 'Empty.'

The dowager opened it, and a glint of gold winked up at Freddie. 'Full,' the dowager murmured. 'You lose, girl. I name Lara as your dominatrix.'

Freddie bowed her head, as usual avoiding the stern green gaze.

'Double or quits?' the older woman whispered.

Freddie glanced up. It was the ultimate wager - freedom to walk out into the traffic of Ladbroke Grove, or servitude beneath the lash of the beautifully vicious strawberry-blonde. She took a deep breath, and nodded.

'*Heads* I win,' the dowager stated, and spun the golden coin in the air, and *heads* it was.

Freddie paled, and then began weeping. Hours of humiliation stretched out before her into days and nights of unmitigated torment.

The dowager opened her palm. On it, gleaming softly, Freddie saw her double-headed sovereign. 'I'll cure you, my girl, you can bet on it.'

CAUGHT BEHIND

The late summer breeze sighed at the bedroom window, wafting the drawn curtains and making them shiver. Lying on her bed in the darkening room, Susie dug the rubber spiked fingers of the stolen cricket gloves into her wet pussy, parting her labial lips. Shiny wet with her arousal, they too shivered. She grunted impatiently and dug deeper, pinioning and punishing her slit with savage tenderness. A single spike skidded up her slippery flesh, catching her clitoral thorn, and she squealed softly. Grinding her buttocks frantically into the prickly surface of her green candlewick bedspread, she grunted in response to the sweet burning ache between her thighs.

Out in the deepening dusk, high up in a shivering elm, an owl hooted, a soft, sorrowful note. On her bed her legs lewdly spread, Susie dragged her gloved hands up through her tightly coiled bush, across her pale stomach and up to her naked breasts. At each trapped globe of flesh the cruel gloves squeezed, and her nipples rose thicker and harder than the red rubber spikes pleasuring them with sweet pain.

Behind her tightly closed eyes Susie squeezed out images of the village cricket team, man by sinewy, sweaty man. The *Cocks*. The team took its name from the pub where she worked as a live in barmaid. The *Cocks* were a virile bunch, very virile, and to the dismay of anxious sisters and jealous wives, Susie served many of their number with more than a foaming pint. Peter, who kept wicket, possessed such wonderfully skilful hands, hands that held tightly and gripped fiercely. Terry, the Cocks's spin bowler, never failed to deliver fast and furiously. And Greg, the lithe, dark-eyed gamekeeper's assistant, was so versatile in the field...

The spiked gloves squeezed harder. In the field... her groan melted into a naughty chuckle. The rubber spikes raked across her stubby nipples, and then painfully dimpled her tender orb. She gasped, clamping her thighs closed to contain the juice flowing from her hot pussy. Greg in the field... twisting her face into the bedspread, she tongued the rippling cotton embroidery. Greg had taken her to the secluded paddock behind Lower Grange Farm last Sunday. In the field, bare-bottomed and kneeling, she nuzzled the sweet grass as Greg took her roughly from behind.

Viciously strumming her mulberry dark nipples, she remembered Greg's hoarse gasps as he pounded into her faster and harder, his heavy balls slapping noisily against her wet sex as his hard length filled and stretched the tightness between her clenched buttocks. He came, and his hot seed spilled out of her bottom to scald the crease of her cleft. Still thick and at full stretch, he remained lodged inside as he spanked her, his hand swiping down to deliver a stinging crack across her helpless buttock. She remembered her shrill cry piercing the silence of the dark spinney behind them. He spanked her a second time, and then came the soft slapping of his balls again as, faster and faster, he shafted her between her smouldering cheeks. Smothering her full-throated scream of raw pleasure, she was forced to bite into a clump of pungent clover just as Greg hurriedly pulled out, and contemptuously shot his sticky load down onto the nape of her bowed neck.

Greg in the field... memories of the paddock last Sunday drew the batsman's gloves down to her wet heat again. Spreading her sex lips wide, she drummed the spikes furiously. Tightening her buttocks, she jerked them up off the bedspread, submitting her glowing clitoris to the firm caress of a spiked index finger.

Greg... she remembered rubbing the shiny wooden bails slowly between her thighs afterwards, slowly and deliberately, as his cooling cum flowed around her neck like a rope of liquid pearls. And recalling the sweet rank smell of his semen in her nostrils, an orgasm welled implacably up inside her. She groaned softly, and twisting her slippery naked body over, she came suddenly, taken almost by surprise by the sweet savagery of her climax. She angled her gloved hand down just in time to thrust a spiked finger up between her tightening cheeks, sobbing with delight. The red rubber spikes bit into her anal passage, rocketing her into a fresh spasm, and opening her mouth wide, she bit her pillow to smother a shriek just as she had bitten into the clump of clover... bitten into the pungent clover as Greg knuckled her pussy tenderly last Sunday in the field.

'Come along, Romulus. Heel, Remus, heel.'

Approaching *The Cock* across the village green, Virginia Emsley, president of the Women's Institute, trod the soft turf firmly down beneath her polished brogues. Beside her, scurrying in her majestic wake, Alice Sneesby struggled to keep pace. And bounding alongside them in the twilight, two red Irish Setters defied the stern commands of their mistress.

'The *Cocks* should take the County Cup from the Stumpies tomorrow,' Alice panted.

'Langley Parva certainly deserves a win,' her companion snapped, the tartness of her waspish tone barely concealing her reluctance to call the home side the *Cocks*.

Alice shivered even though the summer evening was warm. 'Why are they called the *Stumpies?*' she wondered aloud, too timid of her dominant lover to ask the question directly.

'Leave it, Romulus... Remus, come!' Virginia barked, whipping her dog leads smartly against her thigh. 'Damn animals,' she muttered, rattling their chains impatiently. 'Dead squirrel. Why are *who* called *what*, my dear?'

Alice repeated her question, this time directly.

'The village of Selston once boasted a beautiful church,' Virginia explained. 'Square Norman tower. Magnificent. Cromwell ordered cannon fire on it and left the tower a mere stump. Hence, the Selston team are—'

'*Stumpies*.' Alice nodded, enlightened. 'I see.'

'Heel, you dogs, at once!' the president of the WI commanded, shaking their leads.

'The *Cocks*—' Alice began.

'Langley Parva, *please*.'

'*Our* side,' Alice amended quickly, 'will certainly look well even if they don't play well.'

Virginia followed her companion's pointing hand. A long clothesline pegged out at the side of *The Cock* met her gaze. On it, cricket whites danced in the gentle breeze.

'Oh dear,' Alice murmured.

The two women stopped. At the end of the clothesline, Susie's red silk knickers fluttered brazenly.

'Oh dear indeed,' Virginia Emsley muttered.

'I *do* think the barmaid ought to be a little more discreet,' Alice stated with marked disapproval. 'Red silk knickers up on display like that. Really! I wish she would take them down.'

Virginia gripped the jangling leads fiercely in her gloved hand. 'I'd certainly like to make Susie take her knickers down...'

Back from their knock up in the nets, the *Cocks* were downing pints and pies as if they were at their victory supper already.

'Steady lads,' the landlord warned. 'Got to keep your strength up for tomorrow.'

Behind the pumps Susie worked busily, her cleavage deepening invitingly as she bent over her tasks. It was warm work. Perspiration darkened her blouse at the armpits and glistened at the swell of her brassiere-bondaged breasts.

'Bloody odd,' the opening batsman was heard to remark. 'Could have sworn I'd packed my gloves for practice.'

Susie blushed, and between her thighs behind the wispy lace at her pubic bush a deep warmth moistened her pussy lips.

'I found your gloves,' the *Cocks's* opener announced, downing his third light ale. 'Bit damp and smelly, though. Bloody odd.'

'Scent of victory?' the landlord chuckled.

Susie bit her lower lip as she concentrated on pouring out a pint, her face now as hot as her pussy.

A contented silence settled over the boisterous men for a few moments, and then they began discussing tactics. Selston's strength was remarked upon. If only the home team's middle order could stand up to the *Stumpies's* mean bowlers.

A scraping of chairs signalled the departure of several players, and Susie brought a tray of drinks - a round of cautious halves - over to the table. Peter, Greg and Terry had grown morose. The *Stumpies*, she overheard, were in fine fettle - damn fine fettle.

Back at her pumps she ate a bag of salted crisps, sucking her red nails after popping each pale cracker into her mouth. The gloom from the cricketer's table spread throughout the bar. What if Selston snatched the County Cup from her fine boys? The taste of defeat would be sharper than the salted crisps in her mouth. Defeat... she shivered at the thought.

Later, when a towel covered the pumps and mice, emboldened by the darkness, emerged to nibble at peanuts on the beer-stained boards, Susie stood before her bedroom mirror undressing slowly. Her red fingernails rasped at the straps of her bra, slowly peeling them down over her smooth shoulders. In the glass she saw the cups heave, and proudly watched her breasts spill out of them and quiver enticingly, glad to be free of the strict cotton bondage.

Shrugging off her bra, she absently thumbed her left nipple, peaking the stubby pinkness in pleasurable pain. Unzipped, her tight skirt slithered down over her nylon stockings to form a soft puddle over her shoes. Stepping out of it, and then kicking it gently aside, she slipped off her shoes and stood before the large mirror wearing only stockings and a garter belt.

She gazed steadily at her reflection in the glass. The twelfth man... tomorrow she would step in and save her boys. The scent of victory grew strong between her legs as she smiled and mentally went over the tactics she had come up with to secure the Cocks's triumphant victory.

'But Selston simply walked away with the best village gardens—'

'Cheated! Know it for a fact. Grew everything under glass, and then potted out and planted on the morning of the judging,' Virginia Emsley muttered, struggling with a tight white corset that bunched her buttocks together fiercely, rendering her cleft a mere crease between her swollen cheeks.

'And their summer jams scooped up gold and silver,' Alice whined. Already naked, she slipped between the sheets embroidered with pale violet periwinkles.

'No medals for Langley Parva there,' Virginia agreed, easing her quivering bosom out of the corset's balconette cups. 'Not even an honourable mention. But Selston's was bought gold.'

Alice gazed devotedly up at the naked woman beside the bed. 'Bought?'

'Of course, bought. Got it all from the verger's sister.' She tossed her rolled up stockings aside impatiently. 'Romulus and Remus penned up?'

Alice, inching her thighs open a fraction beneath the sheets, nodded.

'Jolly good. No, Sneesby,' the president of the WI barked as she tightened the black leather straps of a softly jingling harness firmly across her buttocks, 'Langley Parva never cheats. When we lift the County Cup tomorrow, it'll all be fair and square.'

'Mm,' Alice said, thrilling to the sound of the harness.

'No cheating,' the president of the WI whispered, deftly guiding the seven-inch ivory dildo into the socket harnessed to her pubic mound, 'or I'll want to know the reason why.'

A few minutes later, spread-eagled facedown on the bed, Alice Sneesby moaned as her anal rosebud puckered and softened. The tiny whorls fluttered, and began to unfurl as her sphincter opened with shy eagerness to accept the ivory dildo's forthcoming thrusts.

'After all,' Virginia murmured, fingering petroleum jelly along the length of the gleaming phallus, 'cheating just isn't cricket. Now open up, Sneesby,' she commanded, dimpling the mattress as she straddled the cheeks below her. Virginia eased back onto her ankles, and then lurched forward, briskly gripping and spreading her lover's cheeks to allow the tip of the dildo entry into the dark little hole between them. 'Come along, my girl, or it'll go hard for you. My strap is under that bolster, and if you don't get your bottom up right now I do believe you'll be begging me not to use it.'

Alice cried out softly as, offering her buttocks up obediently, the lubricated phallus slid between them.

'Good girl,' Virginia murmured, jerking her hips to drive the thrusting ivory deeper. 'Play up and play the game.'

By two-fifteen the heat in the tea tent was stifling. The egg and watercress sandwiches already cut and quartered lay hidden under dampened tea towels. Wasps visited the raspberry jam oozing from Victoria sponges. Brushed away by busy hands, they dipped down inquisitively to buzz over the buttered scones. Susie wandered between the linen-covered trestle tables, utterly ignored by the equally starchy women of the parish.

'Trollop!' hissed the schoolmistress, struggling to thumb open a jar of crab paste.

In a humid corner of the tent a silver urn steamed in preparation for the production of endless cups of tea.

The *Stumpies* had arrived just after noon in a dusty convoy along the rutted, late summer lanes bearing them from Selston to Langley Parva. Losing the toss, the *Cocks* went in to bat. The openers were stepping up gamely to sky and six the best efforts of the visitors' bowling.

Susie was cold-shouldered out of the tea tent. So denied access to the communal ritual of sandwich making and cake cutting by Virginia Emsley's WI stalwarts, the spurned barmaid wandered away, her cheeks ablaze. Out in the bright sunshine she saw the first wicket quickly taken, and her white-sandaled feet took her to the steps of the pavilion, where the smell of liniment, sweat and linseed oil greeted her... and the smell of defeat. The *Cocks*, shielding their eyes from the sun's glare, were watching their demise in gloomy silence. She skipped up the wooden steps, and an impish gleam lit up her dark eyes. Bending down, her soft breasts nudging their shoulders, she began whispering into the ears of the middle-order batsmen, first Peter, then Terry, and finally Greg.

As she ran jauntily back down the pavilion steps and glided across the lawn towards the boundary bushes, three pairs of hungry eyes devoured her impudent bottom swaying and rolling inside the tight sheath of her rose-print dress. Despite disaster out at the crease, the *Cocks's* spirits and manhoods rose.

Following the game from behind a thick hawthorn bush, Susie plied the buttered cucumber she'd stolen from the earnest sandwich makers in the tea tent. Kissing before sucking its blunt snout for several minutes, she lowered and levelled it between her parted thighs. Gripping it tightly as she ground her soft bottom cheeks into the prickle of the sedge beneath, she brought the slippery tip of the greased vegetable an inch from her naked pubis.

Out on the pitch the first of the middle-order was taking his stance at the wicket. The leather whistled softly and the willow barked loudly in response. Something seemed to have stiffened the *Cocks's* resolve. Terry, who usually returned a decent eighteen runs, was knocking up a very useful thirty-one.

Out of sight behind the hawthorn bush, Susie's pussy juiced and her sticky labial lips parted in a welcoming smile to receive the first four inches of the cucumber. Rotating the thick shaft with a wrist trained at the beer pumps, the dark-eyed barmaid pleasured herself brutally, while on the pitch Terry reached forty-three. Then a ragged cheer rose as his incautious clip was snatched out of the air by an agile *Stumpie*, but Terry did not walk back to the pavilion. His grass-scuffed boots took him directly to the late flowering hawthorn in the outfield where Susie, aroused by the cucumber's solid length, received and rewarded Terry for his sterling work at the crease.

In silence they knelt face-to-face, their knees just touching. He rolled slightly on his padded shins, and reaching across to unbutton his white shirt and tweak his left nipple, she steadied him against her. Her hand dropped to his fly and she slowly unbuttoned it. After teasing out the awkward box and tossing it aside, she fingered out his thickening cock. Lowering her face, she tantalised his shining glans with the tip of her tongue.

Swearing softly, Terry stretched out his gloved hand and forced her head over his erection. Electrified by his gloved touch, the barmaid sucked hard as he clenched and unclenched his gloved fist in her hair. Sensing his imminent release she tossed her head back, rapidly bared her breasts, and captured his engorged shaft in her deep cleavage. It twitched, aching for the spurt that would ease its sweet pain, and she bunched her breasts around it. The captive penis pulsed and exploded savagely, drenching her chin and throat. Then the warm semen flowed down into a silver puddle glistening between her heaving breasts.

She cupped and squeezed them, forcing the puddle of cum to spill down in a slow trickle over her peaked nipples. Terry, muttering a soft obscenity, slumped forward, and straining towards her bunched breasts he moaned as he struggled to kiss their shiny curves. The wet nipples raked his cheek, and he took a pink bud between his teeth, sucking it devotedly. She bit her lip to suppress a cry of raw pleasure, and then he collapsed, utterly spent, against her wet cleavage, his white cricket shirt absorbing his spilled seed.

Sprawled out on the grass, his head resting on the comfortable warmth of her soft breasts, he squinted up through the sun's glare at the lovely barmaid.

'And how many sixes did you hit?' she purred.

'Only two,' he whispered hoarsely.

'Then that's two I owe you,' she replied, giggling. 'A promise is a promise.' Leaning down, she peeled the cricketer's glove from his right hand and donned it. 'Doesn't he want to play?' she teased, passing the rubber-spiked forefinger firmly down along Terry's flaccid penis.

'Good for another knock,' he grunted. His shaft twitched, slowly thickening in response to the rubber spikes dancing along its developing length. Soon the dark glans winked wetly in the sunshine and Susie straddled her mount, catching his thighs between her knees, and he surrendered, spreading his arms wide. 'Bowl me a leg break!' he laughed.

'Full toss,' she whispered, gripping his erection within her gloved fist and pumping him slowly. The soft spikes raked him ruthlessly, and only moments later his muffled shout of delight sent a jay wheeling in alarm from the upper branches of an overhanging elm. His chest heaving, he gazed open-mouthed into the cloudless blue sky as his hot seed rained down, soaking the white shirt over his belly.

Peter loped from the wicket to the hawthorn with the spring of expectation in his every step. His creditable thirty-seven had included a brace of boundaries, and Susie had promised pleasure for every big hit. Sprinting into the outfield, to the puzzled frowns of the village womenfolk peering out from the tea tent, he skirted the screening hawthorn and tumbled, sprawling, into Susie's lap.

Gathering him up and cradling him in her left arm, she guided his mouth to her right breast. The deep pink of her engorged nipple raked his lips like a lipstick as, cupping and controlling her soft orb, she tantalised the spellbound batsman. He buried his sweaty face in her pillowing flesh and nibbled at her teat before enclosing it within pursed lips and sucking on it viciously. She squealed, and tweaked his nipple through his shirt in revenge. He nuzzled a muffled apology into her cleavage and eased his face back a fraction.

'Gently, Tiger,' she murmured.

Nodding into her breast, his lips at her hard nipple again, he sucked tenderly this time.

Deftly fingering his bulging shaft free of his tight white trousers, she slowly palmed the head of his urgent erection as he squirmed. 'Peter,' she said in a warning tone, a controlling squeeze of his balls brought him obediently back to her breast, and she sensed he was close to his release.

'Please...' he begged.

'No, not yet,' she teased, cruelly denying him his ejaculation. 'After all, you took your time hitting that first boundary. You may come when, and only when, the umpire signals play.'

'Bitch,' he groaned devotedly, and his sweet suffering drove him into a frenzy. Taking as much of her right breast into his mouth as he could, he nearly choked on the captive flesh as she knuckled his exposed glans furiously, and silenced by the soft mound filling his mouth, he swallowed his yell of pleasure as he climaxed. His long liquid spurt splashed her face, momentarily blinding her as his sticky seed sealed her eyes closed, so bending she nuzzled his chest, wiping her face on his shirt.

He remained flat on his back for his second promised reward as she rose and hitched her rose-print dress up over her hips, and then squatting, she guided her naked buttocks down onto his upturned face. She moaned as his nose probed between them, and groaned as she sensed his warm exhale at her anal whorl. She loosened her thighs for comfort, and shuddered as his lips and tongue greeted her hot pussy.

Kneeling astride her pinioned batsman, rocking gently on her knees and toes, Susie rode his face, gently at first. His cock stiffened, rising to salute this new delight, and his frantic whispers of gratitude tickled her pubic fringe. She squeezed

34

her thighs together, silencing him, and then loosened them again, allowing his tongue to rasp repeatedly at her parted labia.

'You need training, my boy,' she muttered, her words darkly affectionate. 'Let's see how you cope with the seam.' She began bouncing down onto his helpless face, spreading her cheeks apart with her hands to reveal her cleft. 'Lick,' she commanded.

His tongue strokes were strong and sure, the juice flowing from her cleft shining across his smothered face while at the base of his belly, his cock was as hard as his bat.

Settling her soft bottom down over his features, smothering and silencing his protest, she giggled. 'Time to knock your bails off, boy.'

Peter's grunt was inaudible through the ripe flesh cushioning his mouth.

Walking two fingers down his chest from button to button, she stalked his quivering flesh spear. At its base she teased him by scratching her nails gently through his dark pubic hair. She felt him writhe beneath her, his lips protesting under her soft buttocks, and promptly punished him by grinding them down firmly, forcing him to remain perfectly still.

'That's better,' she purred, approaching his erection with eager fingertips. 'Middle stump,' she declared triumphantly, flicking his nodding glans skilfully six times in rapid succession. He came explosively, showering semen all over his shirt. Her dark eyes gleamed with pride watching the spreading stains. As twelfth man, she was playing well with the *Cocks*.

Peter stirred beneath her. His tongue, a thickly muscled specimen, drove deeply up through her sphincter just as it did when she served him a scotch egg with his pint. He would scoop out the salted yolk within the savoury meat in one go, and now, his tongue's curled tip raked her tight warmth with similar gusto.

'Middle stump,' she giggled, squirming deliciously down over him, 'but not a maiden over.'

In the sweltering tea tent, Virginia Emsley frowned. An egg and watercress sandwich had left dark green leaves between her perfect white front teeth, and she sucked at them in mounting irritation. 'Sneesby,' she barked, patting a pocket for her dog leads.

Alice looked up from the cups and saucers she was unnecessarily rearranging.

'Pity to keep Romulus and Remus penned up on such a splendid day. Slip along home and take them for a stroll.'

'Oh, but the cricket,' Alice protested peevishly. 'I shall miss the match.'

The president of the WI tossed the leads across the tent. Alice caught them, and held them awkwardly against her bosom.

'A brisk scamper down to the churchyard, I think. I suggest you come back across the green along the outfield. Pay particular attention to that hawthorn bush. It would appear it holds some fascination for our middle-order batsmen, don't you think?'

'But the game...'

'The hawthorn, Sneesby, and then report back to me. You may find some unofficial games being played there, I suspect.'

Greg played like a windmill on a March day at the crease. He left the match with a handy twenty-four notched up, hitting four massive sixes that drew loud applause even from the *Stumpies*.

Behind the hawthorn he tossed down his bat and gloves eagerly. Kneeling, he kissed Susie harshly, dominantly taming her tongue with his own. Brushing aside her hands from his trousers he pushed her gently but firmly down onto the soft turf.

'Four sixes,' he grunted, knuckling her pussy. 'I've done well at the crease, girl, so I think I'll have a go at this one.'

Her print frock rode up her slender thighs and he gazed down at her soft pubic bush. Seeing the wet sheen on his knuckles and the glint at her juicing slit, he quickly undid and pushed down his trousers. He was astride her, and inside her, before she could catch her breath, his chest crushing her cushioning bosom as his thick length filled her. Gripping her buttocks he lunged into her, his fingertips meeting at her deep cleft and splaying the captive cheeks painfully apart. Her stretched anus became a sweet, maddening torment, another hot hole needing to be filled. She sucked hungrily on his neck, and then bit it as his throbbing shaft sent ripples of pleasure up into her belly. In minutes they came together, both almost blinded by the stinging perspiration of their brutal exertion.

'Hell, my bloody shoulder,' Greg muttered.

'Susie kiss it better,' she whispered, mounting him carefully and angling her seething pussy at the shoulder he was ruefully rubbing. Pressing her wetness into his tough flesh, she climaxed again wiping her labial lips against his cotton shirt.

Monday morning was very wet. It rained steadily, filling the rutted lanes with brimming puddles. The tea tent on the village green, silent since Sunday at sunset, sagged.

Virginia Emsley sipped her cup of coffee, her eye fixed expectantly on the back door. The kitchen was perfumed with chicory from her beverage, which she took very strong, and with the smell of pungent sulphur fumes from the partly burnt fuel.

The garden gate creaked. She placed her cup down on the saucer, and its rattle betrayed her suppressed excitement. The back door opened. Alice entered the kitchen backwards, turning and bumping the door closed again with her bottom. Her wet Wellingtons squeaked on the flagstone floor.

'Well?' Virginia demanded.

'I took those empty soda siphons back to *The Cock* on the pretext—'

'Never mind all that,' her lover snapped impatiently. 'Did you manage to get at the laundry basket?'

Alice nodded. 'No washing today in all that.' She nodded through the kitchen window at the pouring rain, and then unzipping her glistening waxed raincoat, she shook free several sets of cricket whites.

'Are you sure you got the middle-order's kit?'

'Oh yes, quite sure. Name tags sewn in. It was easy, just as you said it would be.'

'Terry's and Peter's?'

'And Greg's.'

The president of the WI snatched the trousers up from the flagstone floor, and peeling them open under her nose, inspected them intimately.

'Salt, they say, shifts grass stains,' Alice remarked pleasantly.

'I'm not looking for grass stains.'

Alice blushed pinkly.

'And you are quite certain you saw that little slut of a barmaid behind the hawthorn yesterday?'

'Oh yes. Fast asleep she was. Quite exhausted. Perhaps a touch of the sun, too.'

'Touch of *someone's* son,' Virginia growled. 'Hmm... nothing suggestive on these. Throw me those shirts, Sneesby. I'm damn sure I'm on the right track.'

Bending, Alice gathered up the three white shirts.

'I knew it!' Virginia declared shrilly. 'There, smell that... and that.'

Alice obediently dipped her nose into the stained shirts, and wrinkled it in apparent distaste.

'Semen!' Virginia cried.

Alice shuddered, but her nose remained plunged in the stained cotton, sniffing deeply.

'Better get those back to the laundry basket in *The Cock* before they're missed.' Virginia spoke over her shoulder from the sink where she was rinsing her fingers. 'Looks as though it's going to clear up.'

Alice clutched the semen-stained shirts tightly to her bosom, and while Virginia checked the sky through the window as she dried her hands, Alice risked a darting lick of the soiled cotton.

'Sneesby!' Virginia caught the surreptitious act reflected in the kitchen window. 'By God, my girl, it's the dog lead for *your* arse tonight.'

Sunbeams danced in a spindling shaft lancing the windows of the village hall. Rows of empty wooden chairs waited patiently for the buttocks of the impending WI committee. When they were filled, a little after four o'clock, Virginia Emsley called for order.

'I have convened this extraordinary meeting to discuss events at the match on Sunday,' she announced.

The wooden chairs creaked in quiet disappointment as their occupants groaned inwardly. None of those assembled wanted an inquest into a match lost and best forgotten. The visitors had taken the County Cup back to Selston with them, and that, unfortunately, was that.

'I have asked the barmaid at *The Cock* to be present,' Virginia continued. 'I believe she may be able to shed some useful light on our downfall.'

Something in her tone caused the WI members to stiffen. Their chairs squeaked sharply as the entire committee leaned forward with sudden interest.

'Ah, right on cue. Come in girl. Close the door, Sneesby, and the curtains too, please.'

Susie stepped into the sunlit village hall, grimacing at the stern black upright piano and at the pale faces of the committee.

Alice closed, and locked, the door.

Susie turned, uncertain and a little afraid.

'We pride ourselves on matters of privacy,' the president of the WI informed her evenly.

The sunbeams ceased their silent dancing as Alice Sneesby suddenly closed the heavy plum curtains.

Susie froze. Yellow naked light bulbs glowed overhead, illuminating the dour faces of the silent committee, nine impassive masks of disapproval. 'What do you want me for?' she asked in a small voice.

'Just wanted to thank you, my girl, for encouraging our boys at the crease on Sunday.' Virginia kept her brisk tone pleasant.

Susie, wary as a perch amongst pike, fiddled with her fingers over her pubic mound. 'Always happy to cheer on the *Cocks*.' She attempted to smile.

'Langley Parva thanks you for your efforts, I'm sure. So kind of you to encourage the men and reward their efforts.'

Susie was silent. The click of the door being locked still echoed loudly in her brain.

'Oh come girl, we're not all jam and Jerusalem, you know.'

Susie flushed.

'No, we're jolly good sports, aren't we girls?'

The committee, a little bewildered, nodded in assent.

'We are not here to condemn you. The middle-order hit big sixes for you, didn't they?'

Susie giggled, and relaxing a little, she dropped her hands down to her thighs.

'What was it, my dear, a kiss, perhaps? A kiss for every six?'

The lovely barmaid half assented with a shy nod.

'Or a little more than a kiss, maybe?'

She suddenly wondered why the curtains were drawn. It unsettled her...

'Speak up, girl. No secrets here. All girls together.'

She bit her lip. The buttocks filling the polished wooden chairs belonged, she knew, to indignant aunts, sisters and jealous girlfriends of the middle order batsmen. Village life was like that. A girl went with one man and immediately made several females her enemy.

'We could hardly be cross with you for encouraging our boys to score, now could we?' Virginia ploughed on doggedly, sweet reason dripping from her every word.

Susie remained silent.

'Speak out, slut,' Virginia lost her temper abruptly. 'We're waiting.'

Susie blushed furiously, and the air inside the village hall crackled with tension. Then the silence was shattered by the scraping of a wooden chair against the floor as the president of the WI rose majestically, and strode over to a highly polished wooden table.

'Come here, girl,' Virginia commanded, tapping her straightened forefinger dominantly down onto the wood.

Susie shrank back, but willing hands - those of Alice Sneesby and the village schoolmistress - seized and propelled her forward. Frogmarched to the edge of the table, she was forced facedown across it. Alice and the lissom schoolmistress then skirted the table, took up positions at the far corners, and grabbing the barmaid's wrists, pinned them down against the smooth wood.

The soft tread of the president's approaching brogues filled Susie with mounting dread. She writhed and twisted in an attempt to glance over her shoulder, but the hands pinioning her wrists gripped her even harder. She was helpless, face down and bottom up before the silent committee.

A shocked gasp, mixed with a murmur of delight, rose from those watching as Virginia pushed Susie's skirt up over her thighs and buttocks, arranging its pleats across her back. Her panties bared, she shivered and tightened her buttocks defensively, squeezing her thighs together to conceal her pubic plum.

'Don't be so shy, slut. If the men can see it all, then so can we, hmm?'

Susie hated the skimming fingertips lightly tracing the generous curves of her cheeks through her tight panties.

'Ah, scarlet, the colour of sin.' Virginia Emsley took a deep breath, savouring her moment of victory by dominantly fondling the proffered bottom. Then, just as slowly, she plucked the elastic waistband of the red silk panties away from the barmaid's soft warm skin. Susie's cleft, a thin, shadowy crease between her pert bottom cheeks, was gradually revealed. She jerked her hips in a vain attempt to retain her undergarment, but Virginia simply laughed and yanked them down with a flourish, her cruel eyes narrowing hungrily as they took in the uncovered flesh.

'No, please don't!' Susie wailed, grinding her belly into the table. Pinned down ruthlessly at each wrist, she abruptly sensed the horror of her absolute helplessness. Naked and bent over submissively she was in her dominant tormentor's thrall.

Virginia delayed the moment of punishment, nudging the exposed cheeks and dimpling their tender mounds, perfect twin peaches poised for impending pain.

Leaving the red panties in a tight restricting band of stretched silk just above the barmaid's knees, the president of the WI slipped a shiny red cricket ball from one of her pockets, and holding it aloft between her fingertips, showed it to the assembly. 'As your president, I propose to punish the slut.'

The committee growled with appreciative, impatient, approval.

'I propose to punish the slut until her bare bottom is as red as this cricket ball.'

Susie groaned, and her warm breath clouded the polished wood.

The committee grunted their unanimous pleasure at the prospect of severe punishment.

'It is,' Virginia went on, placing the red ball on the table, 'my painful duty. But,' she added in a whisper, gently scraping her thumbnail down the length of Susie's cleft, 'it will also be a *pleasure*.'

The ball trembled upon the dark sphere of its own reflection a few inches from Susie's eyes. It gleamed like an overly polished apple offered up at the harvest festival.

Taking her stance against the barmaid's left thigh, the president of the WI placed her left hand, palm down, on the buttock she proposed to punish. Controlling the quivering cheek to her complete satisfaction, she delivered three ringing spanks with the firm palm of her right hand.

Gasping aloud, Susie kicked her foot up and trod the empty air. Four more crisp spanks, vicious caresses of firm flesh upon soft curves, exploded across her quivering cheek. The punisher's left hand remained firmly in place throughout, squashing the punished buttock down into total surrender before smacking it again.

Susie squealed and squirmed, her rapidly reddening cheek dancing and jiggling beside the creamy unpunished orb beside it.

Massaging the girl's ravaged flesh slowly and firmly with the hand that had just tormented it, Virginia spoke in a soft but vehement tone as her audience watched, spellbound. 'The slut pleasured the batsmen with her hands and then allowed them the use of her trollop's flesh. Her behaviour was an offence to all the members of this WI and all the womenfolk of Langley Parva.' Snatching up the red cricket ball, she pressed the polished sphere in against Susie's spanked cheek. 'Capital! An almost perfect match.' The cold leather dimpled the hot curve, tearing a gasp, which melted into a moan, from the barmaid's dry lips.

The committee, many taking their strumming fingers from their pussies, clapped with loud approval.

Susie, weeping silently, stiffened against the table. Then a fresh ignominy caused her eyes to widen and her face to blaze as red as her bottom when she suddenly sensed something soft touching the knuckles of one of her clenched hands. She managed to look up, and could not believe it when she saw Alice Sneesby using the fist she was imprisoning to knuckle her fanny. Susie bucked rebelliously, crying aloud as she tried to retrieve her hand from Sneesby's pussy.

Virginia spanked her again. 'Be still and silent, slut. I've your other cheek to punish yet.' She smacked the barmaid's soft white buttock five times in quick succession.

Blinking through her tears, her face pressed down to kiss its own reflection in the highly polished wood, Susie repeatedly suffered the scalding impact of a vicious hand against her upturned rump while the committee sat in spellbound silence. Across the table Alice gripped the captive wrist fiercely, and furtively raked the barmaid's clenched hand up and down across her moist labia.

A final flurry of seven severe blows left Susie sobbing loudly, and at last the cricket ball was drawn up to kiss the blazing cheek.

Virginia sighed with profound satisfaction. 'A perfect match,' she judged, setting the red ball back on the table. Then she knelt down, rubbing the radiant palms of her hands together. Her face a mere few inches from the bare bottom she had just spanked, she gazed at it almost tenderly. Then she turned her face upwards and delivered a terse lecture on the merits of modesty and maidenhood to the whimpering barmaid while the committee nodded approvingly.

Finally the president of the WI fell silent and chairs began creaking uneasily, but unperturbed by the signals of growing impatience in the village hall, Virginia continued to gaze steadily at the spanked bottom. She licked her lips twice, and swallowed hard. Her eyes became narrow slits of fierce fascination. Susie's buttocks dimpled as she squeezed them self consciously, and Virginia's hand rose to rest lightly across the upper curves of the proffered cheeks. She tenderly thumbed the bottom she had just beaten, and then, shuffling closer on her knees against her victim's thigh, she pinched a finger and thumb full of punished flesh and twisted. Susie yelped.

'Silence,' Virginia commanded.

The barmaid began sobbing quietly again, and as their president stood up, steadying herself briefly against the table, the committee stirred and sat up expectantly. Enthralled, they gazed at the scene in unblinking silence.

'You may think my punishment of the slut a trifle harsh,' Virginia began. 'She did, after all, in her own sordid way, try to secure honour and victory for Langley Parva.'

Susie's mind seized on the words, and she dared to hope full penance had been paid and that her pain and humiliation were over. But as her tormentor continued speaking, her hope vanished.

'But the truth is that this barmaid, I am reluctant to say, with her own hands

40

brought dishonour and defeat to the village.' Launching into a scathing tirade, Virginia Emsley explained how Susie's debauchery had unwittingly exhausted the batsmen, sending them spent and useless in to bowl and field. The outraged aunts, furious sisters and speechless girlfriends of the middle-order batsmen gave full verbal vent to their fury. Baying for vengeance, they rose in unison and pressed forward, encircling Susie's bare buttocks.

Virginia Emsley held up her hand. 'Be seated,' she ordered sternly. 'This is a formal committee meeting of the Langley Parva WI Ladies. Pray be seated.'

They obeyed her, muttering angrily.

'Yes, dishonour, for which she has been chastised, but defeat, as well. In rewarding the batsmen, she ruined them. Greg missed four chances behind the wicket. The slut handed Selston the County Cup,' Virginia concluded, and then added in a feral whisper, 'which is why she has still to suffer our wrath.'

As the full magnitude of the barmaid's crimes - and their consequences - dawned upon the outraged committee members, their president knelt once more, and producing them from her pocket, unfurled her dog leads. The first was carefully threaded around, and then between, Susie's ankles, drawing and binding them tightly together. Her flesh whitened where the stern leather bit deep. The second dog lead was secured around her trembling thighs a couple of inches below the spanked buttocks, and the crimsoned cheeks bulged invitingly above the restricting band of hide.

'Miss Inchtipp,' Virginia said, calling over her shoulder to the verger's sister. 'Did you remember?'

'Oh yes,' Miss Inchtipp replied. 'I plucked them from my raspberry bushes.'

'One apiece, if you will.'

Excitedly, the verger's sister distributed yellow whippy canes to the eagerly outstretched hands of the committee. Virginia, accepting and closely examining her bamboo rod, placed it on the table. Susie, glimpsing the eighteen inches of cruel wood through tear-spangled eyelashes, jerked and wriggled violently. The cane rattled eerily as it was jolted and rolled towards her, coming to rest teasingly against her lips.

Miss Inchtipp had miscalculated, leaving herself without a cane, so improvising she started to unbuckle a vicious looking belt.

'Miss Inchtipp, would you be good enough to sit at the piano?' Virginia requested firmly. 'Play for us during the slut's whipping. Something spirited, I think. She is certain to be loud. *Jerusalem, fortissimo*.'

The verger's sister sat at the upright and fingered the bass notes powerfully. As the village hall echoed to the stirring tune, the WI committee rose and approached the terrified barmaid bent across the table. It was an orderly if impatient line as they shouldered their quivering canes and awaited the signal for the chastisement to commence.

Virginia Emsley snatched up her cane. Thrumming it twice down, practice strokes to test the suppleness of her whippy wood, she remarked almost casually to Alice and the schoolmistress, 'Hold her tight, girls. Very tight.'

Alice nodded vigorously, lust flashing in her eyes. The air around the table was heavy with the musk, with the raw scent, of female arousal.

The cane glinted as it sliced down, and Susie shuddered as her bare bottom received the stripe. 'There, I've opened the scoring. One stroke apiece to redress the dishonour,' the president instructed the assembly.

With the piano thundering out *Jerusalem*, the brigade of cane-wielding matrons and young women stepped up one by one.

Swish, whack! Swish, whack!

Pinned and helpless against the table the barmaid begged for mercy, but the piano drowned her pleas beneath its majestic swell of notes.

Swish, whack! Swish, whack!

The whippy wood hissed, cane by flashing cane, lashing down to slice the red striped buttocks below.

Swish, whack! Swish, whack!

A fifth, and then a sixth crisp cut kissed the naked cheeks, decorating their round curves with searing stripes; thin red welts that gradually turned a pale purple shade of intense suffering.

Standing beside the cane striped buttocks, the president nodded her satisfaction as each member of the committee stepped up to ply the bamboo. The final blow, delivered by Terry's mortified aunt, caused Susie to scream, a rising A-sharp note that beat Miss Inchtipp's efforts at the piano.

After each outraged committee member had administered a stroke apiece across the barmaid's bare bottom, they stood in a semi circle, panting slightly and nursing their canes affectionately. Two verses of *Jerusalem* were sung with gusto, Virginia Emsley joining in.

'No, please do not sit down,' the president urged. 'Keep playing, Miss Inchtipp, you are quite splendid at the keyboard.' She turned and once more knelt at Susie's bamboo striped bottom. Lingeringly, her face a warm breath away, she inspected the severely whipped cheeks, then briefly, for a fleeting second, she appeared to lurch forward accidentally and press her stern face into the warmth of those punished cheeks. Then kissing each one openly and mockingly, she stood up. Clapping her hands she attempted to speak, but Miss Inchtipp, in a rapture of her own, ground her heavy buttocks into the leather seat of the piano stool and hammered out *Jerusalem* until the rafters nearly shook.

At last an eerie silence settled over the hall, which was broken only by the snuffling sobs of the beaten barmaid.

Virginia plucked up her thin bamboo cane and tap tapped the upturned cheeks. 'Like Langley Parva, I am afraid your efforts with the wood must be bettered, girls. Insufficient stripes scored.' She flashed her audience a smile, and the committee, as they always did, laughed dutifully. 'You have, with your canes, avenged the dishonour, but not the defeat.' All assembled nodded. 'So now, like our team last Sunday, we are obliged to follow on. Two strokes apiece, please.'

As before Virginia opened the scoring, delivering two vicious cuts with her cruel cane. Susie grunted, dulling the wood's sheen with the warmth of her anguish, which had only just begun.

La Via Inglesa

Nine centimetre spiked heels. Katie waggled her bare bottom. Perched on the high-heels, her rounded cheeks were thrust out, proud and pert. The heels also straightened the curve of her sinuous spine, drawing her shoulders back and causing her breasts to lift deliciously. She glanced down at their budding warmth. Not much of a cleavage, not yet, but then she was only twenty years old.

The shower next door was turned off. Peeping anxiously over her shoulder in case Charlotte caught her vainly preening before the ornate looking glass, Katie staggered slightly, spreading her arms out to regain her teetering balance. She drew her thighs together, bunching her soft buttocks.

The sandals were definitely too much, the softest goatskin dyed an outrageous shade of parboiled lobster. And they had cost three hundred pounds. Charlotte had absolutely forbidden the extravagance, but Katie slipped the leash, returned to the exclusive shop in Milan's *Via Montenapoleone* and bought them. She could have purchased more sensible silver mules for less than half the price, and she bit her lip now gazing down at the outrageous pink high-heels. She had better hide them until they got back to London. If Charlotte found out about them she would administer a severe spanking that would leave Katie's bottom rosier than the sandals prompting the punishment.

She sighed. It was warm and humid. It had rained in Milan for the first three days of their holiday, but here in Naples - *Napoli*, she corrected herself, frowning, determined to improve her Italian - it was *molto amido*. She liked the word *amido*, which meant moist and warm. Bending her right knee and bringing the soft goatskin shoe up to kiss her naked bottom, she reached down and tugged it off. Grasping the supple sole she brought the tip of the slender spiked heel to her pubic nest. Probing delicately, she teased her sticky labia apart. Her shiny flesh was a shade darker than the heel probing it, and she sensed the heat at her damp slit. *Amido, molto amido.* She closed her violet eyes and imagined the feel of the other spiked heel sliding up between her cheeks. Her buttocks clenched and her anus shrivelled in delicious dread.

'Better try the *Museo del Mare* this afternoon,' Charlotte announced, entering the bedroom from the bathroom clutching a large white towel to her wet hair.

Startled, Katie opened her eyes, which darkened to indigo with fear. Briskly stepping out of her other pink sandal she snatched them together at her bottom and, blushing slightly, turned to face the older woman. Her dominant lover.

Charlotte, now sitting on the edge of the bed in a black bustier and sheer black denier stockings, angled her elbows and fixed the towel, turban like, on her head. Her large breasts rose, threatening to spill out of the bodice's constricting cups. As her fingers tucked in the towel she languorously drew her legs together and crossed them. The sheer denier whispered as her slender thighs kissed and caressed each other.

'The *Museo del Mare?*' Katie repeated, suppressing her panic.

Charlotte nodded. The towel threatened to topple, but capable fingers pinned it sternly back into place. She glanced across at the reflection in the ornate looking glass, and her brown eyes narrowed suspiciously as they spotted nervous fingers twisting around pink sandals in the glass... pink sandals pressed up against naked peach coloured cheeks in a pathetic attempt to conceal them. She stretched her left foot out, arching toes sheathed in glossy black. She studied them carefully, twisting her foot slightly.

Katie relaxed somewhat. Opening her legs, she planted her feet apart.

Adjusting her towel again, Charlotte glanced into the looking glass. Her full red lips tightened imperceptibly as she saw the supple soles tap tapping silently against the naked girl's widening cleft. 'It's going to be hot tomorrow,' she remarked. 'Sweltering. We'll stick to the beach.' Her tone was casual, almost bored.

Katie tried to judge how many steps it was to the bathroom. She could temporarily stash the sandals in there out of sight. 'Hot tomorrow?' she echoed, feigning interest.

'In July and August,' Charlotte murmured, thumbing her bustier to ease the bulge of her swelling breasts, 'the butcher's shops here in Naples—'

'*Gli mascellerias*,' Katie translated to herself automatically.

'Are forbidden by law to sell pork.'

'No chops, then.'

'And every night after sunset the mosquito swarms—'

'Mosquito, *zanzara*,' Katie said as she inched towards the open bathroom door.

'*Tu parli italiano molto bene*,' Charlotte complimented her.

'*Grazie*, but,' Katie simpered, 'I'll never be as good as you are.'

'And,' Charlotte purred dangerously, tossing her towel aside, 'do you lie well in Italian, too?'

Katie froze while at her bare bottom the sandals dangled from her anxious fingers.

'I saw you in Milan in the *trattoria* by the railway station. She had scarlet nails and was old enough to be your—'

'No, that was nothing,' Katie protested. 'I swear!' And it *had* come to nothing. The beautiful red nailed matron in the yellow dress had simply crushed a brown sugar cube into Katie's milky espresso. No words had passed between them, only a mutual longing.

'She gave you a little present, hmm?' Charlotte, thoroughly enjoying herself, teased sadistically. 'Gloves, perhaps? No, let me see... a handbag, perhaps?'

'We didn't speak,' Katie whispered. 'I swear, we—'

Three smart taps at the double doors silenced her. They opened slightly and a musical female voice enquired, '*Permesso?*'

'*Avanti*,' Charlotte drawled.

A deliciously lovely maid uniformed in the lemon-and-cream tunic and apron of the *Hotel Amalfi* staff entered the room, and paused to adjust the little white cap perched precariously on a riot of dark, glossy curls. Then she went perfectly still when she saw Katie standing before the bed utterly naked. '*Mi scusi, signorina*,' she gasped, crushing the fresh white towels against her bosom.

'*Avanti, avanti*,' Charlotte beckoned.

Still clutching the pink sandals behind her in a desperate bid to conceal them, Katie could not modestly cover her breasts or pubic mound, and the maid eyed them both appreciatively as she walked deeper into the room. Disappearing into the bathroom she deposited the fresh towels, collected used ones from the rush basket, and curtsied briefly before departing.

'Stay exactly where you are,' Charlotte said sternly, detaining Katie's surreptitious progress to the bathroom, 'where I can keep an eye on you. You need watching, my girl.'

Katie twisted around, the sandals still pressed up against her bare bottom.

'No,' Charlotte said more loudly, 'she would *not* give you a handbag. It would, I think, have been a more sentimental gift, like a pair of shoes.'

'No, believe me, she—'

'Yes,' Charlotte nodded decisively, 'an extravagant present, like those impossible pink sandals I forbade you to buy when we were window shopping along the *Via Montenapoleone.*'

Katie bowed her head, blushing. Shuffling forward, she knelt at the black nylon-clad feet of her stern mistress and reluctantly produced the pink heels, offering them up in submissive surrender. 'I bought them,' she murmured. 'I swear I bought them. I can show you the receipt.'

'You bought them, you say?' Charlotte luxuriated in the delicious drama of dominance and contrition about to be enacted, pausing to savour the power she wielded over the submissive naked girl at her feet. 'You *bought* them?'

The blonde head nodded twice.

'In spite of my strict instruction not to do so?'

Katie shivered apprehensively.

'And you can prove it? You can provide me with a receipt?'

Katie nodded again, carefully avoiding Charlotte's penetrating stare.

'Fetch my hairbrush and my hand cream, bitch.'

Katie attempted to rise.

'On your knees and crawl,' Charlotte whispered venomously. 'I said *crawl.*' The brown eyes, flecked with cruel golden lights, followed the soft buttocks as Katie set the shoes down and crawled on all fours across the carpet towards the antique wooden dressing table. She collected her mistress's large hairbrush, along with a tube of expensive unscented hand cream, and then crawled back towards the bed. It was a short but painful journey. Gripping the brush between her teeth, she hobbled back on two knees and one hand, her left clutching the tube of cream. She slipped once, crushing her breasts and grazing her nipples against the carpet. At the bed again at last she lowered her head and placed the hairbrush at the feet of her dominant lover.

'It would have been the strap, bitch,' Charlotte remarked briskly as she scooped up the brush and vigorously tackled her damp hair with it. 'The strap,' she hissed, 'if that red nailed whore in Milan had so much as touched you.'

'No, no, it was perfectly innocent,' Katie whimpered.

'Innocent?' the older woman repeated harshly. 'Nothing is ever innocent with you, my girl. Quite a little string of *innocent* infidelities behind you already, haven't you? I thought we had left all that flirting behind us in London. No, as I say,' she continued suavely, 'it would have been the strap for you, but as you merely ignored my instruction not to buy the pink sandals, we will be quite content with a severe spanking.'

'But—'

'Across my knee, bitch. You have a painful lesson to learn and I am perfectly prepared to teach you.'

'I'm so sorry!' Katie blurted. 'I *will* obey you from now on. I'll do everything you say, I promise!'

'Promises made under the threat of pain and punishment are easily made, bitch. I intend to make sure you keep them.'

'I will, I swear, please believe—'

'I believe in discipline.'

'I won't spend another *lira*, not a single *lira*, I swear.'

'You will certainly have to exercise more discipline, as must I. On your feet.'

Brushing aside the abandoned pink sandals, Katie inched closer to the bed, her naked breasts bouncing softly. A black shiny foot flashed out, arresting her progress. The toes whitened within the dark stockings as they pressed into Katie's left breast, the sole of the foot pushing dominantly and flattening the bulging flesh. The kneeling girl gasped as the foot ground into her suffering orb, rasping the nipple painfully.

'Knees apart,' came the crisp command, and the bed squeaked softly as the woman sitting on it shifted her weight.

Watching the smooth back of the hairbrush tap tapping the open palm of her punisher, Katie obeyed, inching her thighs wider, and then wider still. Her labia peeled apart and she felt her clitoral hood stretch.

'Funny how you're prompt to obey when your bottom is bare,' Charlotte chuckled darkly, tossing the hairbrush down on the bed and squirting some hand cream onto her palm as she brought her toes down to rest in the blonde fluff of Katie's pubic bush. The shiny black nylon crackled slightly as it nuzzled the girl's fuzz and slid between her parted thighs. 'No,' she warned as Katie inched her thighs together in an effort to trap and tame the instep at her slit. 'Open up, bitch.'

'Please, Charlotte, don't,' she whimpered, and began to cry.

'Save your tears until they're needed, and they will be shortly, I can promise you that.'

She snuffled, wiping her eyes with the back of her hand.

'You must be disciplined, my girl. In a little while I am going to put you over my knee and spank your bare bottom with the hairbrush, understand?'

Katie's tear-spangled eyelashes brushed her cheeks and her sulky mouth kept a sullen silence.

'Do you understand?' Charlotte demanded quietly.

'Mmm.'

'It's high time you were severely punished, Katie.'

The naked blonde flickered her sorrowful gaze up to meet her chastiser's stern regard.

'Flirting like that in Milan. How many times must you be told? If you want to belong to me, my girl, it's time you began to tow the line.' She raised her foot slightly, studying the wet sheen on her stocking. 'Why, I do believe my sweet little bitch,' she murmured approvingly, bending down to briefly finger the damp patch, 'that you are almost as pleased by the prospect of your punishment as I am.'

Katie, closing her eyes, moaned a soft denial.

'Up with you, come along, I want you across my knee.'

Slowly, with awkward reluctance, the girl rose and obediently bent over the waiting black nylon-clad thighs. A firm hand, the fingers still slightly sticky from the hand cream, alighted at the nape of her neck. She squirmed, snuggling down across the soft warmth of her mistress's legs.

'Over a little more.' The controlling hand at the nape of her pinioned neck propelled Katie the required angle across her lap, and she sighed as her breasts spilled down and Charlotte's free hand came to rest, the knuckles turned inwards, upon her buttocks. Then the velvety palm moist with hand cream turned to cup and squeeze each ripe, upturned cheek with a sure grip. Her captive flesh suffering sweetly, Katie cried out softly as a dominant thumb tip ravaged her yawning cleft.

Two polite taps sounded at the double doors again.

The thumb tip tapped three times in sharp succession at Katie's tight little sphincter.

The double doors opened a fraction, as did the anal rosebud, in response to Charlotte's, '*Avanti!*'

'*Mi scusi,*' the pretty little maid said breathlessly, her eyes widening in shock even as they glimmered with delight.

'*Avanti,*' Charlotte beckoned imperiously. 'Put it down there, *per favore.*'

Blushing as she stumbled in a dizzy confusion of voyeuristic pleasure at the sight of the bare-bottomed girl bent across the knees of the stern English signorina, the young maid carefully deposited a silver tray bearing two glasses and an uncorked bottle of Chianti on a nearby table.

Charlotte briefly inspected the label for the little black cockerel - the DOM seal of excellence - nodded her approval and gestured to the girl to pour.

Uncertainly, shyly peeping down, and then quickly averting her gaze from Katie's naked bottom, the uniformed domestic carefully poured out a brimming glassful. As the dark, purplish wine filled the sparkling glass, the silver etched insignia of the Hotel *Amalfi* grew visible - a leaping swordfish.

Charlotte looked closely, and saw there were in fact two sleek creatures cresting the waves in tight formation. '*Due, per favore,*' she smiled, absently caressing the naked buttocks lying across her black thighs.

Katie blushed furiously as she squirmed beneath the pretty maid's open mouthed gaze.

'*Grazie,*' Charlotte nodded.

'*Signorina.*' The maid bowed gracefully, her nervous fingers clutching the Chianti bottle tightly.

'She has been very naughty.' Charlotte lightly spanked Katie's bare buttocks and the taut cheeks quivered under her palm. 'Wicked. *Molta cattiva.*'

The maid pressed the Chianti bottle against her bosom.

'*Molta cattiva.* You understand?'

The pretty young woman blinked and nodded vigorously, trying desperately, but failing, to drag her wide dark eyes from Katie's pink cheeks.

'I am going to punish her the English way,' Charlotte announced casually. 'And the English way to punish a naughty female is to spank her bare bottom. Spank her bare bottom severely.' She reached out to put down the glass she had just drained and to pick up the second one.

Mincingly slipping one white pump behind the other, the Italian began retreating towards the double doors.

'What is your name, my dear?'

'Elisabetta,' she whispered.

'Elisabetta,' Charlotte repeated, savouring the syllables in her mouth just as she had savoured the dark Chianti. 'And are you a good girl, Elisabetta?'

Elisabetta gazed at Charlotte's wine wet lips as if mesmerised. 'Ah, *si, signorina*, always I am the good girl.'

'Always? Surely not. Life would be too dull, no?'

Elisabetta fiddled with the scalloped trim of her apron.

'And when you are naughty, Elisabetta, how are you punished? What is the Italian way, hmm? *La via Italiana?*'

Elisabetta blushed becomingly and her soft little bottom bumped against the door as her hand scrabbled frantically for the golden handle. Then with a shy, '*Mi scusi!*' she disappeared and the doors clicked closed behind her again.

Crack! Crack! The sharp sounds of savage discipline, of the back of a hairbrush swatting against soft buttocks, were slightly muffled by the doors at which Elisabetta knelt, listening. She closed her eyes tightly as she imagined the scene in the room she had just left.

Crack! Crack! Again the savage blows rang out and Elisabetta's dark nipples thickened, straining painfully as they grazed the cotton cups of her black lace bra. *Crack! Crack!*

The stern older woman, the punisher, was *la zia*, and the beautiful young blonde being beaten was *la ragazza*. That was what they called the English couple down in the hot kitchens of the *Hotel Amalfi. La zia*, with cruel red lips, lips wet with wine now and pursed in concentration. Elisabetta recalled the swollen breasts swelling half out of the tight black bustier, and moaned softly. She recalled the long, slender legs sheathed in black nylon and the bare-bottomed blonde, the pretty little *ragazza*, lying across the shimmering black thighs.

Crack! Crack! Elisabetta removed her frilly apron, and after unzipping her skirt with trembling hands, she eased the lemon-coloured cloth up over her hips.

Crack! Crack! She shook her tumble of black curls away from her face and placed her warm ear to the door.

Crack! Crack! And then the sound of an anguished sob followed by a squeal of protest from *la ragazza*. Elisabetta was listening to the punishment of a naughty female the English way, and between her plump bottom cheeks, parted where they nestled against her pumps, her cleft ached sweetly.

Crack! Crack! Her ear pressed against the door, eager for the sound of the vicious hairbrush stinging the bare buttocks helplessly exposed to it, the maid fingered her wet pussy frantically through her moist cotton panties.

Crack! Crack! The *ragazza* was sobbing openly now, no doubt squirming and writhing under the cruel brush as Elisabetta tongued the door hungrily, sensuously lapping the glossy paintwork. In her mind, behind her tightly closed eyes, she was licking the back of the warm hairbrush and then tonguing the hot curves of the blazing red buttocks.

Crack! Crack! Elisabetta drove a finger, swiftly followed by a second, into her wet heat. Adding a third digit she climaxed, shuddering in the throes of an intense, silent orgasm, after which she collapsed, spent and helpless, against the doors.

Charlotte walked straight past the large green glass tank while Katie stopped to stare into it. Within the sealed unit a delicate little seahorse floated, suspended in eternal silence. She reached out and tapped the glass. The exquisite little creature seemed to wink its orange eye before spindling slowly around. She screamed softly as she watched it turn. It had been spliced cleanly in half, split from the tip of its nose to the flourish of its curled tail. She stepped back, horrified, as the creamy-white exposed skeleton twisted into view.

'*Signorina?*' a smartly uniformed female attendant raised a concerned eyebrow. 'A glass of water?'

She nodded faintly and staggered backwards into an empty leather chair. Seconds later the *Museo del Mare* guard was kneeling by her side offering her a glass of iced water, and nimble gloved fingers quickly unbuttoned her silk blouse. Then the attendant bit away her right glove, leaving it dangling from clenched teeth, and Katie murmured softly as she felt the touch of cool knuckles dimpling the soft swell of her exposed breast. The hand turned, and the firm palm cupped and squeezed her tender orb soothingly.

'Leave her to me,' Charlotte snapped, advancing menacingly across the polished marble floor in a staccato of quickening footsteps.

The guard shrugged, pouting sulkily, and slipped her hand out of Katie's unbuttoned blouse. '*La signorina* is unwell.'

'Nothing the matter with her,' Charlotte growled. 'And should there be, I have a sure and certain cure.'

That night, a little before nine o'clock, they left the hotel and strolled through the warmth of the gathering dusk to the *Ristorante del Pesce.*

'Criminal not to eat fish when in Napoli,' Charlotte remarked briskly. She was always cheerful after a session of punishment. 'Let's see what this one has to offer.'

Thigh-to-thigh and hand-in-hand, *gli paia Inglesi* scanned the menu cards posted outside the glass doors.

'*Triglia rossa,*' Katie enthused, executing an excited little dance, and the sudden display of unsophisticated eagerness pleased Charlotte immensely, making her feel completely in control.

'Red mullet, is it?' she said. 'I dare say they'll do a decent mullet in fennel sauce for you here.'

The restaurant was thronged, and they were surprised to see Elisabetta, now in the regulation black and white uniform of a waitress, weaving through the crowded tables towards them.

Katie reddened, and her eyes cast down, she whispered her order for the mullet.

'*Triglia?*' Elisabetta waved her stubby black pencil. 'No, no, *signorina*, you must have the swordfish. Very good, very fresh.'

'How fresh?' Charlotte quizzed.

'My father catch him every night.'

'Busy family, hmm? And you work here as well as at the hotel?'

'Everyone in Napoli works all the time. So many taxes.'

Which none of you ever pay, Charlotte thought to herself, and agreed to the suggestion of swordfish steaks. Elisabetta assured them of their freshness again, suggesting they have them grilled with fresh garlic and herbs.

'Sweet meat, swordfish,' Charlotte opined, and Katie, her eyes still averted, fiddled with a breadstick.

'The swordfish,' Elisabetta sighed passionately. '*Molto vero in amore*. So faithful in love. How you say it, please? Fidelity, no?'

'Yes,' Charlotte nodded, flashing a keen glance across the spotless linen tablecloth. 'Fidelity. Isn't that what we say, Katie?'

The young English girl blushed furiously and the breadstick snapped in her twisting fingers.

'Ah, si, fidelity. The swordfish is so loyal to its partner. When my father catches one, all he has to do is wait.'

'Wait?' Charlotte asked, perplexed.

Elisabetta tried not to remember kneeling at the double doors, her ear pressed against the wood, playing with herself as the stern *zia* punished the beautiful, bare-bottomed *ragazza* with the hairbrush. 'Wait,' she nodded emphatically, 'for the partner, the other swordfish. Always they swim as *una paia*. How you say? As a couple, due. When one is caught, the other swims and swims around the boat until it is dead. Then my father, he takes it from the water. They live and they die together, like Romeo and Juliet.'

Later Katie said she did not care for the garlic. It left a sour taste in her mouth.

'Sweet meat,' Charlotte pronounced, swallowing her final mouthful with relish.

The next day was very hot. They went, as planned, down to the thin strip of silver beach. Charlotte dozed, her brown eyes protected from the glare of the sun by the twin panes of her large black sunglasses. Katie, still sore from the previous afternoon's chastisement, lay tummy down across a blue towel. Cupping her chin in her hands, she thought about the last turbulent twenty-four hours. The painful discovery of the pink sandals, bitter accusations of flirting, the bare-bottomed punishment and Elisabetta, the lovely dark-haired maid witnessing her humiliation.

A statuesque German spread a silver and gold coloured towel down across the scorching sand alongside Katie's. She was slender and supple and her buttocks were deliciously tight.

Fidelity... Katie remembered the hairbrush and closed her eyes. Behind them she saw the seahorse floating in its glass tank and suddenly recalled the wave of nausea that had seized her. Then she remembered the gloved hand unbuttoning her blouse, and the warm palm cupping and squeezing her exposed breast followed by Charlotte's stern indifference, which masked a fierce jealousy. Later, Elisabetta again at the restaurant and the sour taste of garlic... Elisabetta tossing her dark, tumbling curls over her shoulder...

'*Bitte.*'

Katie turned her head and saw the bronzed German sun worshipper holding out a bottle of lotion.

'*Bitte.*'

Smiling, and then swiftly checking to make sure Charlotte was still asleep, she rolled over, wincing as the hot towel kissed her sore bottom. She collided gently against the German's sleek thigh, wearing only a tight white bikini, and the woman's eyes devoured her cleavage. Softly cupped and subtly under-wired, the swimsuit's top lifted her breasts deliciously, causing them to bulge invitingly.

Up on one elbow and accepting the proffered lotion, Katie studied the foreign beauty, who had squeezed her voluptuous breasts and fleshy buttocks into a green and gold spangled bikini with a daringly strapless bandeau top through which mulberry nipples strained, and a bottom that was a mere thong disappearing between the taut bronze cheeks.

'*Bitte*,' the woman repeated, thumbing off her top and offering her naked breasts to be oiled.

Katie shot a sly glance at Charlotte before squirting the richly scented lotion into her open palm and then wiping her hands together.

Slowly and firmly, she greased the German's full bosom, working the oil deftly into each quivering mound and teasing each budding nipple with her fingertips.

Two seagulls squabbling over a ragged piece of bread up in the blue sky screamed raucously, and caused Katie to look up in alarm. The woman arched her back up off the towel and spread her thighs a little. '*Bitte*,' she persisted.

Katie returned to the fleshy bosom, kneading and knuckling the deliciously firm yet pliant pillows of warm skin. At her pussy, a drop of arousal darkened the crotch of her white swimsuit.

The German grunted suddenly, turned over onto her belly and jerked her buttocks up. '*Bitte!*'

Straddling the sunbather's thighs between her knees, Katie rode the slender limbs of the woman beneath her. Squirting the expensive lotion lavishly over both bronzed buttocks, she tossed the bottle aside, splayed her fingers and oiled each tender cheek in turn. A daring thumb jerked the thong to one side, and she saw the dark little pinkish-brown anus wink up at her.

'*Bitte*,' the woman sighed.

Oiling the anus with a lotion coated forefinger, Katie became engrossed in her task, and shuddered as she felt the rectal muscles tighten, grip and retain her probing finger. So engrossed did she become that she ignored the renewed screaming of the squabbling seagulls overhead, and failed to notice Charlotte's brown eyes narrowing and flickering, lizard-like, as she carefully raised her sunglasses.

They never rowed in public. It was not the English way. It was not their style to make a scene. Jealous passions and the tears they provoked were always spilled behind closed doors. So Charlotte warned Katie of her awakening by exaggerated sighs and stretching, and then merely commented upon the heat before politely enquiring of the German beauty if she was staying at the Hotel *Amalfi*.

'Ja, in room three-sixteen,' came the instant reply. Busy thumbing her thong back between her oiled buttocks, she directed her answer to Katie.

'I see,' was all Charlotte said; two simple words but they frightened Katie, instantly quickening her pulse. Caught in the act, she feared the strap.

Donning an airy white cotton shirt over her swimsuit, Katie stood up, stretched and announced her intention to go for a walk. Charlotte remained silent, and the German settled into a doze.

She walked down the beach towards the waves breaking gently on the shore. As she trod the hot sand she knew Charlotte's angry eyes would be devouring the sway of her buttocks, judging their ripe roundness in readiness for the punishing strap. The thought tightened her sensually quivering cheeks, rendering the cleft between them a mere crease into which her swimsuit sank.

A gentle breeze brought the myriad smells of Naples to her nostrils. Not the aromatic mix of lemons, basil and extra virgin oil, but of open drains and uncollected refuse. Ugly smells from the hectic, heaving city huddled against the sea.

Katie shivered. Afraid of the strap awaiting her bottom she paced the sands, deserted now after sunset. She was cold. No, not cold, just afraid of her impending pain and punishment. She hugged herself and her shirt rasped against her nipples, budding within the stretchy cups of her matching white bra. The shirt's scalloped hem tickled the pert swell of her buttocks like teasing fingertips, and she shivered again. The crisp Swiss cotton had been nice in the fierce afternoon sun, but in the moonlight it afforded little warmth.

The staccato crackle of a Vespa roaring along the seafront esplanade broke into her consciousness. *Vespa*, the Italian word for wasp. The scooter's snarl faded and died off in the distance. *Vespa*. The sting of a wasp could be so painful - as painful as the sting of a leather strap. She glanced up, her anxious eyes scanning the floodlit expanse of the hotel. Up in their room was the cruel strap; the cruel length of leather awaiting her bare bottom.

The strap. Charlotte had bought it in Bonn two-and-a-half years ago on their first trip abroad as a couple. It was never used lovingly, in pleasure or in play. The tip of the strap had never been raked against her nipples or used to tease her clitoris, to tantalise and deliciously torment. The strap, Charlotte had decided, was to be used for the single and sole purpose of discipline. It was kept out of sight furled up in a yellow suede bag. She only need mention it and their bickering would suddenly cease, giving way to Katie's whimpered apologies. Charlotte need only take it out of the drawer and dangle the yellow suede bag from her fingertips, and Katie would fall to her knees mumbling apologies into the musky warmth of her mistress's pubic mound. The strap was a potent symbol of their relationship - the dominant and the submissive, the punisher and the punished.

From time to time the strap was taken out and stretched at full length. At such times Katie would peep anxiously as Charlotte thumbed vitamin E cream into the dark leather to keep it pliant - pliant and supple. Katie hated the strap. She hated its sharp bite and the burning pain across her bare buttocks as the broad pink welts it created deepened into a crimson blaze. She hated even more being arranged over her stern chastiser's lap, being pinned down dominantly, bare-bottomed and utterly helpless. She hated being bared and prepared for her punishment like a naughty schoolgirl across the knee of the gym mistress subjecting her to strict discipline. She hated the slow administration of the stinging strap across her naked cheeks; cheeks that tensed tightly at the thin whistle of the lashing leather, cheeks that flattened under the broad width of punishing hide, cheeks that wobbled slightly beneath each fresh blaze of scalding pain.

Then afterwards the humiliating ritual. 'Kiss the leather,' Charlotte would insist, and blinded by tears of shame and torment, Katie would be forced to kiss the doubled length of leather dangling before her lips. She would be forced to kiss and taste with her tongue the tang of the dead hide.

'*Signorina.*'

The velvety whisper startled Katie out of her troubled recollections. She turned and saw Elisabetta, apparently returning to the hotel after her evening stint at the *Ristorante del Pesce*.

'I always come along the beach,' the Italian explained. 'It is so beautiful, no? Look.' She pointed, stretching her arm towards the surging waves. They stood side by side, their thighs touching. Then the pert waitress curled her small hand over Katie's hip and they nestled closer. 'Look,' she cried again excitedly, 'the fishing boats! My father!'

Katie, pressing hard into the other girl's soft warmth, strained up on tiptoe. On the dark band of the horizon she could just make out tiny pin points of red, silver and green dancing lights.

'There are three boats tonight,' Elisabetta informed her proudly.

'Are they fishing for swordfish?'

Her small hand slipped down to lightly caress Katie's left buttock. 'No, tonight they fish for tuna.'

The two young women turned towards each other. For a full minute they just looked into each other's eyes, then sank slowly to their knees, their breasts bumping together gently. Then the waitress bowed her head submissively and rested it in Katie's lap. 'The tuna is not like the faithful swordfish,' she whispered.

'No?' Katie murmured, the fingers of her right hand dominantly raking through a riot of dark curls.

'The tuna, it lives for the moment, for a new love with each change of the tide. A fresh pleasure every night.'

Katie bent her head and kissed the waiting, sulky mouth with vicious tenderness. They rose up off their heels and ground their pubic mounds together, and the English girl grew more dominant, pinioning the Italian down firmly against the sand. Unbuttoning Elisabetta's uniform feverishly she sought and found the delicious breasts, exposing them to the silvery moonlight.

'Kiss them,' Elisabetta pleaded.

Katie fondled the lovely bosom savagely before pressing her parted lips at each eagerly proffered nipple and sucking hard, very hard, grunting her raw pleasure as Elisabetta wriggled like a netted tuna and squirmed her buttocks against the sand.

'I want—'

'What?' Katie teased. 'What do you desire?'

'Punish me.' She twisted her face away shyly. 'I want to be punished the English way.'

Katie felt the pulse in her throat and further down at the wet heat between her thighs. Punishment, the English way. Her mouth felt dry and her head spun with dizzy delight. Elisabetta had asked to be spanked!

The pretty little Italian's bottom was delicious. The soft peaches dimpled to the firm touch of a dominant fingertip and danced beneath Katie's caressing palms. Parting the round cheeks she watched, holding her breath, as the dark cleft deepened in the ghostly moonlight. Resting her spanking hand briefly against the obediently proffered buttocks, she ran her free hand up the spine of the supine young woman until it was buried in the dark tumble of curls at the bowed neck. Her fingers flexed around the soft nape, and then gripped tightly. Elisabetta mewed like a kitten at its cream, inching her thighs open and exposing her glistening pussy to the moonlight. Katie then let her hand sweep slowly down over the naked swell of flesh, and resting it lightly across the girl's thighs, she angled her thumb-tip in at the wet slit. The pretty little Italian wriggled impatiently, jerking her soft cheeks up in eager expectation.

'The English way,' Katie whispered.

The sharp sound of three hard smacks rang out in the moonlight, rising over the sound of the tide. Elisabetta squealed, and then nestled deeper into her punisher's lap. Katie, a little uncertainly at first, quickly thrilled to the task of punishing the bare bottom beneath her, and after six rapid blows she paused to caress the warm cheeks. The girl across her lap sighed contentedly, crooning a tuneless song beneath her breath.

'So,' a harsh voice suddenly snapped, 'this is where you are.' Charlotte's stern statement froze Katie's hand an inch away from Elisabetta's hot bottom. 'Do not disturb me when you creep back into the room. Stay out of my bed and sleep on the floor tonight, you understand?'

Avoiding eye contact with her angry mistress, Katie nodded in contrite silence.

'And,' Charlotte's voice was dangerously low, 'you will remain in the hotel tomorrow morning. I shall be going out after breakfast. I must do a little shopping, but I shall expect you ready and waiting for your punishment when I return.' Turning abruptly, she strode away into the darkness, her quickening footfalls silent upon the sand.

A little shopping... vitamin E cream for the strap. Katie shivered in dread at the prospect of the punishing hide slicing down across her naked buttocks, but unconcerned by the brief drama that ended so abruptly, Elisabetta jiggled her spanked cheeks invitingly.

'Stupid little bitch,' Katie whispered fiercely. 'I'm going to get it good and hard now, and it's all your fault.' Her hand rained down with vicious force across the girl's bottom. 'All *your* fault,' she accused, ignoring Elisabetta's cries.

Katie tiptoed around their hotel room the next morning. They did not speak. Breakfast was a wretched affair, the silence deafening.

Charlotte showered, towelled herself dry, and then went back to bed. Propping herself up on her pillows she covered her breasts with wild strawberries, spliced and iced, which arrived as instructed with the breakfast tray. It was her way of combating the effects of the Italian sun.

The treatment lasted an hour, during which time she ostentatiously read yesterday's English newspapers, holding the broadsheets aloft to deny Katie any reassuring glances. Tossing the paper aside finally, she plucked up the wild strawberries, threw them away, wiped her bosom, dressed and left the room in silence.

Once she was alone, Katie searched frantically for the yellow suede bag. Haunted by the image of the curled hide within it, she desperately sought to unearth the strap from Charlotte's hiding place. Just to hold it. Smell it. Examine it. Somehow she thought finding the strap, holding and touching it, would reduce her terror and torment. But apparently Charlotte suspected this was what Katie would do and hid it well to make sure her submissive young lover passed an anxious, troubled and ultimately fruitless hour.

Charlotte returned to the hotel carrying a curious green canvas bundle, tightly wrapped with waxed cord. She placed her purchase on the bed and instructed Katie to strip and shower. 'You know how I want you, properly washed and prepared.' These were the first words she spoke since their encounter on the beach the previous night. 'I prefer to punish a nice clean, freshly washed bottom. And you need not bother with talc or body lotion after your shower. Now hurry up.'

'No, please,' Katie mumbled, rising out of her chair. 'Please don't—'

'Into the shower at once,' Charlotte commanded curtly.

Katie sank tearfully to her knees and shuffled awkwardly towards her dominant partner. Once at her feet, she stretched her fingers out and clutched the polished shoes before her.

'That will get you nowhere,' Charlotte said impassively.

Katie crushed her breasts into the carpet as she inched towards the impassive shoes. Craning, she kissed the shiny leather. 'I'm so sorry!' she gasped. 'I truly am so sorry. And I'll never look, never touch...'

Charlotte lifted her feet one at a time, extricating them from the lips of the penitent blonde sprawled across the carpet.

'Oh Charlotte, please, not the strap. I beg you.'

'Into the shower, and if you are so averse to the taste of leather across your bare bottom, so be it. No strap.'

'No strap?' She could scarcely believe she'd heard right.

'I shall not use the strap to punish you,' Charlotte repeated patiently, and Katie practically skipped into the shower. Stripping quickly, she stepped under the hot downpour and reached for the scented shower gel.

'No gel for you.' Charlotte, similarly stripped and naked, stepped into the shower behind her and snatched the bottle from her hand. 'A brisk flannel will get you clean enough for me.' She snapped open a coarsely textured cotton flannel sponge and held it up under the water. 'Legs apart,' she barked.

'No, don't, *please*,' Katie whimpered.

'Arms out.'

Katie spread her arms obediently, pressing both hands against the pale blue tiles, and as Charlotte flicked the wet flannel up between her thighs her fingers spread out in agony. The cloth punished her exposed pussy, making her squeal in torment. Charlotte delivered a withering sermon to her victim as she next ravished her breasts with the rasping flannel, concentrating on the sensitive nipples. Katie hung her head in shame, her silence a loud acknowledgement of her guilt.

The cruel sponge, doubled up in Charlotte's avenging fist, was knuckled up savagely between Katie's parted thighs, forcing her to beg for mercy. 'I'm sorry!' she gasped. 'I love you! I love you!'

'Nobody else?' Charlotte hissed.

'Nobody else!' The penitent gulped. 'Please forgive me.'

'Forgive you?' Charlotte echoed as the punished blonde sank to her knees. 'But of course I forgive you. I always do.'

'You forgive me?' She looked up beseechingly, blinking water out of her eyes.

'Yes,' Charlotte spoke decisively, 'I forgive you.'

'And no strap?' she whispered, still scarcely able to believe it.

Charlotte squatted behind her, forcing the flannel between the wet, slippery cheeks to rake the sensitive cleft between them. Katie moaned softly as the cruel cotton was dragged across the tight path of dark velvety flesh buried between her buttocks. Then she sighed, and thinking her cruel punishment with the leather strap a danger now removed, she offered her bottom submissively.

Back in the bedroom she towelled herself dry, and on Charlotte's command donned a special item of lingerie - a seamless translucent body-liner in peachy flesh tones that clung tightly to her soft nakedness like a second skin. The fit was so severe she had to finger the suit away from where it bit lovingly into her flesh, bunching and lifting her breasts whilst sculpting the ripe swell of her buttocks. Each plump cheek wobbled as the thong cut into her cleft. Thumbing the taut crotch from her moist labia, she looked very sweet and very vulnerable in her bare feet.

Charlotte, in a slightly brooding mood, selected a clinging black tulle top. The padding at her pubis narrowed severely, rising up past her pussy to bury itself deeply between her buttocks. Cut very high at the hip, it allowed for maximum freedom of movement. She looked athletic and sinuous and very, very powerful in matching black high-heels.

The green canvas bundle remained unopened upon the bed. Katie approached it inquisitively. Bending down, her breasts bulging, she fingered the bundle. 'What is it?'

'A present,' Charlotte murmured. 'You'll see. All in good time.'

'A present? What for?'

'Just a little something to ensure we remain a couple and truly together from now on.'

Katie's fingertips stroked the canvas-wrapped bundle lingeringly, but they could make no sense of what lay concealed within.

Charlotte picked up the phone, and speaking in faultless Italian gave an order to room service. Several minutes later, three smart taps at the double doors broke the somewhat tense silence.

'*Permesso?*' Elisabetta's voice asked uncertainly.

'*Avanti,*' Charlotte replied.

Katie turned, her face suddenly pale and anxious. Remembering how she had been discovered with the maid on the beach, she blushed as Elisabetta entered the room bearing a silver tray. There were, she noticed, no glasses to accompany the bottle of exotic Italian liqueur. A thick wedge of *ciabatto* bread rolled gently across the tray as it was placed carefully down on a small cherry wood table.

'Close and lock the door, Elisabetta, *per favore,*' Charlotte requested firmly.

The maid smiled timidly, her eyes darting from Katie's body-liner, through which her blonde nest and dark nipples peeped, to Charlotte's bold, figure-hugging sheath of black tulle. 'No glasses, *signorina?*'

'Non, *grazie.*'

'I lock the door when I go, no?' the pretty maid asked.

'You lock the door, si, but then you stay.'

Katie's eyes widened anxiously, their soft violet deepening to a concerned indigo. Something, something indefinable yet palpable in Charlotte's tone, alerted her to danger. She froze like a gazelle hearing a twig snap beneath the predatory paws of a lioness.

Elisabetta remained where she was, looking beautifully puzzled.

'The door,' Charlotte insisted.

Katie shivered, but then she remembered her mistress saying there would be no strap. 'I shall not use the strap to punish you'. Those had been her very words.

After retreating to the double doors and turning the key, Elisabetta turned, approached the tray on the cherry wood table again, and stood docilely beside it.

'We are relaxing in our lingerie, Elisabetta. Why don't you do the same? Come,' Charlotte gestured, 'take off your uniform.' Her tone was one of steely politeness. Nevertheless, the maid understood it had not been an invitation, but an instruction.

'*Signorina...*' she murmured, anxiously fiddling with the hem of her apron.

'At once.'

Katie watched in awe as the lovely maid wriggled and squirmed out of her blouse, apron, skirt and stockings, and as an afterthought, kicked off her white pumps.

Charlotte padded slowly across the carpet towards the small table. Its polished surface reflected the swell of her breasts bound tightly within the stretchy black tulle as she stood above it. 'How very appropriate,' she murmured approvingly, intimately inspecting the nearly naked servant shivering slightly in her white lace bra and panties.

Elisabetta shrank slightly from the caressing knuckles of Charlotte's inverted hand. Her olive hued bosom whitened as the dominant fist firmly depressed the cupped flesh of her breasts. The snow-white bra was lightly under-wired, the exquisite cups individually formed and fashioned to capture and contain each brimming breast. And the delicate white straps bit lovingly into the pretty maid's slender shoulders.

'*Bellissima!*' Charlotte sighed, dappling her fingertips just below Elisabetta's taut belly. The panties, severely cut away to expose both sumptuous bottom cheeks, were of a matching snow-white satin, and the trembling maid's dark pubic bush rasped slightly against the lacy weave as she nervously trod the carpet. 'So pretty,' Charlotte said approvingly, her thumb-tip returning to torment a peaking nipple. The fine interweaving of the bra and high cut panties gave them a delicious, stretchy sheen, intimating the olive flesh bound within their snowy embrace was at once pliant and soft, obedient to the touch. 'Delightful,' Charlotte murmured, stroking the suspicion of a seam dividing the pubic mound and the labial lips below with an idle fingertip. 'Take them down for me, if you please.'

Elisabetta stepped back, her dark eyes widening as they filled with wonder. Then suddenly tossing her head back impetuously, she quickly palmed her panties down to her thighs. The stretchy fabric drew her slender legs together, binding them tightly above her knees.

Charlotte smiled, nodding her satisfaction with the maid's prompt submission to her stern command. 'What a beautiful bush, my dear,' she remarked, taking a finger and thumb full of the tightly coiled fuzz and teasing it out with delicate dominance.

Elisabetta, her toes digging into the carpet, inched forward a fraction. Bound at her lower thighs by the restraining stretch of her panties, she stumbled and bump kissed her pussy against Charlotte's levelled fist. As her pubis collided with the gently clenched knuckles, her fleshy bottom cheeks wobbled.

Katie moaned a low, jealous note. Charlotte's brown eyes narrowed, but ignoring the blonde, she gazed directly at the dark-haired girl's bosom. 'Such exquisite breasts, Elisabetta. Show me.'

But before the maid could obediently slip away the white straps to bare her breasts, Charlotte, still rhythmically knuckling the exposed pussy, buried her face down between the cups. She kissed the satin tenderly over each soft mound before sucking both nipples fiercely, and when, some minutes later, her mistress's head rose from the maid's cleavage, Katie glimpsed the darkening wet stains left by the cruel lips at the snow-white cups. 'Noooo!' Her sharp protest rose to a shrill whine.

'So?' Charlotte hissed, spinning round. 'Now you feel the pain of jealousy, the pang of betrayal? Now the hurt begins to make *you* moan?'

Katie shook her head. She did not speak, but remained sullenly silent.

'Oh, but you *do* feel the pain, don't you?' Charlotte insisted.

Katie, bowing her head, blushed and nodded.

'Here in Naples they use the same word for fishing and flirting.'

Elisabetta agreed. 'Si, *signorina*, it is exactly as you say. To fish is the same as to flirt.'

Charlotte, now at the bedside, scooped up the green canvas bundle and plucked open the wax cords binding it. To Katie's utter surprise, the green canvas disgorged four pieces of a fishing rod - four lengths of whippy cane, a reel and an unruly ball of fishing line. Each segment of the rod was delicately tapered. The thickest section, which held the reel, had a cork handle and narrowed to a hexagon approximately six centimetres in diameter. The whole thing was varnished, giving the yellow whippy wood an evil sparkle.

Charlotte selected, tested and discarded the first three segments of the rod, but when her fingers curled around the most slender, supple length, they tightened. Then she crossed to a door of the large fitted wardrobe, and opened it. A brass hook, for bathrobes or some such garment, was affixed to the white door. 'Come here,' she commanded, and Katie moved meekly forward. 'No, face me.' Katie turned and pressed her back and bottom against the inside of the open door.

When satisfied, Charlotte returned to the bed, picked up the fishing line and bit off a short length. Then returning to her submissive victim, she ordered Katie to present her hands together at breast height. The fishing line quickly bound her thumbs, reddening them as it bit gently into the flesh, and then forcing the bound thumbs up, Charlotte used the hook to pin them to the door above her wriggling captive's blonde head. 'Fishing, like flirting,' she said ominously, 'is a pleasure that brings pain. There is to be no more. No more fishing. Do you understand me?'

'You said you would not punish me,' Katie protested.

'No, I didn't. What I said was that I would not use the strap to punish you. Try to pay attention. You really must listen to what I say, my girl.'

'But that's not fair,' Katie protested again.

'Not the strap,' Charlotte confirmed. 'No, I have chosen something far more appropriate to beat you with, my dear Katie. No fishing. No flirting. I think once I have finished with you, you will remember that.'

'No, please,' Katie begged, writhing in her simple but devastatingly effective bondage.

'Bring me the *ciabatto*,' Charlotte ordered, and Elisabetta pulled up her panties and brought the hunk of bread as instructed.

Charlotte took it, pulled it apart into equal halves, and unceremoniously forced each piece into the two girls' mouths. Katie petulantly tried to spit it out.

'No, don't you dare do that,' Charlotte warned. 'Bite into it; it will silence your screams.' Elisabetta's fingers fluttered up to her lips, but the tip of the cane flashed and swept them away. 'No, *bambina*, you too must bite hard.'

Above the bread stuffed obscenely into her mouth, Katie's eyes widened as they filled with trepidation, but Elisabetta snatched the *ciabatto* out of her mouth and darted towards the locked door of the apartment.

'Come back here at once,' Charlotte commanded ominously.

'No, *signorina, per favore*,' she begged breathlessly.

'Bite the bread.'

Elisabetta remained standing uncertainly before the locked door.

'Do as I say, or I will make you wish you had never been born, *bambina*,' Charlotte threatened, and then smiled cruelly as the maid faltered, and then retrieved the chunk of bread and awkwardly pressed it between her lips.

'Now bend over. At once.'

Hugging her bra-encased breasts, Elisabetta obediently bent, her dark tangle of curls curtaining her tear-filled eyes. Charlotte flexed the thin bamboo cane and tapped the taut buttocks twice. Elisabetta dropped her hands from her breasts. One cupped her pussy while the other drifted to her bottom in a pathetic attempt to protect it from the terrifying tap tap of the cane.

Charlotte swept the fingers away, ordered the maid to touch her toes, and then lashed the proffered bottom eight times in swift succession.

Elisabetta squealed through the *ciabatto* and stumbled forward two paces after the fifth stroke. She let the bread drop from her mouth after the seventh blow, and squealed breathlessly as the final swipe sliced viciously down across her poor buttocks.

Then running the length of bamboo through the tangle of tumbling curls, Charlotte stood supremely triumphant above the sobbing girl, and angling the tip of the quivering cane under her chin, she forced her to raise her head obediently.

Bound and helpless against the door, her stretched arms twisting as they hung from the hook above, Katie writhed in an ecstasy of anguish as she watched, wide-eyed and fearful, as Charlotte discarded the cane and knelt beside the sobbing maid. She peeled Elisabetta's panties down, and eight pale pink cane strokes were slowly revealed as the lacy material slipped away from the whipped cheeks - eight cane stripes gradually deepening into livid lines of crimson pain. Rolling the delicate garment all the way down the girl's slender legs, Charlotte pressed her face against her exposed bottom.

Grinding her bottom against the unyielding wood behind them, twisting helplessly in her bondage, Katie was forced to watch as her mistress lingeringly licked each cruel weal, tonguing the whipped cheeks of the weeping maid in a delicious display of tenderness.

Gradually Elisabetta ceased sobbing and inclined her scalded buttocks to her chastiser's mouth. Suddenly gripped by the erotic alchemy that transforms pain into pleasure, she mewed as Charlotte's firm tongue continued to lap at her reddening welts, and then began moving up and down the dark crease between her severely caned bottom cheeks.

Blinded by her searing jealousy as much as by the tears it prompted, Katie writhed in her bondage. Slumping back against the door she sobbed and nearly gagged on the hunk of *ciabatto* wedged between her clenched teeth, soaking up the saltiness of her meandering tears.

Charlotte turned her head, and gently rested her chin on the maid's reddened buttocks. 'Excellent,' she murmured, noting Katie's anguish. 'It is so important you feel the pain of jealousy, too.'

Katie, impotent in her bondage, sobbed breathlessly, and Charlotte's eyes narrowed as they scrutinised her sub's misery. 'And after the pain of jealousy, you will experience the pain of my cane.' Rising and leaving Elisabetta, who promptly slumped wearily and curled up on the carpet, hugging herself and moaning beneath her breath, Charlotte approached the young blonde pinioned to the door.

As the menacing punisher neared, Katie jerked with renewed apprehension in her helplessness.

Charlotte plucked something from the package on the bed - something small and sharp that glinted between her fingers.

It flashed as she swept her hand up, and Katie had just enough time to make out the silver fishhook and cower slightly before it sparkled and looped towards her breasts.

There was a brief but brutal sound of torn fabric, and the taut stretch of her bodysuit shrivelled away as the hook glanced and ripped, leaving both her breasts utterly naked and vulnerable. As they spilled out, bouncing gently, Charlotte retreated to scoop up the length of whippy cane. Gripping it firmly, she advanced once more upon her squirming victim.

'Punishment, Elisabetta, the English way. Observe.'

The maid, whimpering, pushed herself up onto her knees and turned to face the bare-breasted blonde, in bondage against the wardrobe door.

'*La via Inglesa*,' Charlotte whispered sinisterly, and the bamboo also whispered sinisterly as it sliced through the air into the exposed breasts, just above the nipples, three times in swift succession.

Katie's feet threshed as she wailed into the *ciabatto* gagging her.

Charlotte aimed the cane down, planting the next three vicious strokes across Katie's upper thighs. Each slice bit deeply into her soft flesh, leaving livid welts visible through the nearly transparent bodysuit. 'The English way,' she murmured, and on the carpet behind her, Elisabetta covered her face and moaned into her cupped hands.

'Compose yourself, my dear,' Charlotte told her, 'and get up.'

The maid scrambled to her feet.

'Take it,' Charlotte ordered, and Elisabetta, her fingers trembling, accepted the length of supple bamboo.

'A dozen strokes to commence with... yes, we will open the account with a crisp twelve cuts,' Charlotte pronounced, and turned Katie to face the door. 'Now begin.'

Elisabetta raised the cane, paused a moment, and then whipped the beautiful buttocks before her. A thin red weal instantly appeared on Katie's cheeks, attesting to the ferocity of the kiss bequeathed by the cane.

'As hard as you can, Elisabetta,' Charlotte urged quietly. 'You must understand; no mercy can be shown when punishing a female with a cane the English way. No mercy whatsoever.'

GRADUATION DAY

Ariadne Soames Ayr frowned. Squirming her bottom on the leather seat of the mahogany chair outside the dean's office, she snatched a fifth impatient glimpse at her watch. Her breasts rose and fell as she sighed aloud, their swell rippling the sensuous silk of her clinging blouse.

Three-thirty. What could the dean possibly want with her? Tomorrow was graduation day and there was still so much to be done; fresh panties and stockings to select and a final steam ironing of her black graduation gown. It was going to be a scorcher tomorrow. She wondered if she could risk just a black, demi cup bra, a thong, a garter belt and black seamed stockings under the flowing gown. She shivered with mischievous anticipation at the thought of the cool gown rasping her nipples and tickling her stocking-clad thighs. She would glide up to the podium and receive her degree in delicious near nakedness before the assembly. She squeezed her bottom cheeks together imagining the thong biting into her moist cleft as she stood before the bishop and the sheriff of the county. She grimaced at the thought of her family, who would also be there, arriving in the Volvo, her father undoubtedly fussing about parking and her mother proudly tearful in a ridiculous hat. And her aunt...

Ariadne blushed, and beneath her wriggling buttocks the leather squeaked softly. Her aunt... the blush became a slow blaze spreading across her face just like the reddening glow of a freshly beaten bare bottom.

She swallowed hard, almost gulping, as she tried to suppress the sudden sense of unease triggered by the memory of her aunt; a sudden memory that, though vague and instantly suppressed, left her feeling distinctly queasy.

Closing her eyes she concentrated on the dean. Why had she been curtly summoned to 'Old Fashioned's' office? And what an office it was - a jumble of astrolabes, dog eared textbooks, yellowing parchment scrolls dating back to Isaac Newton, pencils scattered across the dusty carpet and sprigs of thyme sagging from sticky, unwashed sherry glasses. Chaos and disorder everywhere. On the wall opposite the large desk, a sepia print depicted early designs for a computation machine designed by Charles Babbage, predating and upstaging the microchip and laptops by over a hundred years. The dean even used log tables instead of a calculator. 'Cheating', Dr Hilary Mellstock would sniff dismissively, thumbing her battered old book of log tables until she came to the cosines.

Cheating... Ariadne squirmed again uncomfortably... and then it all flooded back to her, leaving her with her head bowed and gripping the sides of the chair so fiercely her pink knuckles whitened.

It was the day after she completed her last A-level maths paper. She was out on the tennis court all afternoon, and returning home hot and perspiring, she dashed upstairs to shower and change. It was a Friday evening. Father had taken mother away to the Cotswolds for the weekend, leaving Aunt Julia, who was staying with them for a while until she sorted out some personal problems, in charge. Aunt Julia, never auntie; she had always been so strict and stern.

Ariadne recalled the surprise of hearing the click of the bathroom door opening while she was in the shower relishing the downpour of deliciously hot water. Then she heard the door being closed again... and locked.

'Have you finished yet, young lady?' Aunt Julia's firm voice enquired from inside the steamy bathroom. 'I trust you have.'

Startled by her aunt's sudden presence, Ariadne almost slipped on the wet tiles.

'Well, have you?' the woman demanded sternly.

Blinking through the fierce stream of water plastering her hair over her eyes, Ariadne pawed frantically for the tap and then for her towel, wondering what on earth Aunt Julia was doing intruding upon her ablutions.

'Have you washed properly, young lady?'

The opaque plastic shower-curtain stuck to Ariadne's left buttock as she edged away from it instinctively, the towel clutched over her breasts, tummy and thighs.

'Show me, my girl.'

'Aunt Julia!' Ariadne gasped, utterly bewildered.

'At once,' came the terse command.

'Aunt, please, I'm having my—'

But before another word of protest could be uttered Aunt Julia flung the curtain aside and snatched away the scant modesty afforded by the towel. Startled and dumbfounded, Ariadne skidded slightly on the wet tiles in the cubicle, and she was no match for the capable hands that caught and pinned her wrists to her sides, and after a brisk visual inspection by the woman, spun her around.

'Aunt Julia!' Ariadne gasped. 'Wh-what on earth are you *doing?*'

'What am I doing? I am inspecting you, my girl, to make sure you are thoroughly washed. I never punish a dirty girl.'

'P-punish?' she stammered in disbelief and alarm.

'Punish,' the older woman confirmed humourlessly, and then a ringing smack echoed in the tiled bathroom and left a pinkish blotch on the bare buttock her hand had visited so abruptly. 'Very good,' she concluded. 'Here.' She offered Ariadne the towel. 'I want you dried and out of there this instant. Quickly, girl, the sooner you've been punished, the better.'

'But, Aunt Julia—'

'Dry your bottom, girl, at once.'

Ariadne obediently, if sullenly, dabbed the towel against her pussy, and then, burning with shame, she passed its gentle roughness into the warmth of her anal cleft.

Aunt Julia moved silently across the tiles to the wicker laundry basket, flipped open the lid, and fished out a crumpled blouse; Ariadne's white uniform blouse; a crisp cotton shirt that always seemed to emphasise rather than conceal her budding breasts.

'And what have you to say to me about this, young lady?' she demanded, following the length of the left sleeve down to the cuff and folding it back.

Ariadne saw the dark squiggles scrawled inside the cuff. She saw the tiny mathematical formulae she had inked onto the inside of the cotton cuff just before going into her A-level exam. She blushed furiously as she remembered sitting on the toilet ten minutes before the exam scribbling the four equations of motion. 'N-no...' she protested, shaking her head, 'no, you don't understand...'

'Oh, but I think I understand all too well, my girl. You were cheating; it's as simple as that. But what I fail to understand is why. Can you explain that to me? When I quizzed you four days before the examination, you recited the laws of motion and their attendant equations perfectly.'

'Yes, but...'

'But?'

'But the pressure,' Ariadne said, without conviction. 'There's so much to remember. It was just a little bit of insurance against—'

'It was just a lot of cheating,' Aunt Julia cut in abruptly.

'No, I didn't even look. Honestly.'

'Honestly?' Aunt Julia snorted. 'After I find this,' she waved the cuff and the scrawl of incriminating evidence in Ariadne's flushed face, 'you dare to use the word *honestly?*'

'But I didn't cheat!' the shamed girl insisted desperately. 'I didn't even do the laws of motion question on paper three. I didn't need the equations.'

Aunt Julia raised a hand to quell the outburst of pleading. 'Nevertheless, you cheated. Not by actually using the copied formulae, but by scribbling it on your cuff in the first place. Now come here, girl.'

'But Aunt Julia, I swear—'

'You are to be punished, my girl, and deservedly so. What your poor parents—'

'Oh no, please, Aunt Julia,' Ariadne pleaded. 'It would break mummy's heart! She wouldn't understand. And daddy, he fusses so. He'd never be sure I hadn't—'

'Then we will keep this matter strictly between ourselves,' her aunt promised solemnly. 'I will spank you, spank you very severely on your bare bottom, and we will consider the episode forgotten. Understood?'

Her head bowed, her frightened eyes lowered, Ariadne shrugged silently.

'Are we agreed, my girl? A severe spanking on your bare bottom, and the ugly matter of your dishonesty will be closed. Are we agreed?'

Knowing there was no other way out of this shameful predicament, Ariadne slowly nodded, still avoiding her aunt's accusatory stare.

'Head up, girl, and look at me,' Aunt Julia pressed, and the naked young woman's breasts rose and fell as she took a deep breath, and lifted her worried countenance.

'Now quickly, hands behind your back,' the older woman ordered, and Ariadne's pert breasts quivered vigorously as she hastily obeyed.

'Now kneel.'

Her hands clasped above her bare buttocks, Ariadne winced as her knees pressed down to the hard tiles.

'Keep your head up,' her aunt commanded, 'and look at me.' Reddening even more with shame, she obeyed.

Hands on hips, her full bosom heaving, Aunt Julia towered over her penitent niece. 'Do you admit it now?' she demanded insistently. 'Do you admit you cheated by writing those equations on your sleeve, whether you used them or not?'

'Um, yes...' came the contrite whisper.

'And are you sorry?'

'Yes, aunt, truly sorry.'

'Sorry and ashamed?'

Ariadne nodded.

'And you *will* be sorry, my girl, very sorry and deeply ashamed when you're lying across my knee having your bottom spanked.' Tossing aside the incriminating blouse, Aunt Julia unzipped her black skirt and palmed it down over her hips. It slithered down to the tiles, completely burying her shiny court shoes. Stepping out of the skirt's dark puddle, and then out of her shoes, she stood resplendent before her young niece in sheer pearl-grey hose.

Peeping up timidly, Ariadne could discern the gentle swell beneath the stretchy sheen where white knickers sheathed her aunt's pubic mound. The shy peep became a sustained, mesmerised gaze as she watched her stern relative unbutton and roll up both sleeves of her blouse. Then she rubbed her palms together slowly for a full minute before removing two rings from her right hand. Her spanking hand.

'On your feet, girl.'

Ariadne stood up slowly.

'Come along. Across my knee with you.' Seating herself on the lowered lid of the toilet seat, her plump buttocks splayed within the clingy hose, Aunt Julia summoned her naked niece to her.

Ariadne reluctantly approached the grim woman, then bent over and positioned herself for punishment. Easing herself across the waiting softness of the older woman's thighs, she whimpered as a firm hand gripped the nape of her bowed neck, forcing her naked body fully over her punisher's lap.

'Hands down... no, not like that,' her aunt's voice snapped waspishly, 'arms forward. Touch the floor with your fingertips.'

The pre punishment preparations seemed endless, heightening Ariadne's shame and humiliation. Stretched helplessly across her aunt's glistening hose, her face blazed as her pubic nest crackled against their taut sheen as her warm fingertips touched the cool tiles. The sudden rush of blood to her head left her giddy, her bare bottom rising up in utter helplessness while her toes supported her tautly braced legs.

A dominant fingertip dimpled her left buttock's tender swell. 'Open your legs for me, girl.'

She clamped her thighs even more tightly together, but then cried out as her aunt spanked her, and instinctively spread her thighs wide to avoid another punishing blow.

Aunt Julia drew her thumb up and down across the girl's exposed cleft several times in swift succession, before dipping the fingers of her spanking hand into the shadowed warmth. A brief but blistering lecture on the merits of honesty and the futility of attempting to cheat then followed. It was a very stern sermon, and the drumming of the fingertips at her cleft, and then upon her vulnerable anal whorl, filled Ariadne with delicious dread, and before her aunt's lecture was over she found herself almost wishing the spanking would begin. She was growing strangely confused, and she felt warm and moist in her most private places.

Then, at last, the punishment began, exploding across her upturned cheeks with a savage staccato of spanks, eight blows in total followed by a pause. She held her breath and squeezed her tear filled eyes tightly closed as the palm revisited her warm flesh to rhythmically smooth and caress her punished cheeks. Then her aunt recommenced the chastisement with a flurry of harsh smacks that made Ariadne's bare bottom bounce. Her squeals escalated to shrill shrieks before transforming into broken, muffled sobs as the strong hand ravaged her increasingly red buttocks. The blows were swift and searing, crimsoning every square centimetre of her helpless cheeks as they quivered beneath the blistering onslaught. Then another pause followed, during which she clenched her buttocks tightly as the heat and pain spread down to her wet quim.

Afterwards Ariadne tiptoed gingerly along the landing, and as she passed the spare bedroom into which Aunt Julia had withdrawn, leaving the door slightly ajar, she paused to listen, and heard low moans emanating from within. Daring a quick peek, she saw her aunt stretched out naked on the bed, masturbating furiously by rapidly skimming her knuckled tights over her sex.

Then later still, in the darkness of her own bedroom, Ariadne thrust her sore bottom up against its own reflection in the full-length mirror by her bed. And as her reddened cheeks kissed their own cool image frozen in the glass, she came uncontrollably.

The large old bell in the tower overlooking the quad struck the half hour. Ariadne Soames Ayr blinked, wriggled on the chair and out of her reverie, glancing at her watch again. It was almost four o'clock. She sighed. She would miss her dreadful tea and bun now, and it was her last chance to partake in the time-honoured tradition. Tomorrow was graduation day. After that, London and a career. Actuarial work, perhaps, or fund management. Or had the dean secured something a little bit special during last month's 'milk round' when the multi nationals had come to cream off the brightest brains? Could it even be the Treasury itself? Had 'Old Fashioned' squared it with the men in grey to secure her star pupil such a plum post? Ariadne flushed with pleasure at the thought. She had, after all, got a double first with honours, achieving the highest marks. It would mean a terrific salary, she realised suddenly, absently plucking at the cotton panties over her pubis through her skirt, panties now wet from her recent recollection of Aunt Julia's spanking.

A post at the Treasury would command an excellent salary and secure her a small flat just off Sloane Square. She would settle for a bed-sit, for anything, even a broom cupboard, so long as it had the desirable SW3 tag. She smiled, easing the gusset of her tight panties from her hot cleft by inching each thigh up from the seat a fraction. The leather creaked beneath her rippling buttocks. Yes, a bed-sit within the golden triangle of Peter Jones, Hans Crescent and the Lower Brompton Road visible from her room, but not a flat share. No, definitely not a flat share.

Her pulse quickened at her throat. Flat share... she shivered in sudden delicious dread as more buried memories bubbled up from their deep well of shame. Seconds later, images flooded her mind...

She found herself at the start of her second year - late parties, never any milk and always someone hogging the payphone - living in town in a flat share with two third year girls above a kebab house. The flat share and the two third-year girls; a bossy blonde and a silent brunette, both always chivvying and chasing her to wash up the dishes or put the black bags out on bin-day. And she, busy at her books, ignoring them. Too engrossed to shop - the dean had promised a double first if she worked hard - she pinched things from the fridge, swapping those silly little post it notes with *Mine!* scribbled on them from one carton to another to cover up her crimes.

After Christmas, back for the Spring term, red, green and silver decorations wilting in the window of the kebab house below, and the reception committee - the bossy blonde with the brunette bringing up the rear - burst into Ariadne's cramped little room.

'We've decided you're going to get only one more chance,' the blonde informed her. 'There'll be a schedule and you'll do your bit.'

'And no more eating what we've bought or cooked, understand?' the brunette added.

Ariadne had been flippant, defiant, which was a bad mistake. The blonde grew furious. Kicking the bedroom door closed, she produced two table-tennis bats from beneath her jumper, gripping one and tossing the second to her friend. The dark-eyed girl caught it, and thumbed its red rubber surface menacingly.

'One beating and one more chance,' warned the blonde. They overpowered her easily, and choosing not to fully undress her, they yanked their struggling captive's jeans and cotton panties down to her knees. 'Get her hands and tie them.'

The brunette thrust her table-tennis bat between Ariadne's thighs, and then used a single nylon stocking on her wrists. The nylon burned slightly as it bit into her flesh, leaving her hands helplessly bound behind her.

Stumbling as she screeched in protest, Ariadne was propelled facedown across the narrow bed. As she fell, her bared buttocks shamefully exposed to the punishing bats, she saw her teddy bear tumble tipsily down from his perch on the pillow.

Crack! Crack! Crack! The blonde proved brutal with the small round bat. A blistering triple echo broke out as she swiped it down urgently, vehemently, across the upturned cheeks. As the bat barked the buttocks flattened, wobbled and trembled in their sudden crimson glory. *Crack!* A telling swipe jiggled the poor cheeks, fleetingly depressed beneath the rubber coated bat. Nine strokes were administered in a ragged staccato of three, three, one, and a final flurry of two. The blonde was panting from the exertion, her heavy breasts rising and falling swiftly, while beneath her on the bed Ariadne sobbed brokenly.

After the ninth stroke the blade of the bat was placed down with tender dominance across the swell of the beaten buttocks. Then the cruel punisher, tucking her disarrayed hair deftly behind her ears, angled the rubber surface of the warm bat against Ariadne's lips. The punished, bare-bottomed girl wriggled violently, but the red surface returned to dominantly smother her moaning protests. 'Promise!' the blonde hissed. 'Promise to clean and tidy up and follow the schedule!'

Ariadne refused, turning her head away defiantly, but swiftly repositioning the levelled bat under her captive's chin, the blonde gazed contemptuously down at her. 'Promise!'

Ariadne, tears jewelling her sorrowful eyes, finally nodded and panted, 'Okay... okay, I promise.'

'That's better, bitch. Now seal it with a solemn kiss.'

She kissed the bat that had just blistered her bare bottom.

Crack! In her surrender and submission to the rubber prickling her dry lips, she had forgotten the second girl. Straddling her victim by tucking her heels under her armpits, gazing sternly down at the reddened buttocks, the brunette wielded her table-tennis bat competently, briskly delivering four brutal strokes.

Crack! Crack! Crack! Crack!

Wriggling and shrieking, Ariadne jerked and fought with all her strength to dislodge her punisher, but was merely rewarded with a furious flurry of three more harsh blows. Then, twisting the bat in her grip, the punisher aimed the thin edge down between the ravaged cheeks, and with a deliberate sawing motion she administered the most delicious torment to the wet cleft at her mercy.

Ariadne froze. Surely not... surely she was *not* about to come. But the inexorable waves were cresting in her pelvis and her pussy was dangerously hot, her slippery labia blooming open, lewdly creaming and exquisitely tingling. The red rubber dimples of the bat's surface teased and thrilled the inner curves of her punished cheeks as she squeezed and clenched them, causing even more juice to flow from her quim.

Planting a controlling hand firmly down on her victim's back, the brunette exposed her deep cleft. She applied the thin edge of the bat with intimate ruthlessness, skimming the tight little bud of the puckering anal crater. Then it skidded across the velvety skin buried between the clenched cheeks as juice from the opening sex lips lubricated the rubber trim.

The bat was then brought to Ariadne's lips and she was forced to submit to it with a kiss; forced to kiss and lick the bat that had just visited her bare buttocks and the sticky cleft between them; forced to kiss and taste, to taste and smell, her own feral juices glistening wetly on the dimpled red surface.

And as her two flatmates caressed her and stroked her hair and shoulders, licked and softly bit her punished bottom and untied her bound wrists, Ariadne raked her pussy against the now slippery duvet. Crushing her open sex down and wriggling and writhing, she spread her labial lips apart before splaying them deliciously, and her beaten buttocks still blazing, she smothered her screams of pleasure as she started coming...

The chimes in the quad sounded again. No tea and sticky buns today. Sticky... she winced slightly feeling how wet she was from the recent rush of turbulent memories.

The approaching tap tap of high-heels on the polished wooden floor announced the arrival of the dean. Dr Hillary Mellstock swept up the corridor, black gown billowing, steel-rimmed spectacles flashing fire as they caught the afternoon sun pouring in through the window.

'Ah, the Soames Ayr girl. I shall see you presently.'

As the office door closed behind the disappearing dean, Ariadne tossed her head angrily. Girl, indeed! A third year graduate who had achieved so much with honours, and who was about to embark upon an important career, was hardly a mere girl. Then she relaxed, her frown softening to a fleeting smile; 'Old Fashioned' was quite eccentric. Everyone knew that.

After a short time the door to the dean's office opened again and she was instructed to enter. Her mind vaguely acknowledged the sound of the door being closed behind her, but she attached no particular significance to the scrape of the key turning in the lock.

The dean ignored her visitor at first, busily preoccupying herself with the blinds, which refused to come down until bullied into submission, and then with a floor lamp. The four dim bulbs glowed grudgingly in the gloom of the darkened room as she snapped on the main lights. A double fluorescent strip flickered and blazed down from above. Ariadne blinked. The sudden flood of light illuminated the dean's office mercilessly. She saw the dusty leather chair behind the cluttered desk and the disorderly chaos everywhere.

As if indifferent to her presence, the dean continued to fluster about her office, tidying up and arranging things as neatly as possible. Then she opened a deep oak cupboard and produced an abacus, which she cradled gently against her bosom. Closing the heavy cupboard door with her knee, she placed the abacus down upon her desktop and briskly dusted off her large bosom. Ariadne saw the full breasts wobble and bounce.

'Well, girl, what do you think of it?'

'It is a beautiful counting frame, Dr Mellstock,' Ariadne admitted, gazing down at the row of beads.

'Beautiful? Fiddlesticks, girl, it is of unique interest. And why is it of unique interest to the mind mathematical?'

She concentrated hard on the winking line of five red beads flanked at one end - the end next to the wooden frame - by a single silver bead.

'Well, girl, can't you see?'

'There are only five counting beads.'

'Exactly. Unlike the Greek and later Roman counting base of ten, early Arabic arithmetic was founded upon the counting base of five, representing the right hand. Nowadays, only the nomadic tribesmen of the North Yemen use such an abacus. The tribesmen, who herd their goats on horseback, devised this five-beaded saddle top abacus for one handed use. But watch.' The dean's straightened forefinger alighted on the line of beads and flayed them, whizzing them along the taut wire. They rattled almost eerily, and tapped softly as they bunched together in a sparkling huddle at the other end. With a *click* the final red bead sped home, and suddenly clutching and tilting the counting frame, the dean held it aloft, allowing the single silver bead to slide down the wire. 'The northern Yemeni women punish wilful young village maidens in a most remarkable manner,' she remarked. 'I was privy to such chastisement five years ago when travelling from Aden up into the Blue Mountains of A'qaar.'

Ariadne frowned, wondering what on earth the mad old dean was twaddling on about.

'That is, I think, why I purchased this little gem in a particularly noisy market. Observe.' She flicked the silver bead and the single red bead across the stretched wire. 'When a young woman has misbehaved, the rest of the village females take her to a tent on the very edge of the encampment. There they bare the young woman's bottom and beat one cheek - just one cheek, mind you - with a short, cruel whip fashioned from plaited goatskin strips. Very supple goatskin.'

Ariadne felt her tongue thicken in her suddenly dry mouth.

'They whip one cheek until it is quite painfully crimsoned, leaving the other unblemished.' The dean's thumb toyed with the two separated beads, turning over the red against the silver. 'This allows the unfortunate girl to continue with her chores and domestic duties for three days, sitting precariously upon a stool on her unmarked buttock. After the third day,' her voice nearly dropped to a whisper, 'the miscreant is dragged back to the tent on the edge of the encampment and, her buttocks bared, she receives the plaited goatskin whip across her unpunished flesh. It reddens swiftly under the savage lash and a most pretty result is achieved. When perusing such a punished maiden by moonlight, one cannot but appreciate the delightful effect of the whipped cheek against the unpunished twin. The red against the pale cream.'

Ariadne's stomach grew heavy as she watched, spellbound, while the dean turned the fat little red bead against its silver partner, very much like a punished buttock bunched against its unmarked twin.

'This frame allows a herdsman on horseback to count his goats single-handedly.' The voice was perfectly neutral - quiet, calm.

'I see.' Ariadne sighed as the uncomfortable moment passed. 'Yes, I see.'

'Even on a wild stallion, in the torrid heat and swirling, blinding dust, the northern Yemeni tribesman can be sure of a true and accurate count.'

'Yes, Dr Mellstock.'

'True and accurate,' the dean repeated slowly, fingering the little red bead and the little silver bead gently. 'So important to the mind mathematical to achieve a true and accurate tally, is it not?'

'Of course.'

'Indeed, truth and accuracy could be said to be the very basis of the queen of sciences, could it not?'

'Oh, absolutely,' Ariadne nodded decisively. Her sixth-sense warned her to agree enthusiastically with the dean; Dr Mellstock would make a formidable foe in any intellectual discussion. She watched as the woman gently plucked the steel rimmed spectacles from her nose and placed them carefully down on the freshly dusted desktop. They glinted brightly, the lenses reflecting the harsh fluorescent light.

'Warm afternoon,' Dr Hillary Mellstock remarked, slowly unbuttoning the cuffs of her blouse, after shrugging off her black gown.

'Mm,' Ariadne agreed, her eyes seemingly unable to do anything other than follow the fingers over the large bosom within the blouse.

'And it's very warm in here.'

It had become rather hot and stuffy in the study, but Ariadne shivered slightly despite the heat as, bizarrely, the dean finished unbuttoning her crisp blouse and peeled it off. Dr Mellstock was wearing a seamless, deeply cupped, flesh toned brassiere. The satin was slightly dark with perspiration, and Ariadne's tongue flickered out to wet her dry lips as she saw that both the large cups strained to contain the full breasts squeezed within their stretchy sheen. But for some perverse reason Ariadne found the sight of her dean devoid of her blouse far from abhorrent or weird, and the prickle at the watching girl's pussy became a pleasurable warmth as her labial lips juiced and peeled apart, kissing the panties snugly encasing them. Her clitoral thorn hardened as she glimpsed the mulberry-dark nipples pressing against each bulging bra cup as she began to feel more aroused than alarmed. 'Old Fashioned', as everyone knew, was quite eccentric. So she lowered her eyes and pretended not to notice as the dean continued undressing with no loss of her austere composure; after all, it was hot, she reasoned.

The skirt, unzipped, was lowered and discarded, revealing flesh toned knickers and a garter-belt holding up bronze-hued stockings. From beneath her fringe Ariadne surreptitiously watched the shoes being kicked off and tidied away beneath the desk, but surely no more would be removed...

Dr Mellstock raised an accusing finger and pointed it directly at her. 'So, girl, you deign to agree that truth is important in all matters mathematical?'

Ariadne tore her gaze from the carpet and looked up directly at the severe face of the dean, trying to avoid and ignore her odd state of undress. Everyone knew the old bat was eccentric, after all. 'Um, yes,' she whispered, finding even those two short words difficult to articulate.

'Absolutely sure?'

She nodded.

'That is all I need to know. Get undressed.'

'I, um, dean?' Ariadne gasped, incredulous.

'I said get undressed,' the woman repeated. 'There are some questions I wish to put to you as I spank you. Oh yes, girl,' her voice rose imperiously, 'I propose to spank you as you supply my questions with answers. Eventually I will get the truth out of you. And if I deem it necessary, I will then cane you.'

'No!' Ariadne protested. 'You can't!'

'I can, and most certainly will, cane you if it proves necessary. Now get undressed this instant and bend over my desk.'

Ariadne was aghast, and staggered back a few disbelieving paces. 'B-but...'

'If I have to cane your bare bottom, Miss Soames Ayr, you will thank me for having spanked you first. Receiving strokes from a rattan cane across unprepared cheeks can be almost an unbearable experience. Almost. Much better, Miss Soames Ayr, for you to be prepared for my bamboo by being given a warm bottom...

'What, still dressed? Do not provoke me, girl.'

'No, p-please, I mean, I don't understand,' she stammered, her thoughts as incoherent as her tumbling words. She edged back towards the door, and forgetting it was locked, her scrabbling fingers stretched out blindly behind her. They found the handle and twisted but the door remained stubbornly closed, and then, at that precise moment, Ariadne's mind remembered the click of the lock after she entered the stuffy office, remembered and finally attached full significance to the ominous sound.

The dean was leaning on the edge of her desk, her legs crossed, her stockings gleaming in the bright light. 'An anomaly in your examination paper has drawn attention to itself, my girl,' she stated ominously.

Ariadne, her bottom pressed against the locked door, looked towards the desk, her eyes wide and sparkling with consternation.

The dean, slowly stretching out to finger the red beads on the abacus, adopted a brisk, no nonsense tone. 'You wrote out in full, and demonstrated mathematically, that zero cannot in fact be an infinite quantity, applying the Zoll-Zimmermann principle. Now that I found truly amazing since I omitted to explain the Zoll-

Zimmermann principle in my tutorials. Omitted it altogether, I must confess. And yet you anticipated the question in the exam paper and answered it completely.'

'I was lucky—'

'You stole into my study the day before and sneaked a look at the exam paper. Then you went to the library and checked the Zoll Zimmermann principle on the Internet. I have a log of the site.'

'I didn't open the exam papers, they were sealed...!' Ariadne protested desperately, and then stopped herself, too late, as she realised the enormity of her mistake.

'They were sealed, yes,' the dean chuckled triumphantly, 'but you unsealed one, didn't you?'

'I didn't—'

'Then resealed it and slipped it back into the pile. The fifteenth in the pile, to be precise.'

'No...' Ariadne denied without conviction.

'Because you carefully calculated you would be sitting in alphabetical order for the exam, putting you in the fifteenth desk. You planned to receive the resealed paper and, of course, not remark upon it. But you made an elementary mistake, Miss Soames Ayr.'

'Mistake?' she echoed, trying to contain her mounting dread.

'A miscalculation, my girl,' the dean clarified. 'A simple counting error. You forgot the first paper is always placed upon the desk of the invigilator.'

Ariadne, biting her lower lip, reddened.

'Ah, I see you understand me. So, Miss Soames Ayr, you received the sixteenth paper from the pile. The girl in front of your desk was given the paper with the broken seal. Quite properly, she quietly informed the invigilator. The matter was brought to my immediate attention, and the contents of your exam afterwards clearly indicated to me the nature of the wrongdoing and the identity of the wrongdoer. You see, Miss Soames Ayr, how easy it was for me to deduce both the crime and the culprit? Now get undressed this instant and bend over my desk.'

'No, please, Dr Mellstock, I didn't... I mean, I'm sorry...'

'Are you denying your guilt, or apologising?'

Ariadne's silence was self damning, and the dean nodded knowingly.

'Undress, quickly,' she said. 'I want you bare-bottomed and bent over.'

Knowing she was lost, Ariadne's fingers fumbled nervously at her buttons.

'Your guilt in this unpleasant matter places me in a very difficult position - a very difficult position, indeed,' the dean went on. 'Your achievement of a double first with Honours could be deemed to be... hmm.'

Ariadne stripped awkwardly, shrugging off her clothes in clumsy haste. Trembling, she stood before the locked door in only her white bra and panties, her discarded uniform lying in a heap at her feet.

'No,' the dean whispered softly as Ariadne reached behind to unclasp her bra, and the blushing student's hands fell down by her sides.

Tapping the desktop, Dr Mellstock invited her to approach.

'Please don't punish me,' she whimpered, stumbling obediently across the carpet towards the desk.

'Bend over and give me your bottom, you wicked girl,' came the crisp reply.

Reluctantly, and reddening deeply in shame, Ariadne planted her hands down on the desk, her splayed fingers trembling.

'Right over, girl.' The dean loomed. 'Face down, bottom up, if you please.'

Bending obediently, Ariadne crushed her soft bra-encased breasts against the hard wooden surface. She caught the whiff of lavender water as the dean stepped around her, and flinched, shrinking slightly as the woman's stocking-clad thigh brushed against her left leg.

Dr Mellstock questioned her closely between each harsh spank. The required answers were supplied between gulps and squeals. The blows raining down across the proffered buttocks were fierce, but not ferocious. Red-bottomed and squirming, the punished girl blinked away her tears of pain and shame and braced herself for the next flurry of stinging slaps and searching questions.

Smack! 'Briefly but accurately expound for me the Zoll Zimmermann principle.'

Ariadne did so, mumbling the answer into the desktop.

Smack! 'Expound the proximity of absolute zero to infinity.'

The young student obliged, tearfully acknowledging 'theta' as the differentiated axis of projection.

Smack! 'Give me an account of your first chastisement, girl, your first real bare-bottomed punishment. I want the details. The exact details.'

Ariadne moaned softly and squeezed her poor buttocks together, but another sudden, unexpectedly severe spank opened them immediately.

'Answer me,' the dean demanded, so in a throaty whisper, one Ariadne barely recognised as her own, she recalled and recounted the spanking administered to her by Aunt Julia. And at the dean's insistence, no detail of the punishment was omitted. She felt the egg of shame crack against her stomach wall as the dean extracted every detail from her, and felt the yolk of humiliation slither inside her. It was a cold, raw feeling not quite like fear, but more akin to a delicious dread as all the time, relentlessly, ruthlessly and dominantly, the dean's firm palm caressed her punished bottom. And before she finished relating the details of Aunt Julia's chastisement, she sensed the slithering yolk of shame seeping from her pussy in the form of her own warm juices.

The dean's forefinger, fully extended and rigid, stroked the tightened cleft between the girl's crimsoned cheeks. 'And what of punishments since?' she asked softly, almost tenderly.

Ariadne, fearful of the hovering hand above her sore bottom, quickly confessed to the treatment meted out to her bare buttocks by the red rubber bats wielded by her disgruntled flatmates.

'And how did you respond to these punishments, my girl?' the woman probed. 'Did you experience any *reaction*,' the dean emphasised the word, 'to each or either chastisement?'

'Reaction?' she echoed in a faint whisper, clenching her spanked cheeks even tighter.

'Arousal,' the dean explained, her voice neutral, as it was when she was defining a difficulty in Euclidean geometry.

Ariadne hid her mounting confusion with silence.

Smack! Smack! The reddened buttocks bounced and jerked beneath their renewed torment. 'I mean to know everything, girl. *Everything*. So tell me, at once.'

'But I'm not sure I understand what—'

Smack! Smack!

Ariadne squealed. 'Yes, yes!' she cried, reaching back in an effort to cup and protect her scalding cheeks.

'Hands back across the desk, young lady,' the dean ordered sternly. 'No, right across. Further...'

Ariadne's fumbling fingers sought, and found, the desk's far edge. She gripped, swallowing hard as her stomach stretched and her breasts moulded against the unyielding wood, threatening to burst free from her straining bra. At her ankles her stretched panties prevented her from kicking her heels to relieve the pressure.

The dean maintained a meditative silence. Then, abruptly, she snatched away Ariadne's panties. Moving quickly, bending over her victim she unclasped and tore away her bra, instantly and painfully unburdening the cups of her breasts' warm weight. The girl shrieked, confused by the new onslaught, writhing in renewed shame and distress.

Then towering over her naked, punished student, the dean demanded to be told how Ariadne responded to corporal punishment, and utterly broken, the young woman spoke haltingly but truthfully of her sensations of excitement and arousal when receiving bare-bottomed discipline...

A brief silence settled over the woman and the naked girl across the desk, which was eventually broken by Dr Mellstock, who delivered a short sermon in words that burned deep into Ariadne's whirling brain. 'The case against you has been proved, my girl,' the dean concluded. 'I believe you deserve your double first with honours. You have a first class brain but only third class morals. You have been previously punished, and most deservedly so, for your dishonesty, and you have responded, to some extent, to such punishment. There is hope for you yet. At university,' she continued, caressing the spanked cheeks before her, 'we consider it our duty to turn fully rounded young people out into society. You, Miss Soames Ayr, remain somewhat deficient in matters of probity. As such, you must remain here until that deficiency has been thoroughly corrected.'

'*Remain* here?' Ariadne could not believe what she was hearing.

'Be silent. You will graduate tomorrow.'

Ariadne sighed her relief aloud, her cheek still pressed to the old desktop.

'But you will return next term to participate in my research project. I shall be your personal supervisor.' Gripping and squeezing Ariadne's taut yet beautifully malleable buttocks, she continued in almost a conspiratorial whisper. 'I propose to supervise you closely, my girl. I shall be keeping a very sharp eye on you from now on.'

Ariadne quietly moaned her alarm and dismay into the desktop, clouding the wood with her sweet breath. Then the soft rustling of papers quickened her senses and, twisting slightly, she craned her neck to see the dean rummaging through an open drawer, unearthing a sheaf of forms.

'Your application for postgraduate work here at college has been accepted, Ariadne.'

'But I—'

'All that is required now is your signature.' The dean placed the completed paperwork down next to her face, and then moved the abacus gently so its wooden frame nudged her naked shoulder. 'But before you sign, I will cane you.'

Ariadne gabbled her protest and began pushing herself off the desk in an effort to escape the threatened punishment, but the austere dean, serenely unruffled, levelled the length of rattan cane she was gripping against her student, almost effortlessly taming and controlling her lovely victim. A consummate dominant, she stilled the spanked girl against the wood by depressing the cane's quivering tip down against the nape of her neck.

Mysteriously, the touch of the yellow wand stilled and silenced Ariadne into complete submissive surrender. Bamboo had never visited her flesh before. But she knew its first kiss would be excruciatingly potent, and she shivered in delicious apprehension. Pinned down and rendered motionless, she whimpered helplessly. It was an ambiguous whine; part hunger for and part dread of the dark delights to come. The tip of the rattan cane left the nape of her neck and traced a tremulous line down her spine before tap tapping and dimpling the left cheek of her hot, spanked buttocks.

'What is the fifth perfect number, girl?'

Frozen beneath the light pressure of the cane against her bottom, Ariadne's brain failed her.

'Come, come, the fifth perfect number, if you please?'

Ariadne's brain whirled. Flinching from the dominant touch of the bamboo, she quickly calculated aloud. 'Nought plus one, one. One plus one, two. Two plus one, three. Three plus two, five. Five plus three, eight.'

'Eight?' the dean echoed. 'Quite sure?'

She nodded mutely.

'Eight strokes it is, then. Bottom up a fraction more, if you please.'

Swish, swipe!

The first cut of the cruel cane was applied immediately. It whistled down to slice swipe Ariadne's vulnerably exposed cheeks, Judas kissing their helplessness with a thin crimson weal. The caner grunted softly as she administered the stroke, while the caned girl squealed aloud as her bare buttock received the cruel lick.

Taking a step back from the lovely young body across the desk, the dean quelled the writhing buttocks with a light touch of the cane that had just lashed them. 'With my whippy stick, I will correct the tendencies towards dishonesty and cheating your behaviour manifests so blatantly, Miss Soames Ayr. Brilliance of intellect, I so often discover, is frequently found to be morally flawed.'

Swish, swipe!

The cane rose swiftly, sparkling in the harsh fluorescent light, and lashed down for the second stroke.

Ariadne hissed like a scalded cobra, bucking her whipped bottom in a frenzy of delicious pain, and jamming her pussy and breasts down against the wood. Abject beneath the quivering cane, she pressed her belly and pubis into the hard surface, rasping her clitoral thorn into the wood. Across her whipped cheeks the cane had bequeathed a second livid line of torment.

'I will correct you, my girl. And punishment with my whippy stick,' Dr Mellstock purred, raising the cane high for the delivery of a third stroke, 'shall play a prominent part in your post graduate experience under my strict supervision. A prominent part.'

Swish, swipe!

Ariadne screamed and gripped the far edge of the desk even more tightly. The fierce heat across her beaten buttocks melted and merged into a warm rivulet of arousal that seared down along her cleft.

The caning continued at a slow, measured pace. Between each vicious stroke, the dean adopted the practice of levelling the cane down at the abacus to deftly flick a single red bead across the taut wire, tallying each lash with maddening precision and mathematical exactitude. And as she did so, she enunciated each stroke aloud. 'Four!' *Swish, swipe!*

Despite the hot blood singing in her ears, Ariadne heard the fourth click as the bead sped home.

'Five!' *Swish, swipe! Click.*

'Six!' *Swish, swipe! Click.*

A slight pause between the administration of the sixth and the seventh stroke of the rattan cane caused Ariadne to whimper pitifully.

'Patience, my girl,' the dean chuckled darkly, momentarily pausing to rub the tip of the cane down against her pubic mound.

'Seven!' *Swish, swipe!* And yet again the dreadful *click* of the tallying bead.

It was a cruel cut. Ariadne kicked out, treading the empty air with her foot, and the tip of the cane angled down instantly to quell the movement into stillness. Then the tip of the cruel bamboo travelled slowly up over the smooth curves of her leg. Arriving at the almost invisible crease where her upper thigh melted into the swell of the buttock above, it probed inwards between the caned cheeks, aiming directly at the partly exposed glistening fig within. The tip of the questing bamboo darkened as it made contact with the wet heat shimmering at Ariadne's plump young labia.

'My goodness, girl, it would appear you have turned my whippy stick into a sticky whip,' the dean quipped, sniffing as she scrutinised the moist tip of her yellow cane before once more savagely lashing the supple bamboo down across the crimson-striped buttocks. 'Eight!' The final stroke was duly tallied by a little red bead whizzing across the stretched wire.

But Ariadne scarcely heard it. Still gripping the far edge of the desk as though hanging on for dear life, she ground herself wantonly and frantically against the polished wood.

A few moments later she climaxed with a soft scream, and as she did so, the dean flicked the cane in against her parted thighs. The whipped girl whimpered her delight, and shuddered as a second orgasm engulfed her.

'Kneel,' the dean commanded gently, after giving her student time to recover. 'Kneel down on the carpet, my girl.'

Ariadne's perspiring breasts slid back across the slippery wood as she collapsed drunkenly on her knees before the desk.

'Use your hands and fingers,' the dean urged. 'Go on, girl, you have my full permission to achieve absolute satisfaction.'

So keeping her recently whipped bottom cheeks just above her heels, Ariadne lowered her fingertips to her smouldering pussy and caressed her inner sensitive lips mercilessly, deploying both thumb-tips at her clitoral bud. Then suddenly she tensed and collapsed, succumbing to yet another climax that ravished her as ruthlessly as had the cane.

'The pleasures of punishment are something of a philosophical conundrum, are they not?' the dean murmured, pausing briefly to kiss, and then suck, the wet tip of her cane. 'The sweetness of pain. The pleasure of suffering. A sugared sorrow, as the Chinese ancients deemed it. Yes, to be sure, a sugared sorrow.'

Utterly spent and exhausted, the student curled up at the dean's feet.

'Now you know my terms and conditions, Ariadne, are you willing to sign?'

She nodded, swallowed silently, and then hoarsely whispered, 'Yes...'

'Just as I thought,' Dr Mellstock murmured, a glint of triumph sparkling in her eyes. 'Tomorrow, you will receive your double first with honours, but I think we shall both come to agree you graduated with me, bare-bottomed across my desk, today.'

PARSON'S PENANCE

'Be still, little one. You have been sinful and so must be punished. With all sin must come retribution. Retribution, penance and punishment. Be still, I say, or it will go hard for you, my girl. Very hard, indeed.'

Despite the stern warning, the girl continued to wriggle and squirm across the lap of her punisher. She felt the firm hand at the nape of her neck tighten as it forced her bowed head even further down. Whimpering, she attempted to toss away the dark fringe of hair curtaining her eyes. She felt the brutal fingers busy at the buttons of her calico under-drawers, and burned red with shame as, swift and sure in their task, they opened and unfurled the flap of soft material covering her bottom.

'Naughty girl,' the parson murmured, his eyes glinting sharply as they drank in the delightful swell of her plump cheeks. 'No,' his stern voice warned, 'I mean to punish you. Be still.'

The wriggling ceased and the young woman slumped obediently into silent submission. The parson nodded approvingly and relaxed his fierce grip on the nape of her neck, settling her warm weight across his supporting thighs. Pinned helplessly down, the dark-haired penitent remained mute in her surrender. Her fringe tumbled straight down, covering and hiding the tears in her large, sorrowful eyes.

Beneath the warmth of her belly, the parson's cock pulsed. The pulse quickened to a throb. He swallowed and closed his eyes. He groaned softly and whispered a hurried prayer. It was the devil at work, the arch tempter. Trying to ignore what he could not deny, he opened his eyes again and resolved to do his duty, which was to punish.

'Well, Edwina? Come girl, what have you to confess to me?'

'Nothing, sir, truly, sir,' came the whispered response.

'Have a care, young lady. Today being the Sabbath, the time for confession has come. Today is the just and fitting occasion for contrition. Tell me of your wrongdoings and I will shrive you of your sins and mete out your penance.' His free hand alighted on the softness of her sweet young buttocks and began firmly massaging their clenched flesh.

'I have nothing to confess, sir,' she insisted quietly.

'Nothing?' He increased the pressure of his massaging palm, bunching the captive cheeks slightly as he pressed down more urgently upon the bare bottom he was about to punish. 'Nothing? I think that is not entirely true. Speak of your sins. Come, confess all to me. Confess and be prepared to do full penance.'

Edwina whimpered, but the parson remained ominously silent - ominously impassive to her distress. He already knew of her misdeeds. His housekeeper - who conscientiously spied on all three of his distant cousins living under his roof - had informed him of it not an hour ago.

'I am waiting, Edwina. Pray do not add mendacity or insolence to your catechism of woes.'

'I remember now, sir, there was a mouse,' her words spilled out anxiously, 'but I did not mean to err or sin, sir, I—'

'A mouse, you say? What *of* this mouse?' His flattened palm smoothed the curves of the clenched cheeks in his thrall. He asked, even though Miss Strappleton, his vigilant housekeeper, had told him all about the mouse.

'A mouse, sir, it was in a trap, a cruel trap. I set it free.'

'Free, you say?' He lightly skimmed his thumb down between her tightened buttocks. 'How so?'

'It was so piteous to behold, sir, so I set if free.' It was obvious from her tone she believed she had done nothing wrong, at least as far as the mouse was concerned.

'Set it free?' he echoed, grimacing sternly even though her position made it impossible for her to see his face. 'Do you know that just such a mouse, set free in my house, can eat through a whole tallow candle every night at a cost of a full farthing to my beleaguered purse? And,' he palmed the soft cheeks with increasing fervour, 'that just such a mouse can nibble through sixpence worth of cheese each week?'

'I am sorry, sir, I did not know, I am sure. Please do not punish me, sir!'

'A mouse,' he continued suavely, ignoring her fervent pleading, 'is never a single sorrow to a house, child. They, like all contagion, come in vexing numbers. They are legion.'

'I thank you for your instruction, sir, and I promise to think hard upon it from this day forth.'

'Pretty words from a penitent do not postpone just punishment, girl.'

'No, sir,' she sighed, submitting to her doom.

'And what else have you to tell me?'

'Please, sir, nothing, sir...'

'Nothing else?'

'I - I'm sure not, sir.' Her soft cheeks hollowed in mounting dread.

'And are you quite certain of what you say, little one?'

Edwina nodded vigorously, and across the parson's knee her bare buttocks danced seductively. His cock, now hard, rose and thickened with a sweet ache. He breathed heavily, for the moment staying his spanking hand. His housekeeper had informed him of a theft on the night of the heavy rains, a theft of small coals. The silence grew loud between them, during which she wriggled restlessly across his knees.

'In a little while from now, your bottom will be *hot*, girl. Does that word not suggest your misdemeanour to you?'

Suddenly reminded of her sin, Edwina blurted out the details of her wrongdoing. 'Oh I remember now, sir. I stole small coals and took them up to my bedroom. It was for a cat I found out in the rain all shivering and wet, the poor thing. I brought it up to the fire for creature comfort, sir.'

'These are not grave errors, child,' the parson concluded aloud. 'Foolish impulses, no more.' He sensed the body across his moleskin breeches relax as she detected the tone of forgiveness in his stern, authoritative voice.

'Thank you, sir, for your clemency.'

'You have so very much to learn, child.'

She snuggled comfortably across his lap, obviously daring to hope the threat of pain and punishment had passed.

'But even small and slight transgressions have their price and must be paid for in full. Consider, little one. The mouse you set free no doubt ate a good nine pence worth of tallow and cheese, and the small coals stolen to warm the wretched cat add yet another burden to my purse. I have lost a full shilling, girl. Be sure of it. And the cat, to be sure, lived only to catch and kill the mouse.'

She cried out in dismay.

'Small sins, but with still some price to pay. They still require some penance from you. Bottom up, my girl, if you will.'

'No sir, please!' she squealed, stretching back her arms in a frantic effort to cover and protect her naked cheeks.

'Edwina,' the parson snarled softly, 'you must be subject to my will.'

'But sir—'

'Give me your bottom, child,' he ordered, his voice a rising growl.

Timorously, her fingers curled in fearful expectation, the girl drew her hands away before dropping her arms down.

The parson raised his chastising hand above the tensed cheeks. 'And what do we say for our penance, Edwina?'

She maintained a sulky silence.

'Edwina?'

'Out of your charity, sir, chastise me,' she mumbled sullenly. 'Helpeth me repenteth truly...'

'And?'

'And please spank me for my sins...'

His flattened palm cracked down. The smacking blow rang out harshly as the open hand visited the proffered buttocks, which wobbled slightly after being fleetingly depressed beneath the savage impact. And as he lifted his hand again, the parson noted her buttocks reddening as the stinging pain spread across their satin contours.

Smack! A second swipe of his unforgiving hand across her suffering flesh made him grunt and wince as his stiff cock poked up into her tummy. She jerked in response to the second blow, but the pinioning hand planted on her neck forced her to submit absolutely to his will and purpose.

Smack! Smack! The jiggling cheeks bounced as they suffered a sharp double blow from the parson's punishing palm. She twisted in a desperate effort to escape the scalding agony, but only succeeded in causing her bottom cleft to part lewdly.

Grunting his suppressed pleasure on espying the dark path between the crimsoning hillocks, the parson swiftly drew the knee of his moleskin sheathed right leg in against the trembling thighs to further confine and tame them. 'Now you are trapped, my little mouse,' he rasped hoarsely, breathing hard with mounting excitement as well as from exertion. 'Now you shall do full and most deserved penance for your foolish, girlish sins.' He swept his durable palm down four times in swift succession, stinging and scalding the helpless bottom swelling out of the unbuttoned calico drawers. The furious flurry of chastising spanks left his hand tingling and his victim's buttocks ablaze. As the punished cheeks grew hotter their blush of pain and shame burned brighter, and as the blush burned brighter and deeper, the shrill cries issuing from the lips of the writhing penitent grew louder in agonised protest.

Bucking yet again in response to a particularly savage blow, Edwina thrust her scorching bottom up. Tense and swelling in the grip of fierce pain, her cheeks threatened to burst out of their calico frame.

The parson gasped sharply, troublesomely thrilled by the delicious contrast afforded by the white fabric surrounding the crimson of the punished flesh. As her hips rose and her spine arched seductively, her buttocks quivered and her cleft became a sharp crease before suddenly parting. He caught his breath as he spied, deep down in the shadowy space between the spanked cheeks, her tiny pink anus winking. 'Eye of Satan, turn thy gaze from me!' he shouted, gripping the two cheeks he had so thoroughly chastised and squeezing their scalded domes viciously. The pink rosebud of her anal whorl disappeared, and swallowing hard, he brought his hand up to wipe his fevered brow.

Across his fierce erection, grinding her belly down innocently onto its thrusting tip, Edwina sobbed softly in her blazing shame. The cruel fingers of her chastiser relented, relaxing their savage grip at her cheeks. Then, as though ordained to punish the very source and fount of all wickedness and sinfulness in the world, the parson arced his hand down again, and again.

'Let me hear your atonement, little one,' he commanded, a full five minutes after the final blow rang out. A full five minutes during which the palm sweeping smoothly across her hot cheeks formed a fist to knuckle her moist cleft.

Innocently riding the parson's erection, the punished girl craned her head around to gaze up at her stern punisher. 'Thanks be all thine, sir, for the penance you so kindly and in all justice meted out to me,' she whispered huskily, and then lowering her face to his thigh, her dry lips kissed the moleskin obediently.

The parson shuddered and his engorged cock speared up painfully. Pushing the bare-bottomed minx hurriedly off his lap, he spoke softly. 'Only doing my duty, girl. In all conscience, it was only my duty I have done.'

Luncheon was a capital meal. Miss Strappleton served up a whole roasted goose generously stuffed with apple, sage and onion. Carving himself a third plateful, the parson briefly wondered if a plain boiled fowl would not have been the more prudent choice. At either elbow, heads bowed over their earnest task, his three young distant cousins were eating him out of house and home with unrestrained relish. Edwina, to be sure, fidgeted from buttock to buttock, squirming uncomfortably on her chair.

Yes, the roast goose was succulent. Torn between the dictates of his appetite and the inevitable damage to his purse, the greedy parson swallowed his claret and helped himself handsomely to the spiced pears stewed in port the capable Miss Strappleton had brought to the table. As he finished a fourth such fruit, he wished for the sake of his purse it had been an apple apiece for the Sabbath tide dessert, or an even more economical sliver of cheese cut from a truckle of honest cheddar.

After luncheon, he shouldered his fowling piece and strode out into the surrounding waterlogged levels of Spixby cum All Sorrows. Beasts of the field ignored his passing as they trod their steaming dung into the abandoned crop of cabbages. The sweet reek of rotting vegetation pervaded the noisome, clammy air.

An hour later the parson was stamping the damp and cold out of his boots at his back porch. Dark clay soiled the red bricks Miss Strappleton scrubbed religiously every morning. He was in a good humour, having bagged a brace of plump woodcock with a single shot, the ball passing clear through the hen to catch and stun the accompanying cock in mid flight. The cock fell to earth alongside the dead hen, flapping pitifully. Its neck had felt soft to the parson's strangling hands.

In his study he unearthed his tithe books and conned them keenly, the better to calculate revenues and incomes since Lady day last quarter. Since the fields flooded, and the Bain used to drain the levels was still in a state of disrepair, rents and tithes were down and diminishing. The living of Spixby cum All Sorrows was a lean one, and a recent appeal to his bishop had proved fruitless.

The parson, a high churchman of stern Tory provenance, was not in favour with his sleek bishop, a Whig of no marked religious fervour.

'Fellow empties his pews with all that blood and thunder,' the bishop was heard to remark once at a game of backgammon. 'I sometimes think he is a little mad. Had the effrontery to bring a plea against my rural dean, damn him.' When the bishop brought himself to reply tersely to his parson's request, no mention was made of the possibility of an increase in stipendiary support.

'Fripperies and fal de lals, young lady. Vanity of vanities. All is vanity.'

'That is neither fair to me, sir, or true,' Rebecca countered spiritedly. She stamped her dainty foot impatiently. 'You should not see fit, sir, to frustrate me and deny me the smallest essentials.'

Miss Strappleton had dutifully informed the parson that Rebecca, two years older than her sister, Edwina, had squandered housekeeping monies away on ribbons for her shining golden hair and - the temerity of the girl - on a saucy pair of satin slippers.

'My purse cannot support your profligacy, Rebecca. You disobeyed my express wishes in the matter of economies, and now I find you unrepentant as I attempt to remonstrate with you. Very well, I will more than remonstrate with you, young lady. I will speak plain and deal severe with you, understand?'

'Economy is another word for meanness in your book, sir,' she retorted hotly.

'My book, maid, is the Good Book, and therein are many lessons to be learned.'

'Sermons are for simpering schoolgirls!'

'Silence, Rebecca, do not be pert with me. A pert wench is soon brought to sorrow. The sorrow of punishment—'

'No, sir!' gasped the willowy blonde, shaking her head vigorously. 'Pray, I meant no mischief with my wanton words. Forgive me, *please*, sir.'

'Hold thy prattling tongue.'

'Sir, I beseech thee, do not beat me.'

'Silence!' he thundered. 'Be done! I chastised your younger sister before luncheon, and I mean to hear your howls before sundown. Come here, baggage.'

Emitting a shrill squeak of alarm, Rebecca backed around the study, putting a polished mahogany table between herself and the wrathful parson. But despite her agility and his heavy luncheon, he gained upon and grasped his struggling charge. She wrestled pathetically in his fierce embrace before slumping abjectly down to her knees before him.

'How much were you emboldened to squander, my girl?' he demanded to know.

She shrugged, tossing her golden ringlets insouciantly over her shoulders.

The parson, smouldering with rage in the knowledge - supplied by his prying housekeeper - that Rebecca had squandered a couple of pennies short of a half sovereign on her fripperies, demanded a full answer from her. 'How much, harlot?'

Flinching, she swayed and sank back, shrinking from his anger. Resting her round buttocks on her heels, she bit her lower lip before whispering her remorse.

'Like the whore of Babylon, your contrition comes too late,' he sneered. 'Remove your skirts, petticoat and farthingale, young lady. I propose to punish you, bare-bottomed, with a most fitting instrument.'

Rebecca rose and steadied herself at the mahogany table. Then she lifted trembling fingers to her bodice and plucked it open slowly, reluctantly divesting herself of her outer garments.

The parson was indifferent to her discomfort. As she bared and prepared herself for his impending chastisement, he peeled away his coat and unbuttoned the cuffs at each sleeve. He approached her, treading softly on the Turkish rug.

He bare buttocks pressed against the smooth wood of the table's edge, Rebecca shivered in her nakedness and shame, cowering before his stern gaze.

His narrowed eyes raked her nudity, glinting at the sight of her pink nipples, and as they took in the golden fuzz of her privy part.

Sensing his searching gaze she covered her bosom with her left arm, squashing her breasts and bunching them up into deliciously full mounds, and hid her cunny with her right hand.

'I am blighted to struggle with a living that yields little profit and less reward, Rebecca,' he said. 'The souls hereabouts prove to be as resistant to spiritual guidance as they are reluctant to pay their tithes. And since last Michaelmass, I have had to bear the additional burden of you three wicked girls. It is, I consider, both unjust and inequitable. But it is my duty, and I will do my duty. Bend over across the table, young lady. Present your bare bottom to me, for I mean to beat you.'

'I am a good girl, in truth, sir, and I thank thee for giving succour to myself and my sisters, but—'

He held up his hand, and then waved it dismissively recalling the day his three distant cousins arrived, orphaned by the Napoleonic wars and quite destitute, in a pony and trap. 'You will obey me, Rebecca. Am I to be rewarded for my charity by impudence, impertinence and improvidence? Across the table, now, my girl, for I mean to do my duty.'

'No, please, sir...'

'You three girls are wanton and most wicked. I will break your venal spirits and instil the righteous fear of God in each of you. Bend down across that tabletop my little sugared whore. Down across the table with you now.'

Abruptly subdued, she submitted to his will. Spreading her naked thighs slightly apart, she dug her toes into the Turkish rug as her nipples kissed the polished mahogany and her full breasts slowly flattened their soft warmth into their own reflection.

The parson stretched out a dominant forefinger and tapped the swell of her right buttock. The flesh dimpled and the whole cheek quivered a little. 'Draw your legs together, harlot. Have you no shame?'

The wet pink of her gleaming fig disappeared as she squeezed her thighs together obediently.

He had snatched away the two blue ribbons fluttering from her twisting fingers before she undressed for her chastisement. Holding them, he stepped up behind her, pressing himself against the naked warmth of her thighs. His urgent manhood, already prompted into thickness by his wrathful ire, stirred and straightened as his taut moleskin breeches kissed her soft flesh. Trying to ignore the tumult building in his groin, he brought her wrists together and bound them tightly against the small of her back with the first ribbon, leaving her hands quite helpless just above the swell of her bare bottom. In his exertion to master her and bind her thus, he was forced to pinion the naked girl down by planting his knee in the small of her back. In doing so, the bulge of his cock briefly but disturbingly rode the ripeness of her naked rump. He swallowed hard to relieve the tightening in his throat.

The second ribbon he brought down to her ankles, tying it fast around them. Her legs and thighs now pressed tightly together, Rebecca's buttocks bulged invitingly. Then he bent over again and snatched up a single satin slipper, thumbing its supple sole.

'A most fitting instrument for dispensing your penance and punishment, young lady,' he decreed. 'Let us see if you will still desire, nay, *demand*, the kiss of a satin slipper at your flesh within this quarter hour, hmm?'

'You are most mean and cruel, sir!' she wailed into the polished wood at her soft lips. 'Mean and—'

'Silence! All I presume to hear from you, my little harlot, are the words of your confession and true contrition. This being the Sabbath, you have sore need to be released from the coils of your wretched devices and dark desires. Speak.'

'No sir, I will not.'

'It is a bold and impudent jade you are, Rebecca. Let us see, shall we, if this slipper applied judiciously to your naked haunches will not spill forth words of repentance.'

'Never!'

During the silence that followed her rebellion, she squeezed her upturned cheeks together while the parson sniffed the sole of the slipper, and then furtively licked its soft suppleness.

'Well, girl?'

The young woman bent over the table remained stubbornly silent.

The satin slipper spoke in her stead, barking sharply as it was brought down repeatedly across her rounded buttocks. She angled her knees inwards as she writhed under the stern chastisement, her skidding nipples raking their pointed peaks into the mahogany.

Swish, crack! Swish, crack! The stinging slipper whispered malevolently as it struck the jiggling buttocks again and again. After the ninth searing blow the parson paused and absently brought the warm sole up to his lips again. He kissed it fleetingly, and then slapped it harshly down against his moleskin sheathed thigh. 'I demand to hear your words of repentance, Jezebel.'

'No. I will defy you, sir. I will defy—'

'Daughter of Gehenna!' he snarled, plying the slipper viciously, and she screamed shrilly as it lashed down to scorch and scald her six more times in rapid succession - rapid, savage succession. And each blow addressed the smooth crown of her scarlet left buttock.

'Speak, girl. I desire, and demand, to hear true words of atonement spill from your stubborn lips. Own your sin and admit your shame.'

Sobbing as she writhed in her bondage, the punished nude trod the Turkish rug awkwardly with her feet, and the parson stood directly behind her addressing the curved right buttock with the slipper's hot sole. 'Repent, girl.'

'Damn you, sir!'

Swish, crack! Swish, crack!

Six blistering strokes ravished her pale right buttock, turning its soft swell a cruel shade of crimson.

Perspiring freely, the parson stood back to peruse his handiwork. 'Now your rump is as red as the lips of a Drury Lane drab, young lady. And, to the grave peril of your soul, a Drury Lane drab is what you will become if you insist on spending my monies on ribbons and satin slippers. What, jade, you seek to speed your passage into licentiousness? Remember, my pretty little whore, that bare feet are well suited to the penitent. Satin slippers, indeed. To quicken your steps to perdition? "*She that runneth hasteneth to her folly and despair*". Luke, chapter four.'

A tiny trickle of wetness glistened at the juncture where her squeezed fig peeped below her crimsoned cheeks. The parson grunted thickly and swiped the slipper harshly against the wet cunny.

'I confess!' she cried, writhing in renewed anguish.

Briefly lost in a trance, he examined the wet stain on the slipper's sole. 'What, girl, you confess?' he asked vaguely.

'Yes sir, I will own all,' she whimpered.

'I await your full contrition.'

She sobbed for a moment, and then rapidly confessed to all of which she stood accused. The frivolity. The vanity. The unpardonable largesse when times and circumstances were so straightened.

'Fair words, young lady. Fair words, and meekly spoken. You have taken unto yourself a bridle and you scold and muzzle your pert tongue most seemingly. I am pleased.'

'As you say, sir.'

'But what remains to be said? What more do I need to hear, girl?'

'I repent me of my sins, sir, and beseech you to rule me with thy rod of righteousness.'

'And?'

'Do your duty by me, sir, and do with my sinful flesh what you deem fit and proper.'

The parson surreptitiously and inquisitively touched his tongue-tip to the wet stain on the slipper's sole, before levelling it up above the squirming cheeks, whilst squirming her engorged nipples into the table's polished surface, Rebecca emitted a series of low, carnal moans.

Taking these to be the true sounds of sorrow and remorse, the parson gripped the slipper fiercely. 'Whisper your penance as I beat you, girl. It will cleanse you of all ungodliness.'

Inching up onto her toes, Rebecca pressed her pubic mound against the table's bevelled edge, and the smooth wood received the slippery crown of her vulva, pressing firmly against her clitoris.

Crack! Crack! Crack!

The parson swiped the slipper down, biting it into the blaze of her punished cheeks. At each remorseless stroke the naked girl thrust the warmth of her juicy fig into the hard wood. With each merciless stroke she rode the smooth mahogany, jerking and tightening her ravished cheeks in mounting ecstasy.

'I will make and keep thee chaste,' the parson snarled, oblivious to her lascivious self pleasuring against the table's edge.

'Beat me, sir! Oh beat me! I am a sinner and must suffer sorrow at full measure!'

The perfume, the very scent of Sodom from her weeping pussy, pervaded the room, stabbing at the churchman's flared nostrils. Snuffing up her feral odours, his hand spasmed and the slipper dropped silently to her naked feet.

Staggering slightly, as if he had partaken of too much claret, he turned away from the naked girl sprawled across the table. Breathing sharply, he clutched his groin and climaxed violently inside his moleskin breeches.

Warmed hare soup, an excellent saddle of Canterbury mutton served with capers and followed by Stilton and port, made a most agreeable dinner. In all conscience, the parson would have accepted a lighter supper of toasted cheese and four penny ale. Stern stringencies, he reflected, pouring out another pint of the capital port, must be more strictly observed.

After dinner he busied himself with the pile of dusty papers concerning the case he proposed to bring against the rural dean at the Courts Consistory in the Spring term following Rogation Sunday. The rural dean was evidencing, the parson felt, somewhat popish tendencies. And what would follow? Schism, doubt and a scandal. The matter of the rural dean's Romish proclivities must be brought to book, no matter what feline wiles the bishop brought to bear as a result. Mindful of the time told to him by the half hunter watch at his elbow, he ploughed on through the thicket of fine theological points he was arranging to place as pleas against the rural dean.

Silence filled the study. The glowing logs settled softly in the grate, sending fierce orange sparks shooting up the wide black chimney. His eyes flickered from the page before him. The half hunter warned the parson it had just passed the tenth hour. Soon it would be midnight. Midnight, and the Sabbath spent.

After rolling up his legal documents and tidying them away in the recesses of his cluttered desk, he snuffed out the candles in their pewter sconces. Rising, he left the darkened study and climbed the stairs. It was his intent and purpose to visit the bedroom of Judith, the elder of the three distant cousins, and discharge his stern duty.

Standing at the door of Judith's bedroom, the parson brought his ear gently to the wood. His throat tightened and his fingers twisted feverishly in response to the low, sweet moans emanating from within. It was just as the housekeeper had said. The wench was wantonly indulging in a bout of self pleasuring. Soiled and stained bed sheets unearthed from the laundry basket told their own tale. He held his breath, wishing his loudly beating heart would be still, the better to hear the young woman at her sins beyond the closed door. Then a soft shriek pierced the dark silence. He twisted the doorknob violently and stormed into the bedroom.

A flickering taper cast a dim glow over the bed. On it, lolling back almost drunkenly against the bolster, Judith gazed up at him in wide-eyed alarm. Wriggling, she tightened her hands over her cunny, and between her squeezing arms, her bunched breasts bulged.

'So this is how it is, girl,' he seethed. 'Not joined in prayer as is meet and fitting for the Sabbath tide, I see your hands have been at the devil's work.'

'No sir, I was just—'

'Whore,' he snarled.

She clutched the hem of her linen shift, which was hiked up around her hips and thighs.

'Cover your maidenhead, girl. Have you abandoned all shame and decency?'

Whimpering softly, she covered her cunny with her cupped hands. Her firm breasts burgeoned within the tight linen binding them. The thin material sculpted the delicious mounds, clinging to the perspiration damp curves. The ripe bosom heaved, rising and falling after her bout of exertion and the tumult of sexual excitement.

'You have stumbled upon Eve's knowledge, whore.' He licked his dry lips as he spied two berry-red nipples peeping boldly through the taut linen. 'The knowledge of carnal sinfulness. You have tasted, nay, you have eaten, forbidden fruit, have you not?' His nose quivered as it caught the haunting whiff of her sweet musk.

'I did not mean to sin, sir,' she whispered.

'Do not lie, young woman. This is not the first occasion you have been so wicked, is it? You have bitten deeply into the apple of abomination, I believe, the wretched fruit of wormwood. And that worm within has entered into thee, wench.'

'No, sir,' she protested weakly.

'I see how you give lusty glances to the waggoners that pass by. It is a canker within you, girl. It burns, does it not?'

'Burns?' she echoed.

'There,' he roared, jabbing a forefinger down at the hands cupping her cunny. 'You must be thrashed.'

'No, please, I beg you, sir!'

'I would be unkind not to punish you, girl. Unkind and unjust if I was to let these sins go unpunished. Turn over this instant.'

'Out of modesty I would *not*, sir.'

'Modesty?' he thundered. 'I mean to punish you. Turn over and present your buttocks.'

Judith squealed and flipped over onto her belly, burying her anxious face in the bolster. The linen shift still rode her hips, fully exposing her beautiful bottom to his stern gaze. He took a step closer to the bed, and the soft cheeks squeezed together in a spasm of dread.

'It being the Sabbath, and you being taken in your sin, it becomes my solemn duty to beat you, Judith, to beat your bare buttocks.'

'No, pray, do not speak of beating me, sir, *please!*'

'It is my solemn duty to beat your bare, brazen buttocks, girl,' he reiterated coldly. 'You shall suffer the full twelve strokes.'

'No, I beseech you!' she wailed, writhing as her sentence was passed.

'The full twelve strokes, and at each stroke you will name one of the dozen apostles. If your memory fails you, the whipping will commence all over again.'

She gripped the bolster between her clench fists and sobbed into its soft whiteness.

'It is well said that idle hands do tempt the devil, girl. So be it. When you have been well whipped, we must make those hands busy, must we not?'

Squirming deeper into the bolster and mattress, her only answer was a muffled sob. As she pressed herself down into her bed of shame, her naked bottom cheeks wobbled deliciously. The parson, gripping the brass bedstead until his knuckles whitened, growled quietly. And as his growl became a soft, carnal groan, she bucked against the bed, lifting her rump as if eager for the taste of pain he had promised to impose upon her nakedness.

'Where is your Psalter?' he demanded. 'The Psalter you should have been attentive to this Sabbath tide?'

Raising her head out of meek submission and twisting her face up to his, she nodded in silence towards her dresser. He turned, followed by her anxious eyes. On the pear wood dresser rested the large black Tewksbury Psalter. He gathered it up solemnly and returned to her bedside with it. Opening the book with due reverence, he thumbed the pages. Grunting softly, he paused to extract the bookmark - a broad strip of pale vellum four fingers wide and some eleven inches long, as strong as it was supple.

Judith shivered and clenched her thighs together as the Tewksbury Psalter was snapped closed. Then she moaned and buried her face in the bolster again as the tip of the vellum bookmark skimmed the curves of her fear clenched buttocks.

'Be still and obedient while I speak to you of wickedness, girl,' the parson said quietly, dangling the length of supple vellum just above her taut cheeks. 'Give your haunches up to my leather and contemplate both the nature of your sins and the penance I propose to meet out to you.'

Obediently, she inched her bare bottom up towards him and her soft cheeks kissed the dangling length of hide submissively. Whimpering softly into the bolster, she stretched at full length across her bed to receive the stinging homily. But then, as the parson's withering words burned a deeper flame of shame into her face, she shrank timorously from the teasing torment of the vellum at her buttocks.

'Bottom up if you will, girl.'

'No, please, sir...'

'And be so good as to recite the venerable names of the sainted twelve,' he commanded, 'as I thrash you. As I thrash your sinful flesh.' He raised the vellum up and whipped it back down again. The first stroke licked her upturned cheeks with a vicious *snap* that left a blazing broad pink band across her quivering bottom.

'Simon!' she cried.

He raised the vellum again, and held it aloft. The second stroke, delivered smartly after a deliberate pause, lashed her quivering cheeks devotedly, burning a second, deeper pink badge of shame into her tender flesh.

'Peter,' she groaned, naming the second apostle.

Resting one bent knee on the mattress, and steadying himself by gripping the brass bedstead with one hand, the parson loomed large over the defenceless, twice striped bottom of the quaking sinner below him. He struck again, relishing her just penance.

'James!' she gasped.

Snap, crack!

'John!'

Snap, crack!

'Matthew!'

All twelve strokes were delivered with equal severity, eliciting sharp squeals and soft moans from the parted lips of the whipped girl, but she somehow managed to name all twelve apostles correctly.

'Philip,' she sobbed as the twelfth searing stroke crimsoned her fiery cheeks.

The parson stood back from the bed and palmed the vellum, squeezing it hard before spreading it across the soft mounds it had just ravaged. 'A moment for you to reflect, girl, to ponder on your penance and punishment.'

Hating the touch of the firm leather across her blazing cheeks, Judith jerked her buttocks up, rebelliously attempting to rid herself of the added torment, but the parson spanked her and effectively stilled her writhing. She shrieked, but her sore bottom, quelled by the harsh hand, submitted to the leather strap draped across her smouldering cheeks.

Gathering up the bookmark again, he fingered each reddened cheek to inspect and examine the effects of the vellum more intimately. He dimpled both crimson buttocks fleetingly as his stern forefinger dug briefly into each hot flesh mound in turn. 'Well whipped,' he murmured, nodding his satisfaction. 'Well whipped, as every whore must be.'

She squirmed as if she hated feeling his dominant fingertip against her naked skin.

After bringing the vellum up to his lips to kiss it, the parson ordered the red bottomed girl to kneel on the floor alongside her bed.

'For prayer, sir?' she asked faintly.

He shook his head and offered her the vellum strap. 'Take it.'

'Sir?' she repeated, even as she obeyed him and knelt beside the bed holding the accursed bookmark.

'The devil,' he grunted, pointing down at the junction of her thighs where her pubic coils glistened. 'The devil tempts idle hands, Judith,' he rasped hoarsely, his voice thickened by his mounting arousal. 'The remedy is pain. The devil must be punished and your idle hands kept busy. Punish the devil, girl. Punish the devil.' Snatching the strap from her trembling fingers, the parson swiped it down, aiming the flickering tongue of supple hide between her parted thighs.

The penitent young woman tossed her head back and screamed as the lash burned her wet cunny.

'Take it, Judith. Take the strap and punish the devil. Drive sin out of your venal flesh, girl. Let me see your hands busy at their work.'

Snivelling, she accepted the strap and raised it until it fell back across her left shoulder. She flinched, causing her linen shift to loosen and slip down to her thighs, shielding her cunny from the lash.

'One moment,' he said, bending to pluck at the hem of her thin garment. Straightening up again, he peeled the linen away from her kneeling body, once more revealing her crimsoned cheeks and glistening pussy. She raised her arms as the shift was pulled free from her shoulders, and her naked breasts bobbed invitingly in their sudden freedom.

The sight of her naked bosom, the nipples thick and proud, provoked the parson into a paroxysm of righteous fury. 'Drive Lucifer from thine flesh, whore!' he shouted. 'Lash Satan!'

Judith, her thighs parted, her ankles supporting her scorched buttocks, whipped the firm vellum down against the base of her belly. The edge of the supple hide stung her cunny and she screamed again, jerking forward and thrusting her naked breasts out in wanton abandon.

'Lash!' came the cruel command.

Dazedly, the young woman whipped the vellum directly down over her vulva again and again, screeching and rocking on her heels as her maidenhead seethed.

'Lash Satan!' he repeated, noting that the tip of the vellum, flickering up and away from the punished cunny, was stained dark with the wetness of the kneeling girl's sinfulness. 'Lash!'

Judith moaned as she obeyed him, and unbuckling his moleskin breeches, the parson sank to his knees behind her. Clutching at her abandoned shift he covered his erect member with the rasping linen and grunted, whilst unbidden by her stern chastiser, she continued snapping the vellum strap down between her thighs, until she suddenly collapsed on the floor, her body convulsing in the throes of a searing climax.

Behind her, clutching the linen around his gnarled length, the parson cried out aloud to Beelzebub as his pulsing release soaked the lovely penitent's shift.

Hanging suspended from the game pole down in the cool pantry, the parson twisted like a crow on a gibbet. Beside him, the brace of woodcock bagged earlier that afternoon spindled slowly from their single chain, tiny drops of scarlet dripping from their gaping beaks. He jerked against his chains, causing other specimens of well-hung game to stir as if coming alive again.

'Be still, good sir. The Sabbath tide is over by some hours, but you have yet to be shriven of thy sins.'

'Purge me with punishments,' he whispered thickly, eyes glinting as if with greed.

'I will purge thee, sir. Pray tell me of your sins.'

'I confess all. I espied the girl's privy parts when punishing her and—'

'The girl, sir?' the housekeeper demanded. 'Tell me,' she quizzed sharply, 'which girl?'

'The youngest.'

'Miss Edwina, sir?' she pressed, studying the tip of the cane she gripped tightly in her strong right hand. 'You speak of Miss Edwina?'

The parson's moleskin trousers, unbuttoned and dragged down, bound him at the ankles. 'Yes, Edwina. As I chastised her, I saw that which is damnation to behold.'

Behind him, Miss Strappleton palmed her free hand down across her pubic mound, and shivered. Her hand paused at her secret flesh, paused, cupped and squeezed as the bamboo cane in her right hand rose and quivered. 'Tell me, dear sir, what was the nature of your sin, exactly?'

'As I chastised the girl, my flesh grew hot and hard.' Stepping back briskly, the housekeeper brought the bamboo cane swiftly and sharply down across his buttocks. The parson gasped and threshed helplessly in his bondage, rattling the chain noisily and causing the woodcock beside him to dance. 'Purify me through pain,' he pleaded.

'You can depend upon it, sir. I mean to do just that.'

'Beat me,' he begged. 'Rule me with thy rod of righteousness.'

'In truth, good sir,' Miss Strappleton purred, kissing the tip of her cane before sucking hard on the shaft, 'I will be your confessor for the Sabbath. For is it not written that the confessor must be made to speak out his sins? Must not the shriver of sins himself be shriven?'

'I confess...'

'Yes?' Her voice was urgent.

He spilled forth his sins, admitting to lewd thoughts and licentiousness at the punishment of Edwina.

'Confess all, sir,' the housekeeper urged whilst dominantly caressing the crowns of his caned cheeks.

The parson freely confessed to enjoying the forbidden pleasures of the spanked girl riding his manhood as she writhed across his lap, and of glimpsing her tiny rosebud deep between her chastised cheeks.

'The jewel of Sodom, you say?' The cane hung interrogatively in the air above his naked buttocks. 'You spied her jewel of Sodom?'

'Verily, I spied her jewel of—'

Swish! The cane cut viciously down again and the parson screeched. 'Silence, sir. You must suffer your penance in silence. No more noise, sir, or I will lash you until cock-rise.'

Slumping in the chains the parson twisted and spindled helplessly, his stretched arms and caned buttocks burning.

'And what of Miss Rebecca? Did her punishment bring about an occasion for sin, sir?'

'Yes, I own that it did.'

The stern housekeeper took a couple of paces back and positioned herself squarely behind her bound captive, and levelling the cane at his bottom cheeks, she slowly brought the tip of the quivering bamboo to his tightened cleft. Smiling as she heard his grunt of surprise, she probed the clenched, striped buttocks. 'Confess,' she commanded.

Tumbling over his hurried words as the tip of the cane annoyed his sphincter, the parson freely confessed to all that had passed through his feverish mind and aroused flesh during the disciplining of Rebecca.

Swish! The sinister whisper of the bamboo broke the silence four more times in swift succession, and four fresh scarlet welts slowly faded to a pale blue tint of pain in the flickering light of the tapers.

'And Judith, sir? What have you to tell me of the chastisement of the eldest girl, hmm?'

The parson remained silent, bowing his head in blushing shame, while standing behind him, the cane resting against her right shoulder, the housekeeper perused the beaten parson. 'Nothing to confess, sir?'

He remained silent.

'It were better to tell me, sir. I cannot abide the silence of a liar, nor can my cane.' Her eyes narrowed as she watched his whipped cheeks clench in mounting dread. Lowering the length of whippy wood down to his thighs once more, she inserted the cane between them to tease, tap and torment his hot sac.

'Satan's stones, sir,' she hissed.

He convulsed in his bondage.

'Did not the chastisement of the little whore cause you to spill your seed of shame, sir?'

'You saw?' he croaked, his parched lips working anxiously.

She tapped the cane upwards, churning his balls. 'I see everything, sir. No keyhole in this house is blind to me. You know that full well, sir. It is my duty to kneel and spy, sir.'

He trembled, discovered in his sin. 'Yes,' he confessed hoarsely, 'I confess. I did spill my seed.'

'So be it,' she responded sternly, her voice potent with menace. 'It shall be six strokes for you, sir. Six strokes from the stick of sorrow that stingeth like a serpent and biteth like an adder.'

Swish, swipe! Swish, swipe! Six times the glinting wood lashed down across his defenceless buttocks. Six times Miss Strappleton grunted with exertion. Six times the chain rattled as the whipped parson jerked in anguish.

'And have you no more sins to speak of, sir?' Her words were mumbled indistinctly as she sucked hard on the tip of the cane. 'No more to confess to me?'

'No, no more,' he managed to reply through clenched teeth. 'Free me now and set me down to kneel at thy feet where I may repent my—'

'Hypocrite,' she snapped. 'You, sir, will remain in your chains until I have heard your full confession. Heard your full confession, sir, and dispensed fitting punishment and pain.'

'But I - I,' he stammered, his voice rising in alarm, 'I have naught to—'

'Silence, sir. Think well before you speak and then tell me of your wickedness. Or must my cane beat out both your confession and your penance?'

His eyes dulled with fear and perplexity, and twisting his head around to face her, he spoke rapidly. 'There is no more, I swear.'

'Liar,' she snarled. 'You dare to lie to me, sir?'

'Good Mistress Strappleton,' he pleaded, his eyes wide with terror.

'Be quiet.' She fished out a roll of parchment from the pocket of his jacket, hanging limply from a pantry meat hook. 'These words will silence thee for my rod.' Thrusting the rolled up copy of last Sabbath's sermon, delivered to deserted pews, between his teeth, the housekeeper rendered the parson silent. Then dropping the cane onto the tiled pantry floor, she circled his waist with her strong, punishing arm - the arm that had wielded the whippy wood - and hugged him to her bosom. 'Remember, sir, I see all that passes in this household. And so now I will tell you of your sin, sir. And when we are both agreed you did indeed commit this sin, I will pick up my cane and use it fiercely, sir, most fiercely, until I see you spill again your seed of shame.' She grimaced as he jerked in his helpless bondage and her firm embrace. 'It was last Thursday evening, sir, a little before supper, the night I served up beef and dumplings. Did you not entertain a visitor, sir?'

Gagged and mute, the parson could not even grunt his protestations.

'Was it not the apothecary's sister from Spixby Magna, sir, Miss Catchpole?' She felt him twist as he writhed within her strict embrace. Releasing him, she positioned herself at his striped buttocks and caressed them slowly, and then allowing her straightened index finger to penetrate between the cheeks and torment the dark cleft with her fingernail. 'In the parlour you two were, sir. I was watching you.'

His hot cheeks tightened, trapping her fingertip as she drove it deeply into the wet warmth of his anus. 'She had come for her music lesson. Learning to finger the hautboy, was she not?'

Pinioned by her firm finger, the parson squirmed.

'I spied upon you, sir, as music is well known to be an occasion for sin. I saw the instrument pass from your mouth into hers. Wet from your lips, it was, sir, all wet and shiny.' Her other hand slid in between his thighs and cradled his sac. 'Straight it went to her eager tongue.' She squeezed.

The parson threshed in his chains. He spat out the roll of parchment from his mouth and begged the housekeeper not to beat him again.

She scooped up the sermon and read the opening words aloud. '*Let the rogue feel the rod and the lecher fear the lash*,' she intoned. 'Fine words, sir. Now, will you not eat them?'

She forced the rolled up scroll firmly back into the parson's mouth, and he bit down into it, his spittle making the ink blotch and smudge.

'It was sinful, sir, you and the apothecary's sister. Susan Catchpole is a Jezebel and I must save you from her. It is a kindness I do thee, parson, a kindness. And afterwards, I will serve thee a handsome game pie and a glass of good claret to help you heal. But it was sinful, sir, thy wet lips and Susan Catchpole's eager tongue. The devil's music was being played betwixt you both, sir, and now you must pay full penance.'

Biting down hard into the choking parchment, the parson tried in vain to blink away the beads of sweat scalding his eyes. The queer note of jealousy in his housekeeper's voice was curdling into the crooning of one quite mad, of one driven insane by jealously. The realisation of his helplessness before her unbridled fury burned deeply in his brain and he began shivering. Then, as his body trembled to the sound of her snatching up the cane from the tiled floor, he began to pass water, and the steaming urine scalded him much more fiercely than the sweat of fear in his eyes.

'Jezebel,' she whispered.

The madness in her voice sent more steaming urine spurting from him, splashing and soaking the curled feathers of the brace of woodcock beside him on the gibbet. As the last golden dribble sparkled in the dancing light of the guttering tapers, a cold thrill of terror crept down his spine that quickly melted into a nameless dread in the heat of his caned cheeks.

She thrashed him savagely, loud in her prayer as she striped him remorselessly. Like his fowling piece earlier that Sabbath afternoon, his manhood cocked and rose. Stiff and straight he was fully primed. The discharge was imminent. Then a final vicious stroke of the evil cane exploded across his blazing buttocks and he squeezed his thighs together tightly.

Dropping the cane and unbuttoning the shirt over her bosom, the housekeeper flung herself upon his groin, cradling his stiff shaft between her full breasts. Gripping his whipped cheeks with her hands she dug her nails into the flesh she had just lashed, and caught the parson's penance as it spurted into her deep and welcoming cleavage.

STAR STRUCK

The gaggle of chorus girls poised for their sensual interpretation of *Scheherazade* trod the carpet with shiny stiletto heels. James saw pale hands reach up to creamy breasts as the dancing girls thumbed their bobbing bosoms into the half cups of red velvet bustiers. Silver feathers, rising provocatively from pert bottoms, quivered expectantly. James noticed the trembling hands furtively reaching down to pluck where seamed fishnets severely divided tender bottom cheeks.

The producer had vanished earlier. Front of House was in charge behind the scenes, and assorted flunkeys were scuttling up and down the warren of backstage corridors like midnight mice before the shadow of a sharp-clawed tabby. Any minute now...

'Fifteen seconds,' Front of House mumbled into his throat mike.

The dancing girls stiffened, thighs pressed together, fishnet-meshed buttocks clenched.

On stage, the Berlioz overture to *King Lear* announced the diva's departure. James nodded. A cunning exit, he thought, very stylish. The music had a brooding resonance that would leave the audience hungry for more after the departing singer's final bow. She was a clever little bitch.

'Five seconds. Places, everybody.'

The chorus line trotted down the corridor, soft bottoms joggling. James watched the last silver tail-feather glint and disappear. He was three feet from the diva's dressing room door. Two feet. His hand touched the white handle and depressed it. Nobody challenged. He felt the door give.

He had thought of a false press pass. Too risky.

Or acquiring a monkey jacket and a bunch of white roses. Too obvious.

So settling for a brown overcoat, bucket, mop and rubber gloves, he made it into the darkness of her dressing room. In all the glitz and glamour, he'd rightly calculated, nobody had eyes for a mere cleaner.

She burst imperiously into her dressing room moments later. He peeped out from behind a hastily drawn blue curtain as she strutted around the room, her fists clenched, taut as a harp string, the sequins on her fish tail gown glinting like flashbulbs at a Three Tenors' photo call. Fitted tightly at her waist and bottom, the dress accentuated her firmly fleshed, superbly rounded buttocks. James felt his throat tighten.

The dresser entered breathlessly, mumbling apologies. The diva was brisk with her, barking orders in a dismissive, domineering tone. The dresser started snivelling. In the end, weeping copiously, she was ordered from the room. Peeled out of the tight fitting gown, the diva strode around dressed in nothing but a peach-coloured thong and a rope of pearls. Locking the dressing room door, she walked to the desk.

'No interruptions for the next hour,' James heard her snap into the intercom. 'And get me another dresser, understand?'

James peeped out at the near naked icon. She had achieved success through much sweat and tears - other people's sweat and tears. He closed his eyes, savouring the moment, the moment that had taken five long years to come. He opened his eyes. He must time this perfectly. Nothing must go wrong. After five long years, he could wait five short minutes. He peered through the slightly parted blue curtain.

Prising open a bottle of champagne, the diva poured herself a frosted glassful, drank it in one swallow, and then refilled the glass. Sprawling elegantly across a beige sofa, she nursed the moisture-beaded green bottle to her bosom. James saw the pink nipples darken slightly as they prinked and peaked at the kiss of the cold glass. He took a deep, silent breath and perused her intensely, taking in the supreme contempt in the proud arch of her neck and the delicious swell of her naked bosom, an imperial, proud bosom still heaving slightly after the two hour concert. Rigorous exercises and controlled breathing techniques had given her a very flat stomach, but he noticed with a flicker of malice in his eyes that her hips were broader than the fish tailed gown suggested, and her buttocks, pressed heavily down against the sofa, bulged slightly. His eyes narrowed as they drank in the shadowed flesh between her parted thighs. The peach-coloured thong bit softly into her pubic mound and the line of her labia was perfectly pronounced. Fat sex lips, and moist, too. Worked herself up during *Turandot*, no doubt. He swallowed hard. His tongue was thick and his mouth dry. His gaze lingered on where the thong just managed to cover her pussy. Then he saw; saw and grinned. He saw that the peach-coloured strip failed to conceal stray dark wisps of pubic hair; dark wisps of coiled fuzz that belied the blonde mane flowing over a crimson cushion above. The unnatural blonde was talking into her mobile phone now, and James listened carefully.

'Not done it yet?' she demanded, apparently bullying her agent. 'I want the pictures out before the CD is released. No, *any* children's hospital, you fool. A hamper of toys, if tax deductible. No,' she continued as if dealing patiently with a moron, 'I'll just be accidentally discovered crooning to some kid in a coma. And no pretty little nurses in the shot, just me.'

His eyes narrowed in anger as he listened to her manipulating.

'We need to use our own man. No agency staffers, okay? No, you fool, not the front steps, shots of me leaving by the back door. I'll look angry and surprised.

Make it all seem genuine. Yes, of course the red tops. Time I milked the tabloids and got bigger coverage.'

Behind the blue curtain, James gripped the handle of the mop and twisted it savagely between his rubber-gloved hands.

'Oh, and about that piece due to come out last Tuesday...' She paused while her agent replied. 'That's what I pay you for,' she snapped. 'Did you manage to get the little creep who wrote it sacked?'

James stiffened.

'Good,' she purred. 'See to it he signs nothing but giros from now on. That's all.' She snapped the mobile shut and sipped her champagne contentedly.

That's how it was done, James realised. It must have been just like that five years ago when he dared to argue with her from the pit, when it was her voice not his violin that could not reach A-sharp.

Taking a deep breath, he stepped out from behind the curtain. He had been hiding in a white-tiled recess for a loo and shower.

She registered neither alarm nor surprise at his appearance. 'Have you fixed the shower as I instructed?' she demanded, not even bothering to cover her naked breasts.

The brown workman's coat had deceived her. James unbuttoned it slowly.

She ignored him, finished her champagne and rose from the sofa to cross the dressing room. Her rippling buttocks sashayed with insolent contempt at him, a mere hired hand in the presence of the naked diva.

'Get out if you've finished,' she barked. 'I need my rest.' She bent down at her dressing table, cupped her breasts, then squeezed and inspected them lingeringly in the bulb-framed looking glass.

He saw the tip of her thumb worrying a captive nipple. 'No, not yet,' he replied softly. 'I've not quite finished in here yet.'

'Then get on with it,' she snapped, her eyes and thumbs engrossed with her nipples.

'Wonder what the red tops would write,' he whispered. 'Good coverage, the tabloids.'

The thumbs froze at the nipples they were teasing. In the looking glass her eyes widened imperceptibly as they gazed into their own cold reflection.

'Wonder if they'd even dare to print half of what I could tell them,' he mused.

The blonde mane flounced as she twisted her head over her naked shoulder and stared at him. 'What the hell—?'

'Always sniffing around,' James added suavely. 'Used to ferret in dustbins. Stars like you used to dread the rattle of bin lids late at night, didn't you? Scared of having all those nasty, stinking little secrets uncovered.'

'Who are you?' she hissed.

'It's wheely bins now, of course. Don't make a sound, do they, those plastic lids.'

'I said *who* are you?' she insisted, her voice sharp with anger and a frisson of fear.

'Get dressed,' he ordered.

The command confused her. She stared at him open-mouthed, as if suddenly realising she was all but naked in front of him.

James strode across to the wardrobe, wrenched it open and snatched out a few items. 'Get dressed,' he thundered, tossing her a black bra, black elbow-length gloves and a pair of black tights. 'You're quite a bitch, aren't you?' he added conversationally. 'Quite a bitch.' The words came thick, fast and obscene. For five years he had scraped a living as a part-time music teacher, suffering as kids scraped violins. She had ruined him utterly in a fit of pique five years ago. A spiteful temper tantrum, and she had flushed his career away completely. Now, finally, payback time had arrived. 'Not dressed, yet?' he asked in a threatening undertone.

Her eyes darted to the door.

'Go on,' he shrugged. 'I'm not stopping you. I've got more than enough. Walk straight out, if you really think it best.'

It was the sweet reason in his voice that appeared to scare her more than anything. She shivered and her hands fell to her pubic bush in a belated attempt to cover it. Her pupils dilated with fear, she knelt and reached for the items he had thrown at her feet.

'Do it, bitch. I'm waiting,'

'Who - who are you?'

'You don't remember? You really don't remember? I might remind you, if I feel like it, when I'm finished with you.'

'F-finished with me?' she stammered.

'When I've finished punishing you,' he confirmed. 'Think of it as a little present from me and all those you've made miserable on your way to the top. And it really doesn't matter if you remember me or not. You deserve what's coming to you, whoever administers the pain.'

'You wouldn't dare—'

'Just get dressed, bitch.'

'I'll give you anything. My cheque book, my—'

'You can't buy your way out of this.'

The bra fluttered in her hands.

'Put it on.'

She struggled into it, easing each breast into the softness of the waiting cups. Slowly, timorously, she slipped the satin shoulder straps into place.

'Gloves,' he instructed.

So absolute was his air of authority that she succumbed to the stern command without further protest. Moments later, she was smoothing the gloves over each elbow with trembling fingers.

'Remove that thong.'

She pushed down the peach-coloured underwear, revealing her glossy black bush.

'Fake blonde, aren't you, bitch?'

Her gloved hands flew up to her face, and covering her eyes, she sobbed aloud.

'Another little juicy titbit for the tabloids if you don't sing to my tune, eh?'

She moaned softly, shaking her head fervently as if attempting to wake herself from a nightmare.

'Thong off, bitch.'

It had slithered down to her ankles, and her breasts swayed as she bent down to drag it over her ankles and step out of it.

'Tights,' he nodded curtly.

'But—'

'Put them on. *Now.*'

Turning her back on him, she rolled up, and then gingerly stepped into, the dark tights. Their sheer lengths sparkled as they sheathed her prinked feet and long legs. He saw her bottom dimple as she flexed each knee in turn, and the stretchy sheen captured and bunched her cheeks together as she tugged the dark band up around her waist.

'Turn around,' he commanded, taking a menacing step closer.

She obeyed him reluctantly, shrinking back from his advance, her soft buttocks pressing against the edge of the dressing table.

'Good,' he nodded, satisfied with her obedience. 'Now strip.'

'But... but I've just—'

'Done what you were told. So do it again, bitch. Strip. Gloves first.'

She lowered her eyes. At her hips, her gloved fingers clenched nervously. 'Please...' she whispered.

'Okay.' He shrugged. 'I'll go now, but then that bit about the kid in a coma will make the front page tomorrow.'

'No, listen, please. Wait, I—'

'Yes?'

'I'll do exactly as you say,' she murmured, her sullen pride fractured.

'Strip then, bitch, I want you naked for your punishment.'

'No, please, not that, I—'

'Naked for your pain, bitch.'

'But I don't understand. If I've ever—'

'You don't need to *understand*,' he echoed sarcastically. 'I could be any one of the victims you've trodden on and destroyed on the way up. Now strip. Nice and slow.'

Her humiliation began in earnest. Previously she had been almost naked in contemptuous disdain of his presence, but now she had to bare herself slowly and intimately beneath his piercing, hostile gaze.

He clapped his rubber-gloved hands together loudly as she brought her right hand up to loosen the strap at her left shoulder. 'No,' he said harshly, 'undo the clasp first. Take it off very slowly. And legs apart, like a slut performing a striptease. You're a slut and used to performing, so do it and get it right. Nice and slow, remember.' He squatted down on the carpet a few feet in front of her, gazing up at her as he swigged champagne from the green bottle she had abandoned by the sofa.

Shuffling her feet awkwardly, and then planting them apart, the diva tossed her blonde mane back and, closing her eyes, drew her hands behind her back to unclasp her bra. The black straps at each shoulder loosened and the cups fell away, revealing her beautifully round, ripe breasts.

'Hands down,' he barked.

Her black-gloved hands fluttered obediently down to her sides.

James swigged noisily from the champagne bottle, belched, and jabbed his finger at her. 'Gloves now. Slowly, and use your teeth like a stripper. Nice and dirty, bitch. Do it nice and dirty.' Reaching across the carpet, he snatched up the abandoned bra and sniffed deeply into the warm, empty cups. 'Orange water,' he pronounced. 'You still use orange water.' He had nurtured that memory for five years.

She whimpered in alarm at his casual disclosure. His knowledge of her - his *intimate* knowledge - was obviously frightening her, and her mounting dread and shame made the removal of the gloves a clumsy business. Then she stood with her head bowed before him.

'Head up, bitch. Don't disappoint your audience.'

A dry sob escaped her lips.

'Look at me,' he ordered.

She met his fierce gaze. Flinching, she drew her legs together, and as her warm thighs met the shiny black material of the tights rustled softly.

'Kneel,' came his curt command.

As she sank to her knees, he rose and stood over her. His right hand reached down and fleetingly, but dominantly, caressed her blonde mane. 'With your success comes a lot of exposure,' he said, 'exposure to the public gaze.' He knelt down beside her. There was still no recognition of him in her large eyes and he grew bolder, thrilling to the sense of having her in his power, having her kneeling and nearly naked, ready for her punishment and his rightful revenge. He tilted her chin upwards and held her face in a ruthless pincer between thumb and fingers before pulling her lower lip down with brutal tenderness. 'So that's where the golden voice comes from, eh?' he murmured, dominantly controlling her face with a thumb pressed into one cheek and four fingers squeezing the other.

Releasing her from his possessive grip after a long moment, he allowed his rubber sheathed fingers to trace the line of her throat, downwards. Soon his rubber digits were busy at her bosom, fiercely punishing both breasts by roughly cupping and squeezing the soft mounds of warm flesh.

She moaned, begging him to stop with her eyes, but her silent, fervent pleading was ignored by the finger and thumb milking first her right nipple and then her left. Leaving her puckered buds red and sore, he palmed each breast and weighed its warmth in his hand. She almost swooned, but he checked and steadied her by gripping her chin again.

'Hold perfectly still while I take a good look at you, understand?' He swallowed his mounting excitement at the prospect of intimately examining her, before punishing her. She whimpered, and to silence even this token resistance, he squeezed her cheeks again. 'Silence!' he hissed, and she nodded her compliance to his stern will.

Satisfied, he relaxed his grip a fraction and she remained immobile. He smiled. He knew he had tamed her completely now. She was in his thrall. 'The public gaze,' he murmured, touching her nipples gently, and then dragging his clenched fist down across her belly. 'Always in the public gaze.' At her pubic nest, his clenched fist paused. 'Tights off now.'

The diva's trembling fingertips gripped the dark band biting into her waist. Slowly, with difficulty, she managed to push the black tights down over her hips and down from her plump buttocks.

'Good,' he said when she stepped awkwardly out of the tights. 'Now kneel. Sit back on your heels and get your hands up where I can see them. No, on your head, bitch.'

She gave him a terrified look.

'Do it,' he snarled, so she rested her bare buttocks on her ankles, and the sight of her full bottom cheeks caused James to grunt. 'Hands,' he insisted.

Submissively, her anxious reluctance clouding her eyes beneath her tear-spangled lashes, the kneeling naked diva lifted her hands, palms down and fingers interlocked, up to her blonde head.

'Open,' James whispered, his rubber-sheathed forefinger dabbling dominantly into her dark bush, and the trembling performer inched her thighs apart a grudging fraction. 'Wider, bitch.'

Snivelling, she obeyed him, and then cried out as he firmly pushed her backwards, forcing her to topple back onto the carpet, her knees spread and her pussy fully exposed.

'Maximum exposure is what you seek, and so maximum exposure is what you get,' he told her.

'No, please...' she begged.

'I said silence, bitch.' He probed her open mouth with one, two, and then a third rubber finger, silencing her sobs. 'Wider, bitch. I'm waiting.'

Grunting into the makeshift gag, she spread her knees further, and keeping his captive effectively silenced with three fingers, he lowered his free hand over her pubic mound. He sneered as he felt her buttocks clench as the rubber kissed her pussy. He withdrew his hand, and caressed his fingertips with his thumb while the diva ground her naked bottom cheeks into the carpet. He visited her slit once more, and she sucked fervently on the living gag in her mouth. A soft, wet sound rose up from where his rubber-sheathed palm cupped her cleft. Fingering her outer labia until the tip of his rubber glove glistened, he worried the wet and fleshy lips methodically. The diva inched her buttocks and hips up in an instinctive physical response to his touch, and gazing down at her sternly, James used his thumb-tip to peel her dark, thick lips apart.

'Maximum exposure,' he whispered. The inner, paler lips of her sex tightened visibly. He used the tip of his little finger to split their wet seam open, and felt her teeth bite into him as he forced the finger inside her. 'No!' he warned, responding angrily to the nip of her teeth on his silencing digits. 'Be still and absolutely quiet for your maximum exposure.'

She was utterly helpless - helpless and vulnerable.

His eyes widened, watching her, the darkness of his pupils large with the lust of revenge. For five long, silent minutes he teased and tormented her slippery pussy, repeatedly fingering and spreading wide her fleshy sex lips. Palming the wet rubber of his gloved hand inwards against her sticky heat, he knuckled rhythmically at her slit until her hips bucked and her bottom ground on the carpet.

'If you dare to come, bitch,' he warned her sternly as he deliberately pleasure punished her wetness, 'I'll shave your head bare.'

Unable to control her response to his gloved hand, the diva wriggled and squirmed.

James watched as her belly tightened and her silky thighs grew taut. 'I'll shave you bare everywhere,' he promised, and sucking fiercely on the three fingers in her mouth, she battled to delay her climax.

He paused, triumphantly savouring his complete authority and control over her helpless naked body. He withdrew his gloved hand from her heat, clenching and holding it aloft above her stomach, struggling to deny the urgent desire to fist her into ecstasy. He must not lose control. Later, perhaps, after the punishment, he might have a little fun with her, but not now.

The hint of her juices pricked his nostrils. He clenched and unclenched his fist above her, and struggled to fully appreciate the intensity of his moment of triumph. After five long years she was his, completely his to do with as he willed. He knew he had already brought her to the peak of both arousal and shame. It was so easy, almost too easy. Another minute and he would have had her creaming into his rubber palm...

No. He was here for a purpose, not for her pleasure but for her pain. He wiped his gloved hand on her thigh, removed his fingers from her mouth, and slowly pushed her legs together. 'Up,' he commanded, and gasping for air, she staggered to her feet. He caught her and held her briefly in a fierce grip. Their eyes met; hers wide and submissive, his narrowed and cruel.

'Now it begins,' he whispered into her frightened face. 'After a taste of shame, a generous helping of pain, bitch.' Removing his hands from her trembling nakedness, he bit off and tossed away the rubber gloves.

She stumbled into him, her bare breasts bunching against his chest, but he straightened her up at arm's length, steadying her. Then he sat down slowly on the edge of the sofa, dragging her down and swiftly twisting her into the desired position - face down across his knees.

She cried out as her feet kicked the empty air. His left hand alighted upon the hollow behind her right knee, and firmly smoothed her leg down into the stillness of submission. It took only the slightest touch of his dominant hand to quell her other rebellious leg into motionless surrender. He slid his controlling hand, palm down, along her legs, lightly skimming the silky warmth of her submissive flesh. At her thighs his hand paused briefly to squeeze, and then the dominant palm inched upwards until it was greeted with the smooth swell of her upturned bottom. Again his hand paused to squeeze, gently depressing the curves of the diva's plump cheeks before resting palm-down upon the bare bottom it proposed to beat.

At her neck his controlling hand tightened its grip. Her blonde mane spilled down in a wanton tumble to curtain her apprehensive face. She squirmed beneath the dominant touch at her buttocks and neck, and James felt the warm weight of her naked breasts against his thigh. His hand sank to capture and give a punishing squeeze, and as he felt an erect nipple graze his palm, he saw her buttocks tighten, rendering the shadowy valley between them almost invisible.

He released her soft breast and returned his hand to her neck to keep her down. 'Discipline,' he remarked. 'No success can be achieved without discipline. And dedication,' he added almost conversationally, 'and skill, and luck, and talent. They're all important. But the most important of all is discipline. Isn't it?'

She wriggled in response, but remained silent.

The thumb of his spanking hand thrust between her cheeks. She clenched her buttocks to force it out, but only succeeded in trapping it between her soft globes.

'Isn't it, bitch?'

She nodded. He felt the unseen response as her neck muscles rippled in his controlling hand.

'I asked you a question and I expect an answer,' he insisted relentlessly.

'Yes,' she whispered hoarsely.

'Yes, *what?*' he demanded.

'D-discipline is - is necessary,' she blurted.

'So glad you agree,' he goaded. 'So glad you agree with me that a successful diva requires discipline.'

She squirmed, subconsciously thrusting her bare rump up invitingly.

'You do, don't you, bitch?' he demanded, milking her pre punishment anguish to the last drop. He felt the question hovering menacingly over her like the threat of his spanking hand above her bare buttocks.

'Yes,' she whispered, sobbing gently.

'I'm going to discipline you, bitch,' he murmured, caressing the mounds of her buttocks with smooth sweeps of his dominant hand. 'I'm not quite sure how many strokes... no, strokes are for caning, aren't they?' he teased. 'Just be content with the knowledge that I'm going to spank your bare bottom very, very hard until your cheeks are cherry-red and blazingly sore.'

'No...' she wailed. 'Please don't beat me! Please don't—'

'Too late, bitch. Your bare bottom is mine, all mine.'

'I'll do—'

'Exactly what I tell you to.' Straining slightly beneath her weight on his thighs, he stretched out his right foot and deftly scuffed one of his abandoned rubber gloves back to the base of the sofa. Then scooping it up he forced the fingers inwards to fashion a ball, which he stuffed into the diva's mouth. 'Don't want you singing too loud during this performance, eh?' he gloated. 'Bite on that, bitch,' he added, his voice cold and cruel. 'Bite on that as the fire burns across your bare bottom.'

Crack! Crack! Crack! Three sharp staccato spanks rang out as he swiped his punishing palm down across her soft and utterly vulnerable naked buttocks. The punishing smacks bequeathed a flame of blushing pink pain across her smooth curves, and he felt her jerk in response, but the rubber glove stuffing her mouth stemmed her cries. The flesh of her bottom felt pliant to his hard palm as he tightened his grip at her neck, forcing her further down into her shame and torment.

Crack! Crack! A severe double swipe of his spanking hand flattened the curved cheeks briefly, and caused the punished flesh to shudder as the rosy blush deepened to a darker shade of suffering.

Crack! Crack! Crack! The rhythm of the vicious melody quickened as James settled into his task. His cock rose painfully hard as he thoroughly enjoyed his revenge. The suppleness of her reddening cheeks delighted him, and his balls churned as he slapped her satin skin. The heat from his punishing hand spread its scarlet agony across her submissively proffered buttocks. He could not hear her silenced screams, but he sensed and relished them through her convulsive jerking and wriggling on his knees.

Crack! Crack! Crack! He was giving it to the bitch severely. No mercy. No forgiveness. She had to suffer. She had to pay the price.

Crack! Crack! Crack! Almost tipsy with exultant triumph over his naked, red-bottomed diva, James slowed the spanking to a blistering sequence of paced blows. Palpably pausing between each searing contact, he deliberately built up her pain and suffering. Like a nomad at an oasis, he savoured every drop of his longed for, and long anticipated, revenge. His cock rose to stab the softness of her belly, which pressed against his helmet, squeezing out his pre cum.

Crack! Crack! Crack! He concentrated hard, ignoring the pulse of his trapped, throbbing shaft. He was careful to spread the spanks evenly across both her cheeks,

100

aiming the stinging rain of scalding pain down across the upper slopes of her supine buttocks before attacking the fleshy crease that defined the tops of her thighs. He really enjoyed spanking that particular part of her bottom. Each swipe really told. But to avoid embarrassing himself and coming from his intense excitement, he had to pause and merely caress her hot rump for a moment.

He took a deep breath, sucking in air. His tight chest loosened and his shoulders eased. Clenching and unclenching his spanking hand, he parted his fingers wide. Then returning the hand to her bottom, he dimpled her crimson cheeks, smiling as her hot red skin briefly whitened when depressed, and reddened again just as quickly when his fingertips left it.

The glove fell out of her mouth. Possibly, James thought, she spat it out. Then her sudden yelling and sobbing made him tense. He promptly snatched up the glove and gagged her again, but the memory of her loud sorrow haunted him. It was exactly what he had waited five years to hear.

Crack! Crack! Crack! The harsh spanking continued undiminished. The memory of her sobbing grew stronger with each blow, and surrendering to a dark fancy, he snatched the wet rubber glove out of the diva's mouth again, and was immediately rewarded with another snatch of her shrill howling. He almost climaxed it was so thrilling, so intoxicating to hear her screaming as he caressed and squeezed her punished bottom. Then he gagged her again and dragged his forefinger down between her blazing cheeks. The hot, dark cleft was sticky, and as his fingertip tapped her puckering sphincter, he felt a molten juice seep from her anal crater.

She squirmed, crushing her body against his leaking cock and almost rocketing him into an orgasm. He gasped and clenched his teeth. The waves of the climax ebbed, leaving him erect and aching. Damn, she would suffer now... *really* suffer.

A smart tap tap at the door froze his hand above her buttocks. 'Shit!' he hissed.

The diva twisted her face up and her tear filled eyes met his angry, uncertain gaze.

'When I take the glove out, tell them to go away,' he whispered.

She nodded mutely, but he felt her inhale a lungful of air just as his fingers found the glove. He knew. He knew she was going to scream for help. So he slipped his hand down between her thighs and tugged hard at her wet pubic bush. She cringed in agony.

'No tricks, or I'll be back,' he warned. 'I promise.' He tentatively removed the glove, keeping it close to her lips.

She obeyed, managing to send the visitor away in a convincing tone that told of her headache and desire to be alone.

James plugged the glove back into her mouth and stroked her blonde mane approvingly. Twisting a handful around his fingers, he painfully controlled her head as he buried his face between her smouldering bottom cheeks and nuzzled the punished flesh. After licking and kissing her hot and tender skin for long moments, he straightened up, his saliva glistening on her sore curves.

'That was a good performance,' he declared. 'And a good performance deserves a round of applause.' Pinning her neck down, he settled her more comfortably into the punishment position across his knees and spanked her severely. His hand clapped her so hard it soon hurt. He paused to blow on his palm in an effort to cool it. She was twisting on his knees, her thighs spread, her dark fig gaping and glistening. He peeped down over the hand at his mouth, saw between her parted crimson cheeks the line of her dark cleft, and within the darkly yawning groove, he made out the wink of her pink sphincter. He mumbled an obscenity, but managed to pull himself together. 'Cheeks,' he blurted, his face flushed and his expression stern. 'Close them up, bitch.'

But perversely she thrust her bottom upwards, widening the delicious valley between them. Her anus, clearly visible now, puckered as if about to proffer an impertinently obscene kiss.

James licked his lips hungrily, but recovered his self control in time. 'Cheeks together, slut,' he barked, angry he was not entirely in control of his voice; it trembled slightly, and almost cracked on a semi-quaver between anger and desire.

She clamped her thighs together promptly, and her instant obedience pleased her punisher.

'Up, bitch.' His cock pulsed violently. 'I want your bottom up.' He felt her weight as she collapsed, sobbing silently, across his supporting thighs. 'No, bitch, I said up. I want your bottom raised.'

After a few rebellious seconds, her buttocks rose obediently towards his hovering hand, and the crowns of her scorched cheeks chastely kissed his unyielding palm.

James shuddered and swore softly beneath his breath. The sweet ache in his shaft became an urgent burning. Unzipping his trousers, he fingered out his veined, twitching cock and pressed it into the passive flesh of the naked diva. His penis had never been so thick, so full and so potent.

Crack! Crack! Crack! Allowing his wet glans to spear and nuzzle her soft thigh, he continued spanking her upturned buttocks, and just before the harsh sound of a fourth smack rang out, he started coming. Lifting his knees, he tipped her facedown across the carpet and swiftly straddled her, his legs scissoring her plump crimson cheeks. Then grasping and pumping his cock, he emptied his molten seed all over the bottom he had just beaten.

Wiping the knout of his spent erection against her thigh, James stretched on the carpet alongside his captive. Using his hot palm - the palm that had blistered the now semen-soaked buttocks - he caressed the smooth curves of each glistening cheek, methodically smoothing his seed into her skin. 'No,' he said, 'stay exactly as you are. I haven't finished with you yet.' He rose unsteadily to his knees, and the glint of the champagne bottle caught his eye.

Leaving the diva moaning into her gag as the carpet grazed her peaked nipples, he drank long and deep from the heavy bottle at his lips. Draining it, he tossed it away and returned to his quivering victim. 'Change your song cycle every six months, don't you?' he demanded.

Her head rose from the floor. She peered up at him, but her eyes were bleary, almost unseeing.

'Change your tune, don't you?'

She nodded slowly.

'Why's that, then?' He removed the glove gagging her so she could respond, but her mumbled reply was inaudible. 'We can't hear you, bitch. Louder.'

'To widen my repertoire,' she said, her voice thick and soft.

'To widen your repertoire, eh?' he repeated mockingly, thrusting the damp glove back between her lips. 'Well, let's see if we can't do a little widening tonight.' He sank to his knees beside her. 'Up,' he instructed. 'Kneel, on your hands and knees.'

She was slow to respond to his command, but a sudden sharp spank quickened her obedience. Her breasts swinging, her blonde mane cascading down her back and around her face, she knelt as instructed before him.

He slipped his right hand between her thighs and inched it upwards slowly, until it touched her wetness. He worked his thumb against the dark heat of her cleft until it grazed the lip of her anal crater. 'Open up, bitch, time to widen your repertoire.'

She shook her head defiantly and grunted into the gag. He thumbed her dominantly, but she squeezed her cheeks together to hide the sparkle of her anal rosebud. James snarled his frustration, and reaching around to her face, he tore out the gagging rubber glove again. 'Do exactly as I tell you,' he spat. 'I'm in charge, now. Me, not you. Me.' But then suddenly he felt queasy, almost seasick. He was losing it - losing control. He knew, deep down, that if he had to say he was in charge, he wasn't. 'Open up!' he barked.

She shook her head, tossing her blonde mane as she cursed him. And with that defiant gesture, with that ripe curse, the balance of power shifted away from him to her.

Crack! Crack! Crack! He slapped the soft lower curves of each of her bottom cheeks viciously, and then dealt a harsh blow to her wet pussy. She shrieked, but her buttocks parted invitingly and his thumb triumphed at her sticky warmth.

A stern lecture followed, but James felt everything he said to explain and justify his punishing revenge was lost on her. So he said it all again, cataloguing her sins and selfishness. He told of her arrogance, of her petty spite, of her vanity and her egotistical ruthlessness. He spoke of the hurt and harm she had done to all those around her. And all the time his thumb-tip, followed by the length of his thick digit, worried and tormented, stretched and filled her anal warmth. 'Widening your repertoire,' he murmured, jabbing inwards repeatedly in a final flourish that elicited a shrill squeal from the diva. Finally he extracted his thumb, twisting it spitefully as it emerged with a wet plop.

She grunted and moaned and collapsed across the carpet, and he stared down at her in fascination as she writhed like a wounded snake, feeling a warm glow of pride implode in his belly. He had achieved all he set out to. The diva had been sternly reminded of her monstrous behaviour and severely punished for it. He had controlled his hatred and contempt for her, and now he marvelled at how it had subsided from blind fury to the cool assertion of his absolute authority over her helpless nakedness. Yes, he had taught her a lesson she would never forget.

James managed to refrain from hugging himself in self congratulation. He had done well. The bitch had been made to suffer. She had been made to suffer shame, humiliation and pain. His revenge tasted sweet, indeed. *Revenge*, he remembered reading somewhere, *was a dish best served cold...*

'Stop that!' he suddenly said furiously. During his reverie the diva had been surreptitiously raking her clitoris against the prickle of the carpet, and the tension in her buttocks betrayed the imminent climax being conjured up by her furtive self pleasuring.

All the cool authority James was congratulating himself on evaporated in a flash of anger. 'You really *are* a stupid, disobedient little bitch,' he hissed, furious with her obvious attempt at masturbation. 'I thought I'd taught you a lesson.' But to his amazement she laughed; a harsh laugh in which he heard the contempt and scorn of one who has by no means fully surrendered or succumbed to strict discipline or stern punishment.

'Silence!' he thundered, then scrabbling for the rubber glove he re-gagged her, and then, hot-faced and furious, he flung himself down onto the sofa. 'And don't move a muscle. Stay right where you are or you'll be sorry.'

He burned with frustration and bewilderment. Where had he gone wrong? He had planned it all so meticulously, every last detail. He forced her to dress and then strip again. He exposed her to the shame and humiliation of intimate inspection. He touched her intimately too, and spanked her bare bottom, subjecting her to the torments of humiliating pain. Then he came all over her bottom. And yet with that single defiant laugh she scorned him completely.

Had she revealed her mettle, the indomitableness of the true diva? Was she indeed extraordinary, irrepressible, possessed of those sterling qualities that are the hallmark of true stardom? Then he remembered his own arousal, remembered how he struggled to fight back his sexual excitement in his attempt to focus and concentrate on the serious task at hand. He remembered how he weakened after coming intensely over her punished bottom; he almost fainted from the pleasure. She, too, must have enjoyed arousal during her discipline. Pain had ignited a powder keg buried deep in her animal sexuality. Perhaps it was the strict tone of his voice that got to her. Or was it the cruel spanking, intended to hurt and humiliate, that illumined the darkest recesses of her primitive libido?

No, he had not succeeded. He had failed. Therefore, he must try again. But this time there would be no inappropriate arousal. No unintended excitation. No talking, only strict silence. No touching other than the kiss of the lash. Pure punishment and pain. He wanted to whip her, avoiding any actual contact between them... but he had no whip.

Rising from the sofa, he paced the dressing room anxiously. A leather belt would do. Applied across her bare bottom and the softness of her upper thighs, it would surely teach her the true meaning of vengeful punishment. Then he remembered something he had seen behind the blue curtain - his initial hiding place on entering the room - where the bleach, dusters, mop and bucket remained concealed.

The curtain hissed open on its brass rings as he wrenched it aside. Yes, there it was, the long feather duster he glimpsed when in hiding - a six-foot length of pale gold bamboo topped with an explosion of fluffy, multicoloured feathers. Grasping it, he snapped it down sharply across his knee, breaking off, and then discarding, the feathered end like a fox tossing aside a dead chicken.

Back at the sofa he knelt and aimed the quivering tip of the shortened length of cane at her neck. He tapped her dominantly and she turned her head to face him. She saw the cane, and her eyes widened in trepidation as they drank in the meaning of its smooth malice.

In silence - a silence he managed to maintain - he placed the cane down on the sofa and motioned the naked diva to rise. She did, but refused to obey his gesture to stand at the end of the sofa, her eyes brimming with contempt, one hand hiding the nipples of her breasts and the other cupping her pubic mound.

He nodded, once more patiently indicating the end of the sofa, but she shook her head.

104

James smiled, and apparently baffled by his mood swings and the silence she undoubtedly mistook for grudging respect, she decided to obey him after all. Once in position she peered over her shoulder as he rummaged in her wardrobe, but quickly averted her gaze as he returned clutching several silk scarves.

The first he rolled into a ball and gagged her with it, smothering her attempt to protest. The second he wound around her head over her eyes. Then he gazed upon her naked helplessness and savoured the balance of power tilting back in his favour. He carefully avoided touching her as, applying the tip of the cane to the nape of her bowed neck, he forced her to bend down across the raised arm of the sofa. All was done in silence; no verbal instructions were given. He used the cane to conduct things as he arranged her to his satisfaction. He tapped her breasts and pubes to keep them clear of the surface, and standing behind her, he edged her feet apart with the tip of the bamboo rod. She stood trembling slightly, adjusting her position obediently as the mute cane gave its instructions. Belly and breasts free of the sofa, she bent over, raising her buttocks and supporting herself with her hands, her fingers splayed across a cushion. Her elbows were slightly bent, the tip of the cane tapped them, and she obediently straightened her arms. The position thrust her bottom up superbly.

He used a third silk scarf to bind her left ankle to the front foot of the sofa, nodding approvingly as he watched her toes curl up in dread. A fourth scarf bound her right ankle to the rear foot of the sofa, and she was utterly helpless, bared and prepared for the rod.

James savoured the moment, gripping his improvised cane tightly. It sprang up, quivering in his fist as if in a smart salute to the soft cheeks it was about to vehemently stripe. He smiled, remembering that amongst the many cuttings he had collected and collated on her journey to stardom, there was one detailing her demanding itinerary; *a punishing schedule*, the article concluded. A punishing schedule... he raised the cane and the ominous whisper made her body tense. He watched her vulnerable buttocks tighten in fearful expectation of the stinging lash.

Then at the last moment, the cane raised for the first stroke, he changed his mind. He wanted to hear her suffer. The reddening stripes would not be enough, mutely eloquent as they would be in attesting to her suffering. No, he wanted to hear her gasps and cries of anguish, and perhaps her pleads for him to stop between each pitiless stroke. He wanted to hear her raw sobs of agony.

So he eased the balled scarf from her mouth and flung it away. Then he poised the tip of the cane on the play button of the nearby CD player, and pressed it. *La Traviata* flooded the room. *La Traviata*; excellent! Lots of anguish in that lurid operatic tale of woe.

Swish! The cane thrummed the air as he struck a practice blow inches from her head to make sure she heard it. He was gratified to see her squirm in her bondage, the scarves at each ankle ensuring her bare bottom loomed up large and inviting. He fingered the shiny cane and, nodding decisively, decided upon a punishment of ten strokes. Ten measured, lethal strokes. Dispensed slowly, the discipline would leave her buttocks well and truly ablaze.

James took his time. He felt calm, unhurried. Nothing must be rushed. Every stroke must be slowly savoured. And every stroke, he told himself, must count.

He aligned himself, spreading his feet slightly apart so the levelled cane, when brought against and then pressed into her defenceless cheeks, bisected her cleft exactly. He craned his neck to study the effect, and saw the thin line of yellow wood dimple the crimson of her spanked bottom. The cane across the cleft quartered her bare bottom precisely. Perfect. The reach was absolutely perfect. Every stroke would count.

Swish! Swish! The first and second strokes whistled down. The naked diva jerked and writhed in response as two thin pink lines were drawn across the blushed crowns of her already punished cheeks. But James cursed himself. Not so fast. He must slow down. He must pace the experience. One searing swipe of the cane at a time, and then count to twelve. Let her suffer each stroke and learn to dread the next one.

Swish! The third blow swept up into the softness of her flesh just where her thighs ceded to the rich swell of her buttocks. The pink weal darkened more quickly than the two above it into a pale blue testimony of torment.

Swish! The fourth blow had her writhing and vainly attempting to squeeze her knees and thighs together, but the bondage at each of her ankles rendered her defenceless to the cut of the cane. Four strokes. James tapped the whipped cheeks with the bamboo rod four times. He found the tormented bottom beautiful to behold. He rested the cane gently upon the tender cheeks. Four strokes. It was a beautiful bottom, and unbidden, his cock stiffened. And as it rose, raking the stretch of his boxer shorts, the length of bamboo skidded down from the superbly rounded cheeks and dangled impotently in his loosening grip.

He must concentrate! *Her pain, not your pleasure!* He was here for her punishment and pain, so denying the stiff erection thrusting uncomfortably within his trousers, he lashed the proffered buttocks twice in quick succession. She cried out, but did not scream. As he had calculated, the soprano belting out La Traviata drowned the diva's distress.

Four strokes left. He levelled the whippy wood against her striped cheeks, planting it across an as yet unblemished band of flesh - flesh still pink from the spanking but unmarked by the bamboo. He played the cane across her bottom as if it were a bow raking the cello of her cheeks. He would lash her there, etching twin bluish welts across the crimson.

Swish, swipe! She bucked and writhed and James stared spellbound as her hips swayed seductively, making her caned buttocks jiggle. He stared as if star-struck, like one of those hundreds of thousands of fans willing to shiver and shuffle in line to catch a brief glimpse of her or beg an autograph. He shook himself out of his reverie, reminding himself she was a diva bitch and deserved her discipline.

Swish, swipe! She screamed softly as the wood bit lovingly into her bouncing bottom. He followed the glinting bamboo down, grunting softly as it sliced her bunched cheeks and she sobbed in anguish.

Then he hesitated, suddenly uncertain. His erection strained painfully for her, for the diva caned in her bondage, and a flood of confusion swept over him. 'Suffer, bitch, suffer like you made *me* suffer!' he hissed, breaking his vow to remain silent as his detestation turned into desire. Then closing his eyes he lashed her across the buttocks five times, inadvertently rocketing her into a shrill orgasm, and the cane dropped from his trembling fingers as he watched her luxuriate in a furious climax, twisting her torso and thrusting her hips and thighs deliciously.

106

His bitterness vanished under a sudden surge of adoration. 'Diva,' he mumbled, quickly kneeling and burying his face in her angrily striped bottom. 'Diva,' his lips mumbled into her writhing cheeks. He remained on his knees, doomed like all her worshippers to adore her. Exposing his erection he curled his fingers around its hot length and pumped fervently, and the explosion of liquid heat erupted to splatter her caned cheeks.

Exhausted, he slumped down, and peering up between her thighs, he saw his beads of semen sparkling against the crimson flush of her suffering. Then his narrowed eyes caught another gleam. Like a dark oyster opening to reveal the fat wet pearl within, the wet pussy lips above parted to allow James a glimpse of the whipped diva seeping the cream of her own climax. He gazed wearily up at her glistening sex and at a disturbing, ironic truth. He was just another star-struck fan. Her legion of admirers brought bunches of roses to her feet. He had merely brought a bouquet of bamboo.

THE SWEET TASTE OF REVENGE

Drifting in and out of those delicious stirrings between sleep and wakefulness, she parted her thighs and the weight of the duvet settled upon her pubic bush. The whispering rustle at her mound brought a slow smile to her lips. It had been a wet dream. The juice from her hot pussy seeped down her crease to tease her cleft before darkening the satin sheet beneath. Her skin sensed the damp spot. Grinding her buttocks against it luxuriously, she crushed the soft warmth of her left cheek into the mattress.

Beatrice felt the rush of excitement prickle behind her eyes and force them wide open. Staring up at the ceiling she recalled snatches of the dream, but the kaleidoscopic fragments remained elusive... a pair of grass-stained tennis shoes lying in a locker, a hairbrush, navy blue serge knickers tickling her cleft and the shrill whistle echoing across the hockey field. It had been another boarding school dream.

Seven-fifteen. She had woken early. Beyond the pink velvet curtains Notting Hill was waking up as well. Not that it ever actually slept. Milk bottles clinked on a nearby doorstep, and the tap tap of stalls being erected in the Portobello Road could just be heard through the thump thump of some neighbourhood reggae.

Beatrice closed her eyes and squirmed into the wet patch beneath her bottom. She decided to enjoy another hour in bed. She had a big day ahead of her - a busy, exciting day. She was scheduled to make a pitch at lunchtime for a lucrative contract. She had no need to worry; all the details were taken care of and everything was in place. A table booked at *Les Yeux Ardents*, verifiable facts and figures keyed into her laptop. Nothing was left to chance. She liked to be in control.

Stretching her naked body out beneath the duvet, she sank back into a blissful doze. The warmth of her buttock was drying the damp stain, but the sharp pleasure of its wake up kiss haunted her... and followed her down into fresh dreams; dreams fuelled by illusive memories...

A decade ago, when she was only seventeen years old attending boarding school, she moved out of the large dorm into her own cramped, single room. She moved away from the ritual squealing and giggling every morning as naked young women struggled into their bras and panties while hurrying to brush their teeth or their tangled hair, bumping bottoms aggressively as they competed for a place at the white dorm basins or the mirrors above them. She moved away from the furtive rustlings and sly whispering of fingers caressing wet pussies after lights out every night. She moved away from the dorm, yes, but not - even in the seclusion of her cramped room - away from the predatory prefect who patrolled from dorm-to-dorm, a slipper gripped tightly in a clenched fist.

Beatrice murmured softly in her sleep. A tube train clattered across the points outside Westbourne Park... just like the brass curtain rings being dragged back in her small room, dragged back by the house prefect for early morning inspection. She was back in her boarding school and the curtains had been parted. Sunlight flooded the room and a hand dragged the bedclothes away. The sunlight played on her bare bottom as she lay face down in the narrow school bed.

The prefect was standing beside the bed, and in her dreams, Beatrice thrilled to the scent of freshly washed schoolgirl; a milky, carbolic smell with a dark, feral undertone - the smell of a freshly fingered sixth form pussy.

In her sleep Beatrice squeezed her thighs together tightly. The prefect was standing impatiently beside her bed thumbing the supple sole of her tightly gripped slipper. The single room was untidy; books and clothes strewn everywhere. Beatrice failed the early morning room inspection, which meant loss of a house point and extra Latin prep. She endured angry words from the prefect, and the curt tone reached her even in her dreams. She was ordered out of bed. Rubbing her sleepy eyes as she shivered in her nakedness beneath the prefect's stern gaze, she gasped at the harsh swipe of the slipper across her defenceless bottom. Her sore cheeks reddened as they quivered, and the prefect bent to examine the bed sheet at close quarters. She fingered a tiny damp patch critically. 'Dirty slut,' she hissed. 'You're in for it now.' Beatrice was ordered to kneel on the bed, her face buried in the moist sheet, her bare bottom thrusting upwards for punishment...

In her Notting Hill bedroom, writhing with mounting excitement and the thrill of delicious dread, Beatrice moaned in her sleep, a sweet, low moan just like the moan she emitted ten years ago when the slipper struck her buttocks mercilessly. 'Dirty little slut!' Again and again the slipper stung her helpless, upturned bottom. Then she felt the cool touch of the punishing prefect's hand circling and caressing her beaten flesh...

Asleep in her bed of delicious dreams, the young woman squeezed her thighs together tightly to staunch the warm flow of arousal from her pussy. Then the squeal of brakes and the loud ticking of a diesel engine a short distance down the tree-lined street made Beatrice open her eyes. Sitting up in bed, she blinked away the dream of memories. A police siren screamed as it sliced through the congealing traffic along Westbourne Grove, and Beatrice, like the rest of Notting Hill, was now fully awake.

She slipped out of bed and, still naked, popped a brace of buttery croissants into the microwave and brewed some coffee. Her thoughts turned to the day ahead as the microwave chimed and her percolator spluttered a final gurgle.

Flakes of warm croissant tickled over her bare breasts as they fell from her lips.

She sat on a leather topped stool that received the warmth of her buttocks submissively. Reaching for the pot of apricot preserves, she felt the flesh of her cheeks peel away from the sensuous hide, but the strong coffee snapped her into wakefulness and sharpened her mind. She thought about lunch, and the pitch, and closing the contract. But the warm crumbs of croissant tickling her cleavage teased her mind away from the excitement promised by the day ahead - back to memories of past pleasures. As she casually brushed the flakes from her breasts, she suddenly recalled the sensation of the prefect's fingers at her nipples. The prefect had held and cupped her teenage breasts before pinching each of her pink buds into peaks of pleasurable discomfort.

Pressing her bottom down and squirming onto the leather topped stool, she deliberately kissed the hide with her slippery sex lips. A droplet of apricot preserve escaped her lips and was caught by her left nipple, and the dark teat thickened beneath the chill of the golden fruit. She idly cupped her breast, squeezing it firmly, and then absentmindedly offered it up as she had all those years ago to the prefect's waiting lips; the prefect with the hazel eyes who cruelly spanked her bare bottom with a slipper. Her mind drowning in the memory of surrender and submission, her fingers worried her sticky nipple as the leather stool grew damp beneath her.

Then impatiently wiping her breast clean of the glutinous jam, Beatrice sucked the tips of her thumb and forefinger. A shower was what she needed to sluice away the beguiling memories of her boarding school days and nights, and to sharpen her focus on the day's business.

In the shower she pressed her buttocks back against the tiled wall and wriggled deliciously under the forceful stream of hot water. Steam drifted around her, clouding the cubicle. She groped for her expensive scented gel and palmed it over her shoulders, breasts, stomach and arms. The fierce cascade of water rinsed her clean, leaving her skin smooth and radiant. She inched up on tiptoe, her thighs slightly parted, and offered her nakedness to the pounding water. The piercing liquid rods raked her belly and made her pussy throb. She then applied more gel to her hips, buttocks and thighs. Her pubic nest foamed and she knuckled it dominantly, as almost slipping on the slick surface, she twisted around and pressed her face and breasts to the hard tiles. The hot shower clawed over her shoulders and spine and drummed at the upper slopes of her bottom cheeks. Parting her thighs, she allowed her labia to bloom open, and the fierce flow deliciously scalded the deep shadow between her buttocks. Then quickly trying to suppress her simmering thoughts and drawing her thighs together she reached back blindly, her groping hand finding the tap and turning it off.

But even the soft touch of her fluffy white towel against her puffy labia caused her to gasp with pleasure. Dabbing gingerly, she dried her naked body before padding back to her bedroom to dress for the important day.

Her deep green gaze met its reflection in the sharp clarity of her full-length mirror. Her eyes flickered down, noting the hard nipples crowning her full breasts, the flat white stomach and the gloss of pale pubic hair. Her eyes continued their cool appraisal, drinking in with both pleasure and pride the narrow waist and generous swell of her hips. It was a beautiful body, untouched by any man's hand, but accustomed to the urgent demands of other women...

Beatrice shook herself, gathered her thoughts again, and attempted to concentrate on what to wear. Nothing too flirty; she already felt too old for such tiresome games, and there were plenty of younger girls out there with MBAs and the killer instinct to cut a deal. No point in competing with the kittens when she was a sleek feline. No, she decided, flirty would be a mistake; she would play up the chic, focussed businesswoman.

Beatrice dusted her soft nakedness with a musk-scented powder, gently brushing away the surplus from her pubic curls. She chose French panties cut a little daringly at the thigh, cream-coloured and trimmed with ivory lace. They were deeply flattering to the taut swell of her bottom and very sensuous, an exact fit with no annoying seam caught up in the heat of her cleft. She knew that in order to be confident she must be comfortable. A matching silk bra was selected and gently encased her breasts. Her nipples were deliciously sensitive, so she eased off the bra and gently anointed each little throbbing berry with a single drop of baby oil. Then back in front of the mirror, she watched as her soft breasts filled each cup again, squeezing together beautifully as she fingered the thin straps over each shoulder. The effect was stunning; the resulting cleavage deeply inviting, the curves roundly contoured, the sheen of the swelling flesh deliciously sculptured.

She sat at the dressing table in her bra and panties, and carefully began calculating which lipstick would be most appropriate for the working lunch ahead. As she mused, her hand toyed with small bottles of nail varnish, lining them up in a neat row. There was pale blue, pink, scarlet and a dark cherry-red... like the welts across the cheeks of a freshly caned bottom. Pale blue like the lightly bruising stroke. Pink like the stinging stripe. Scarlet like the angrier slice that stung, and cherry-red like the burn of a bamboo cane's bite.

An orange-hued shaft of glistening waxy lipstick inched out of its faux golden sheath as she twisted the barrel. Pouting, she submitted her lower lip to the tip of the shiny stick.

No, orange was no good at all, so tossing the lipstick down petulantly she snatched a tissue and wiped her lip. She decided to go to lunch lipstick-free, unadorned, sharp and businesslike.

Back before the full-length mirror, she deftly unhooked her bra and caught the cups in her waiting palms as they fell away from her warm breasts. Then dropping the flimsy garment aside, she eased down her panties and stepped out of them, and stood before the glass naked again, gazing at her baby oiled nipples.

What she needed was a bustier - a bustier and thong and a chic, severe trouser-suit, the black one with the thin pinstripe. No frills. And with a trouser-suit, no need for stockings or an irksome suspender belt. She smiled; suspender belts were strictly evening wear. It was so exciting to enter the bedroom after a night out on the town and have gentle hands pluck away the whispering belt, only to use it to lightly whip her bare buttocks.

No suspender belt and no stockings, and no sheer hose, either.

Once dressed again, Beatrice scrutinised the result. The bustier had an uplifting effect upon her breasts, squeezing and moulding each soft, fleshy mound. Reaching down for the baby oil once more, she lightly soaked a cotton ball and dabbed it over the exposed upper slopes of her captive bosom. The attention left her cleavage gleaming healthily, and her labia pouting as her full lips kissed the stretch of the thong biting between her thighs. She then slipped on the tailored black trousers and the exquisitely cut open jacket, and black high-heeled shoes completed her immaculate appearance. Her lunchtime meeting would definitely be exciting, and she was dressed for the thrill.

Half an hour at her laptop became an hour and a quarter, perfecting the final run through. She was fact and figure faultless and poised for the pitch. She had anticipated everything they could throw at her, and intended to be in control. Being in control was her favourite position in business... although not necessarily in bed...

A taxi called for her at eleven-thirty and whisked her through Hyde Park to Mayfair, where London was ready for lunch.

It felt wrong, all wrong, from the moment she got there. And Monique, the brunette waitress Beatrice had been grooming so carefully, was off sick. An arrogant young Frenchman, Patrice, reluctantly broke away from a pair of chattering blondes he was flirting with at a window table to conduct Beatrice to a secluded, under-lit alcove, and when she requested a larger table, reserved on the phone earlier, she found herself talking to the waiter's back.

'I want a larger table, please,' she repeated more loudly, and even his silence managed to contain a surly tone as she patiently explained she would need more room for her laptop and printouts. Then completely ignoring her request, he handed her the menu, upside down, and returned to the window table and his bubbly blondes.

Les Yeux Ardants filled up quickly. At the table next to hers, a couple of loud-mouthed media bitches kept Patrice on the go, but she eventually managed to flag him down and order a gin and tonic. She studied the menu. It was *à la carte*, with no set lunch today. Patrice shrugged indifferently and her annoyance rose. She had hoped for the option of a set; her experience was that it offered an ease of ordering that always smoothed the path of an important business lunch.

Her drink arrived at last, a frosted tumbler packed high with ice. Generous slices of lime floated on the tonic, but she sniffed and scowled, the victim of an old trick still played on lone women diners; no gin in her glass, just a couple of drops of very dry sherry. An old trick practiced on her by an impudent waiter. She sipped the drink, her frown deepening at the thought of being cheated, but she decided it was better not to make a fuss, but she would watch the wine like a hawk, double check the bill and leave without tipping.

Her lunch appointment was with Cosima, her prospective clients' MD, and her partner, Annunziata. It was a one shot chance as they were only over from Milan for the week. When her guests arrived Patrice paid little attention to them. They were ripe Italian women, thirty-something, svelte and oozing sophisticated allure, but the arrogant waiter only had eyes for the blondes chattering in their window seat and incessantly fluttering their eyelashes at him.

Beatrice led the way through the obstacles of ordering. Patrice, assuming a bored expression of benign patience, gave her little guidance and no encouragement. She chose the grilled sea bass in *beurre blanc*, Cosima selected a red mullet in coriander sauce, and Annunziata played safe with an order for sole braised with artichokes. Beatrice ordered the wine, a white burgundy, 1987 *Chassagne Montrachet*.

The food arrived, not cold exactly, but definitely not hot, and Beatrice noticed too late that she had been served the wrong dish. She blushed as she intercepted the doubtful look exchanged by the two Italians.

'You ask for the sea bass, no?' Cosima queried.

'Yes, but this monkfish is delicious,' Beatrice fibbed, hating every mouthful. 'The sea bass was probably disappointing. So gallant, these French boys.'

At a nearby table, the increasingly racy conversation turned to spanking, and Beatrice saw Cosima's eyes flicker sideways, marking her deepening interest. At their table, lunch was rapidly becoming a desultory affair. Beatrice tried to sparkle, but she knew everything was perched on the brink of disaster. Even the wine - the wrong year - came too late to fully enjoy with the fish it was intended to accompany. Every little thing that could go wrong, went wrong. She was not in control. Patrice was in control with his sullen, arrogant, disrespectful indifference.

Desert was served, and Beatrice started her pitch. But before the third key performance projection was printed out, Annunziata, the accountant of the company, remarked abruptly that what they were really looking for was flair. 'The steel hand in the velvet glove,' she explained.

'Someone who can get things done,' Cosima added. 'Someone who can make things happen.'

'A woman in control,' the accountant stated. 'I need to know that when I am back in Milan, everything here in London is in capable hands.'

Beatrice's cheeks crimsoned and she realised she was talking too fast. A mistake, and the damn table was still cluttered with the debris of the disastrous lunch. Patrice was still neglecting them, even though it was rapidly approaching tipping time, and the plates and glasses prevented her from executing the slick presentation she had planned so carefully. She paused, taking several long, slow breaths. 'Coffee?' she suggested.

'I really do not think...' Annunziata shrugged, flicking her supple wrist in pretence of consulting her watch.

Cosima, staring intently at the retreating bottoms of the two females departing from the adjoining table, did not even hear the suggestion.

'Coffee, and brandies,' Beatrice said desperately. 'I insist.'

The two Italians acquiesced. She had them for another ten or so minutes. Every second counted. After waving Patrice down with amazing speed for a change, and ordering the drinks, she placed the laptop down at her feet, smoothed the white tablecloth twice with her flattened palms and launched into a word-perfect presentation. The key objectives. The core activities. The ballpark figures. Her guests politely gave her their attention, inclining their heads and listening.

Then Patrice, at long last bringing the coffee and brandies to their table, accidentally, or otherwise, trod on the laptop. He cursed in lurid French, completely breaking the spell of her pitch.

'I'll speak to the *maitre'd* and have him reprimanded,' Beatrice mumbled wearily as the waiter walked away without apologising.

'Reprimanded?' Cosima scowled. 'I would settle for nothing less than his tears - his salt tears spilling down in contrition onto my naked breasts.' She snarled the words contemptuously in a strident voice, and Beatrice blushed and acknowledged her own weakness in the Italian matron's powerful scorn. And seconds later, she found herself sitting at the deserted table gazing at the vacated chairs opposite.

Patrice, insouciantly rude, presented her with the bill, but her temper finally snapping, she snatched it up from the white porcelain saucer and scrunched it into a ball, her fist working furiously. 'I'm not paying,' she snapped. 'Bring me the manager.' To which he loftily replied that the manager was busy in the kitchens.

Beatrice stood determinedly, shunting her chair back, and heads turned censoriously as Patrice blocked her way, spreading his arms and positioning himself between her and the swing doors leading to the kitchen. 'No, madam, he is too busy for you,' he insisted patronisingly. So she sidestepped him and stormed across the restaurant, and they burst through the swing doors together.

In the kitchen astonished faces looked up from towers of plates, chopping boards and sizzling pans.

'Where is the *maitre'd?*' she demanded, while beside her Patrice intimated she was drunk by pantomiming a flexed raised elbow, and then draining an invisible glass. Sweating staff grinned and nodded in response, and she stared back furiously at the knowing winks and sneers surrounding her. Then Patrice firmly gripped her elbow and roughly propelled her past the ovens and sinks. She slipped twice on the tiled floor and he spanked her smartly each time, winning a ragged cheer from the onlookers as he bundled her out through the back door.

In the grotty little yard outside Beatrice stood panting in indignation. The bright sunshine momentarily dazzled and disorientated her, and he seized the opportunity to prise a hand inside her jacket and maul her breasts, his lips grazing her throat and his knee pressing between her legs as he backed her against the mossy, crumbling back wall of the restaurant. 'I take my tip now,' he mumbled huskily against the pulse just below her ear as he found and pinched her nipple, but she summoned her wits and determination and pushed him away.

'Bastard!' she hissed, and kicked him twice on the shin. He cursed and raised a hand as if to slap her, but then, tossing his head back in contempt, he simply shoved her backwards.

'Go to the rubbish, bitch,' he said vehemently, and she squealed as she teetered on her heels, and collapsed heavily into a pile of black plastic bags, causing one of them to burst open, oozing fish guts, bloodstained cream and rotten vegetables. She struggled to get up, cringing as her hand inadvertently squelched in the mess as her heels skidded precariously in the sickening spillage. Then as she elbowed herself upright she punctured a second bag, from which rotten eggs sputtered, splashing her chin and impeccably tailored business suit.

Beatrice slumped back into the mess, and started to cry.

The hazel eyes above the lemon icing widened as the white teeth below closed over the slice of ginger cake. The eyes nearly closed in ecstasy. The pungent ginger cake was as moist in her mouth as Beatrice's pussy had been moments before.

Andrea, the punishing prefect from Beatrice's boarding school days and nights, and her passionately intimate companion ever since, licked a stray crumb from the corner of her mouth, and frowned. 'Not eating?' she queried. 'Cherry Genoa's scrumptious.'

Beatrice, naked and resting across some pillows on the bed, shook her head.

Swallowing a final bite of cake, Andrea brushed her fingers free of sticky crumbs, and slipping back into bed, she rested alongside Beatrice, a hand propping up her chin. Her breasts bunched softly as she deliberately crushed them into her lover's shoulder. 'Is something wrong?' she asked softly.

Beatrice, sighing, shook her head despondently.

'You haven't touched your tea.' They always had tea after making love in Beatrice's bed, every Sunday afternoon.

'Not really hungry,' she whispered.

'Not saying much either, are you? There is something wrong, isn't there?'

Beatrice chewed her bottom lip anxiously. It was almost a week after the disastrous lunch and her humiliation at the hands of Patrice.

Andrea sat upright. 'There is something, I can tell. Is it someone else?' she asked urgently, a pang of jealous suspicion sharpening her tone, but once again, Beatrice merely shook her head morosely.

'Tell me,' Andrea coaxed, and Beatrice's eyes filled with tears and brimmed over, but she remained stubbornly silent. 'Then I'll *make* you talk, like I used to,' Andrea vowed, and ten years vanished in an instant and they were prefect and pupil once more - dominant prefect, predatory and stern; submissive pupil, vulnerable and passively helpless.

And before Beatrice could wriggle free Andrea pounced, pinning her naked body down into the soft pillows. Scissoring her legs she trapped Beatrice's between her thighs, rendering her motionless beneath her pinioning weight. Her hands firmly gripping the struggling wrists, she bullied the breasts beneath hers with her own full bosom. 'Tell me,' she insisted. 'You've been off with me on the phone for days. Something's on your mind, I can tell.'

Their lips were only a warm breath apart, but Beatrice turned her face away and closed her eyes.

'I'll make you tell me,' Andrea warned again. 'And you know I can.'

Beatrice made a half-hearted bid to free herself.

'No, my girl, none of that,' Andrea warned, her tone mockingly severe. 'Turn over,' she commanded, but Beatrice shook her head defiantly. 'I said turn over.' Andrea let go of the supine girl's wrists and moved off her, so she could obey, and Beatrice turned over onto her stomach, and closed her eyes.

As it was a decade ago back in boarding school, so it was now. Andrea still had the slipper she used to carry on dorm patrol. It was kept in a white cardboard box wrapped in red tissue paper, and was only brought out and used on very special occasions; birthdays - the last one brought twenty-eight strokes - Christmas and New Year's Eve.

Andrea's hand swept down repeatedly to spank Beatrice's soft, creamy bottom cheeks, turning them from a stinging pink to a deepening shade of crimson. She snarled softly, confused and angered by her lover's stubborn silence. Her resentment flared into suspicious jealousy once more, putting painful force into her punishing hand. Then she paused to survey her bare-bottomed captive. With her arms stretched out and gripping the bedstead, the curve of Beatrice's spine was deeply pronounced. She stroked the crown of each flaming buttock in turn, drawing mews of delight from her willing victim, and then tap tapped the shadow within which her anal rosebud remained tightly furled.

'No,' Beatrice wailed, desperately trying to wriggle her bottom away. 'I'll tell you... I'll *tell* you.' But straightening her forefinger, Andrea twisted and sank it into

114

the heat of her lover's anal passage. It was tight, but she forced her finger a little further.

Beatrice squealed. 'I'll *tell* you...' she cried again. 'I'll tell you!'

'Too late,' Andrea murmured. 'You had your chance, but you chose to cut me out of what's going on - to make me suffer.'

'Suffer?' Beatrice echoed, amazed at the accusation.

'Uncertainty. Insecurity. You made me suffer those, and now it's your turn, my darling. Your turn to feel uncertain and insecure. Your turn to suffer.'

'No, wait, please—'

'I've waited long enough.'

'*Please,*' she wailed.

'For what, to give you time to invent some fib? No, my darling, another even more severe spanking will elicit the truth from you.'

'But you don't understand,' Beatrice protested breathlessly. 'I'll tell you. Honestly, I'll tell you everything.'

Andrea withdrew her dominant forefinger from the muscled warmth of the tight anus and contented herself with a painful pinch of an adorably fleshy buttock.

'Everything!' Beatrice gasped, kicking her feet into the mattress.

'I'm sure you will, my darling, after I've visited your naughty bottom with my relentless spanking hand again.' Her tone was darkening with every stern threat, her voice possessing the unmistakeable timbre of jealous anger. 'I bet it's all down in your filofax,' she mused, and jumping off the bed abruptly, she hurried across the room to retrieve Beatrice's little black notebook. And on her way back she grabbed another slice of the moist cherry Genoa.

Kneeling back on the mattress, upon which her lover remained naked and docilely stretched out gripping the headboard, Andrea sat, squashing her bottom firmly into Beatrice's buttocks, using the submissive nude's soft cheeks as a cushion. She sank her teeth into the cake, and through a mouthful of crumbs began reading the entries in the filofax, pausing to re read the cryptic notes recording the business lunch at *Les Yeux Ardants*. 'And who would A and C be?' she questioned suspiciously.

Beatrice had scribbled the initials of Annunziata and Cosima below the date of the lunch, adding brief but enthusiastic details of their respective charms.

'A and C,' Andrea pondered, then tossed the filofax aside as she slid back slightly to straddle Beatrice's shapely calves. She had saved the cherries from the slice of Genoa, five succulent red fruits she retrieved from the sheets they were already turning pink. She weighed them on her upturned palm, and then fingered them slowly, as she would finger Beatrice's nipples when they were red and ripe. Then inverting her hand down over her lover's bottom, she planted and pressed the five sticky cherries into the satin-soft skin of her tender cheeks. Lowering her face, the tip of her tongue flickering, she chivvied the cherries before capturing them one by one between her even white teeth. Two cherries remained, and Beatrice wriggled her hips, inadvertently tipping them from the crests of her buttocks into the dividing valley between.

'A and C,' Andrea purred, bending to fleetingly nuzzle the glistening cherries. 'And which one took your fancy, hmm? A or C?' She guided the tip of her tongue down to prise out the first, and then the second elusive fruit, pausing deliberately to suck and softly bite Beatrice's succulent flesh. The final cherry swallowed, she licked her lips and eased herself back a fraction, resting her buttocks on her heels. She placed her hands upon the soft cheeks below her, pressing her palms onto each fleshy mound and easing them apart.

Beatrice whimpered, but remained utterly passive.

Andrea spread the cheeks further before once more licking the length of the exposed valley between. Straining slightly, she eased back and peered down to inspect the trickle of juice flowing from Beatrice's pussy, then keeping both cheeks under firm control, she clenched her fingers, squeezing the delicious buttocks possessively. To her delight Beatrice bucked helplessly in response. Smiling, she returned the tip of her tongue to the tight little rosebud of her lover's exposed anal whorl. The puckered little crater shrivelled even more, stubbornly refusing the tongue permission to enter and probe. But Andrea was determined, and soon penetrated the dark orifice to taste the bittersweet warmth within. Meanwhile, she ravaged her victim's pussy with the knuckles of her clenched fist, capturing and twisting a handful of Beatrice's hair in her free controlling hand.

'A or C?' She lifted her head from the delicious buttocks to ask again. 'One of them is the cause of your reticence to talk.'

Beatrice shook her head.

'I'll get the truth out of you, bitch.' Andrea left the bed again a moment, and returned with the boxed slipper. The rustle of tissue paper broke the tense silence with a menacing crackle as the slipper was brought forth.

Crack! Crack! Crack!

The supple sole viciously swiped the crown of both her prone lover's cheeks, until both buttocks shone a bright pink. Eight strokes were administered, and even as she submitted to the rain of stinging pain, Beatrice bucked and jerked in torment beneath the slipper's fierce onslaught.

Pausing briefly, her breasts heaving and glistening with perspiration, Andrea gazed down at the bottom she had severely punished. It glowed a lovely crimson, expressive of pure pain. She then guided the rubber sole of the slipper down to her own glistening labia. The warm rubber kissed her hot lips. She pressed hard, and harder still, and then rhythmically tapped the slipper against her juicing pussy. Again and again, despite the delicious pain, she punished herself with the rubber sole. Jerking her bottom up she changed the angle of attack, her breasts heavy and aching as they swayed beneath her. The rubber sole scalded her sensitive flesh, and teetering unsteadily, almost drunk with lust she ravished her wet heat until her belly tightened, signalling the initial tremors of an approaching orgasm.

Closing her eyes tightly and imprisoning the image of Beatrice's red bottom behind them, Andrea slipper spanked her climax to its peak. It broke with devastating power, with a sweet violence that sent the slipper dropping out of her limp hand. As an orgasm pulsed down from the pit of her stomach into her tightly muscled warmth, she nipped her proud clitoral thorn as carefully as a snake charmer milking venom from a captive cobra. A second wave of blinding pleasure ravaged her body, and she collapsed across Beatrice's back.

Both naked girls tensed as their flesh united. Slowly and deliberately, Andrea raked her hips from side to side, dragging her pussy across the punished buttocks below her as she came yet again, smothering her cries by biting Beatrice's shoulder.

Afterwards she gently caressed her partner's sore bottom, and at last, her eyes averted, Beatrice began to speak. She explained the innocence of the initials A and C, but had to be questioned closely about her disturbing experience at the hands of the French waiter that afternoon at *Les Yeux Ardants*.

Andrea listened to the tale in appalled silence. It angered her intensely to hear how her beautiful lover had been humiliated during an important business lunch, which had turned into an emotional and financial disaster.

'It was terrible,' Beatrice concluded with a choked sob.

'What you've just told me has given me this huge hunger,' Andrea declared.

'Hunger?' Beatrice echoed, her tear-filled eyes widening.

Andrea nodded. 'Hunger pains, or rather, hunger *pangs*, for punishment.'

She tut-tutted at, and adjusted, his velvet bowtie.

The arrogant Frenchman flinched, smouldering furiously beneath her inspection.

'Your hands,' Andrea demanded. 'Are they clean?'

He nodded indignantly.

'Show me.'

He tossed his head back defiantly.

'No show, no big bonus,' she warned quietly. She had lured the waiter to a friend's Barbican flat on the pretext of needing him to serve an after theatre supper. Now she was pretending to make the last minute preparations. *Les Yeux Ardants* had sent Patrice, along with the food and wine, at her special request. 'Show me your hands,' she insisted. 'I cannot abide dirty nails.'

With a shrug of sullen reluctance, Patrice offered his hands, which emerged elegantly from the laundered white linen jacket's sleeves and a white silk shirt with opal cuffs. His skin was nicely tanned and his manicured nails were neat and clean.

'Perfect.' She nodded, and deftly snapped the handcuffs on him before he could react defensively, and the Frenchman's eyes widened in surprise and alarm.

Beatrice drove them back across London. He had struggled, but Andrea's hand cupped threateningly over his balls effectively silenced his protests. As they approached Notting Hill, she blindfolded him.

After taking the food and wine in, Andrea and her lover returned to the car to guide the waiter up to Beatrice's flat. But first they tied two red balloons to his jacket, and passers-by smiled enviously at the sight of two lovely women accompanying a lucky stag to some wild party.

Once in the flat Beatrice retired to her bedroom, leaving her dominant lover to prepare Patrice for his impending punishment.

'Kneel,' Andrea commanded, popping the balloons.

He resisted, remaining rigidly upright by planting his polished black shoes wide apart as he cursed her in both English and French. 'You cannot do this!' he hissed.

'Silence,' she snapped. 'You've been brought here tonight to be taught a lesson, my pretty little bastard, a very painful lesson. And you will obey my orders or I promise you will suffer - and suffer more than was intended.'

He swore again and ducked out of her controlling grip. But blindfolded and handcuffed, his bid for freedom was doomed. He tripped and stumbled, collapsing heavily onto his knees.

'That's right,' she purred, inching closer to him as she spoke. 'You're learning quickly. *Assez bien, garcon*. Lesson number one, *obey*. I told you to kneel, and you did.'

He snarled viciously.

'Be quiet. We'll have no more out of you, *mon petit*, until we give you permission. Permission,' she added silkily, 'to plead with us.' Reaching down for the prepared gag of used panties and a nylon stocking bunched up into a ball, she silenced his curses with it. 'He's ready, my darling,' she called, picking up a pair of sturdy kitchen scissors and snip snapping them ominously.

'Coming,' Beatrice called from the bedroom.

Patrice's head swivelled as he followed the exchange, and then froze as the snapping scissors neared his head.

Snip! His velvet bowtie fluttered down to the carpet. *Snip! Snip!* His fine linen sleeves shrivelled before the greedy steel jaws. *Snip!* The frilled dress-shirt peeled away from his bronze shoulders and slipped off him in elegant tatters. *Snip! Snip!* Before Beatrice rejoined them, the handsome waiter was kneeling bound and naked and utterly helpless, his clothes shredded around him.

Beatrice was naked, too, and Andrea let the scissors fall to the floor as she gazed at her, enraptured.

'Not now, later,' Beatrice smiled, squirming shyly under her lover's intense gaze.

'Sure about the outfit, are we?' Andrea teased.

'I'm dressed for business,' Beatrice responded in a darker, more purposeful tone. 'Strictly for business.'

Andrea nodded. 'Then he's all yours.' She picked up a web cam from the desktop and settled down on the sofa with it, seemingly indifferent to the drama about to unfold before her as she prepared to record it.

Beatrice urged Patrice back up to his feet, and then pulled his blindfold down. The young Frenchman's eyes ogled her bare breasts, her taut belly and her lush pubic bush. Then she caught his chin in her hand and held it dominantly, forcing him to look her in the eyes. He flinched, but she held him silently in her absolute thrall, gazing sternly at him.

He closed his eyes and steeled himself.

'Look at me,' she commanded, but he refused to obey. So she squeezed his face in a fierce grip, digging her fingers into his cheeks until they whitened, tilting his head back. 'Remember me?' she asked smoothly when he finally opened his eyes again.

His frown of concentration resulted only in a slow shaking of his head.

'You will,' she promised. 'You *will* remember me.' She pulled his blindfold up again, covering his startled stare. She left it in place, satisfied with the shadow of alarm she had seen clouding his insolent gaze. 'Perhaps you don't remember me now, but you will, and I can assure you that you will never forget tonight. *Never.*'

He shuffled backwards.

She laughed. 'I'm going to enjoy making you pay the penalty for your arrogance and rudeness. Understand? You humiliated me, so I'm going to humiliate you. And then,' she leaned close to whisper in his ear, 'I'm going to punish you severely for what you did to me.' She allowed her eyes to take in his nicely muscled chest, flat stomach and dark pubic hair. His impressive cock was thickening slightly with fear, but it remained essentially flaccid, potent but passive.

From the sofa, half her face hidden behind the web cam, Andrea murmured a question.

'No,' Beatrice replied, 'they're fine where they are. I'll leave the cuffs like that. He'll go over my knee for a spanking and then for some special treatment.'

Patrice's whimper was smothered by the nylon stockings and panties filling his mouth.

Beatrice, her breasts bobbing gently and her naked buttocks rippling, moved softly with silent, menacing steps as she twice circled her tense captive. Pausing, she swiftly drew her fingertips down the curve of his spine, and probed the crease of his bottom cleft. He rose up on his toes as she fingered his anal bud, buried deep between his taut cheeks.

'Punishment,' she said sternly, 'can be so very pleasurable. For some, it is a duty. For others, it is a privilege. For me,' she continued, her voice a velvet whisper, 'it will be *such* a pleasure.'

He surreptitiously drew his thighs together.

'Ah, *non, ne faites tu cela*,' she purred sweetly. 'You are mine, *mon petit*, all mine. And there's nowhere to hide.' She cupped his bottom cheeks and squeezed them viciously, forcing them apart until his shadowy cleft yawned open. 'No hiding place.' She grinned as she felt the rush of his fear warming her cupped hands, then releasing his buttocks from her fierce grip, she continued prowling around his naked body. She noted the glisten of perspiration at his temples and the way dread tightened his tight buttocks.

'Nappy?' Andrea asked from behind the masking web cam.

'Where did you—?' Beatrice began to ask.

'Sorry, sitting on it,' Andrea giggled, and then squirming, she prised it out from beneath her left buttock and tossed it across the room.

Beatrice caught it in mid air. 'Left foot up, *garcon*,' she instructed, whipping the Frenchman's bottom with the plastic nappy, but he remained immobile. 'Lift your left foot up a little,' she repeated firmly. He hesitated another long moment, but then grudgingly obeyed and she peeled open the plastic and slipped it over the hovering foot.

'Your right one now,' she ordered sharply, giving it a firm nudge with her knuckles, and this time he instantly did as he was told.

'Down now,' she said, savouring his silent submission as she drew the nappy up his stout legs and secured it around his hips.

Andrea rose from the sofa and walked past them towards the desktop workstation. She set the camera down, sat down and began tapping the keyboard. In less than a minute she swivelled around with the web cam nestled in her lap. 'Got it,' she announced, fingering the camera. 'We're live and online to Milan. Should give A and C a bit of an eyeful.' She picked up and levelled the web cam directly upon Patrice's tightly clenched bottom. 'You may begin.'

Beatrice nodded. It *had* begun - the humiliation, retribution and severe punishment of the supercilious waiter who ruined her important business lunch. His male rudeness was being brought to heel by feminine domination and discipline. Her breasts rose, swelling with pride. Her nipples tightened and peaked and their delicate pink darkened. He was all hers, bound, blindfolded and helpless. All hers. She fleetingly fingered her moist labia, and then lightly drummed wet fingertips across his nappy-clad bottom. He was all hers to punish at her pleasure, *for* her pleasure.

119

Bending over slightly, she tugged up the nappy, dragging it even more firmly into position so the waistband bit into his flesh. The heat from his sac clouded the clear plastic, forming an opaque patch at his groin. The rasp of the nappy over his cock caused it to unfurl, lengthen and rise inquisitively, thrusting the swelling knout against the stretched material.

Holding the camera before her, Andrea approached slowly, as if stalking them, circling the pair in silence. Flicking on the zoom button she took in both their faces in vivid close up - the contorted features of the apprehensive Frenchman and the serenely dominant mask of Beatrice's lovely face. 'Bare his bottom slowly,' she suggested.

Beatrice nodded as she inserted her thumbs into the nappy's tight waistband and gradually tugged down the plastic to reveal Patrice's naked buttocks.

Andrea squatted, inching closer, and aimed the web cam upwards. 'Proceed,' she directed.

Beatrice turned away, selected a fork and spoon, and returned to address the buttocks of her victim. 'Punishment is meted out by a disciplinarian or a chastiser,' she informed both Patrice and their invisible audience. 'When that chastiser is a female, she is called a dominatrix. Dominatrix,' she echoed. 'What a beautiful word; a word that sends shivers of delicious dread down the spine of the helpless male.' She let the spoon hang limply from the fingers of her left hand while those of her right tightened around the handle of the fork. Inverting it, she brought the points of the three-pronged utensil to the exposed nape of Patrice's neck. '*Dominatrix*,' she hissed, increasing the pressure of the tines. 'Sends a sudden shiver down the spine, does it not?'

Three little white points of pain appeared where the prongs prinked his skin and the Frenchman's feet trod the carpet anxiously, his toes curling in dread.

Swiftly, with the speed of a heartbeat, she raked the fork down to his clenched bottom cheeks. Then she brought the prongs back to prickle the nape of his cringing neck again. 'But I believe the French have an even more beautiful word to describe the majesty of the dominant female,' she went on. 'Don't they, *mon petit?*'

Patrice lowered his head in abject surrender, and then jerked it up again violently as she raked the fork down the length of his spine, at first fleetingly, and then very slowly and more firmly.

'*Dompteuse*, not dominatrix, but *dompteuse*. Yes,' she cooed as she prodded both his cheeks savagely, 'I like that word. It has a quality of fullness and ripeness. It both suggests and embodies the absolute authority of the female punisher over her victim, *n'est ce pas? Oui, mon petit. Ce soir, je suis toi dompteuse.*'

The plastic nappy had peeled down to bind his upper thighs tightly together. Dropping the fork and capturing his hips almost tenderly, she turned him around as she sank to her knees before him, her eyes level with his cock. She inched the plastic nappy back up, trapping and taming his straining shaft. After teasing his glans through the plastic with the base of her palm, she thumbed the nappy down again slightly. Unbound, his penis sprang up, rigid and quivering. She lifted the spoon to his swinging sac, cradling it through the sheathing plastic, and his gasp was just audible through the gag.

'A good waiter must be skilled at silver service,' she remarked, lightly tossing his captive balls. 'The art of the spoon and the fork?' she murmured. 'Silver service is what I paid for, and what I expected to receive when lunching with my important guests. You failed to deliver that, *garcon*. You failed miserably. Let me teach you the art of silver service.' The prongs of the fork closed over his sac to meet the opposing face of the spoon, and then gripping the fork and the spoon in the classic silver service style, she skilfully trapped and tamed the perspiring Frenchman's balls.

'That's great,' Andrea said excitedly, shuffling closer to get a better shot. 'Shift your elbow, darling... great!' The web cam remorselessly captured the teasing, bullying dominance of the kneeling woman controlling the balls of her victim.

'When serving up the *à la carte* vegetables,' Beatrice went on malevolently, 'be sure to drain them well.' She squeezed gently, and Patrice pawed the carpet with his foot. 'Broccoli and spinach, for example, benefit from this little touch.' The ripple of undulating muscle along her forearm betrayed the slight increase in pressure from the spoon and fork pincer capturing his sac. His feet shuffled and he staggered slightly as his clamped balls bulged.

The spoon and fork followed him in their grip. 'For the waiter who truly wishes to please,' she continued sternly, 'some skilful spoon work is always appreciated.' Releasing the fork, she guided the spoon to the bulbous knout of his erection, and his thighs tensed and he groaned through the gag as she tapped his swollen glans.

'Careful, he's—' Andrea warned, too late, for the tormented erection pulsed, and coated the wrist controlling the spoon with glistening, viscous semen.

'Silver service,' Beatrice whispered, scooping up the glutinous spillage with the spoon, Andrea devouring every detail of the action with the web cam.

Discarding the utensils, Beatrice snapped the plastic nappy back up over the pulsing penis, dismissing it contemptuously. Then she stood up as he sank weakly to his knees. She bent over to whisper something in his ear, the promise of further torment, and he lifted his handcuffed hands helplessly, but she merely gripped a handful of his hair, pinioning the naked Frenchman down. He writhed, attempting to twist out of her clutches, but she quelled his rebellion into stillness and surrender, her knuckles whitening amidst his dark hair.

'*Non, non, non, mon petit*,' she said soothingly, as if placating a naughty child. 'It is time you were spanked - and spanked very hard.' His nappy-clad buttocks clenched as she sat down on the carpet beside him and guided his body up across her lap.

'*Hors d'oeuvres* before the main course,' Andrea threw in, her web cam scanning the upturned nappy of the waiter, now lying helpless across the lap of his stern chastiser.

'A fitting description,' Beatrice agreed, smoothing the palm of her spanking hand across the plastic sheathing the bottom she was about to beat.

Patrice squirmed, but blindfolded and handcuffed and gagged, he remained utterly in her thrall. His face buried in the carpet, he surrendered his bottom, and she acknowledged his submission by firmly gripping the nape of his neck with her free hand.

Circling the cameo of dominance and submission, Andrea captured every nuance of the pre punishment preparations in close up - the pinioning hand planted firmly at his neck; the brief kiss of the dominatrix's breasts against the helpless bottom as she leaned over; the slow, smooth caressing circles of the spanking palm against the captive cheeks; the shine of the stretchy plastic nappy across the clenched buttocks, and the futile threshing of the Frenchman's ankles as he kicked out impotently. Kneeling, she gripped the web cam more firmly as she filmed the menacing palm rise up above the buttocks below.

Crack! Crack! Crack!

Beatrice administered three crisp, severe spanks. Patrice's whole body slumped in surrender, his wriggling and kicking ceasing completely as he tensed in anticipation of more blows.

Crack! Crack!

Fiercer, increasingly savage spanks rang out.

Crack! Crack!

Through the clear plastic nappy stretched tightly across his cheeks, Beatrice saw the pink blush of punishment spreading across them. To her delight the final spank left a distinct crimson palm print right across his cleft, dividing the fingerprints on the one cheek from the palm print on the other.

'Spank him harder,' Andrea urged, her own arousal simmering. 'Make him suffer—'

'He must not merely suffer,' Beatrice interrupted her lover, her voice calm and controlled. 'I want him to learn through his suffering. He must not experience only a sudden pain, but a slow burn that builds to a blaze. And in that blaze there must be sorrow, repentance and true learning.'

Andrea closed her eyes tightly as Beatrice's words caused a knot of excitement to grip her stomach. 'You're right,' she whispered hoarsely, the web cam trembling in her grip. 'You must do it your way. Do with him what you will. He's yours, entirely yours. His bottom belongs to you and no other. Let his lesson be a memorable one.'

'Yes, a lesson learned slowly - slowly and painfully - is a lesson never forgotten.' She swept her hand down with renewed ferocity, the triple staccato echoing loudly around the room.

Crack! Crack! Crack!

The nappy-clad buttocks bounced and bucked beneath the onslaught of vicious swipes.

Crack! Crack! Crack!

The plastic was becoming hot beneath her spanking hand.

Crack! Crack! Crack!

Her breasts bounced as she hammered pain down across the helpless Frenchman's buttocks, and then once more briefly crushed her bare breasts into the delicious heat. He wriggled and squirmed beneath her breasts, and she sensed from the warmth radiating from the nappy that her victim was truly suffering now. The plastic rustled erotically as he writhed across her lap, rasping the nappy against her wet pubic nest.

Crack! Crack! Crack!

Eight times in as many seconds she brought her hand down across his reddened cheeks, thrilling to the sheer satisfaction of her supreme dominance and her ability to dispense such searing discipline.

Then breathless, her breasts heaving, she paused. Her right hand burned. Gazing down, she studied the red buttocks through the clouded plastic. She fingered both punished cheeks through the taut sheen, and then slowly and carefully plucked at the tight waistband, peeling the nappy down a little. She sensed him tense in fearful expectation, and his abject misery delighted her. He was learning his painful lesson. She was proving something of a success as his teacher - his extremely strict teacher.

'Let me see,' Andrea pleaded, rising on tiptoe to point the web cam directly down in an effort to get a direct view of the crimson cheeks.

'All in good time,' Beatrice said.

'Oh, please let me see his red bottom,' Andrea begged, rubbing her pussy unashamedly with her free hand.

'In a moment,' Beatrice promised. 'Be patient.' Her pinching fingers held the elastic waistband up from the crowns of the punished cheeks. She released it, snapping the elastic down swiftly so it bit into the hot flesh. A thin white line immediately appeared, and above it the blazing buttocks swelled. 'I'm baring your bottom now, *mon petit*,' she said softly, gripping the waistband and slowly easing the nappy down to his thighs. 'And now it's completely bare, I propose to inspect it. I propose to inspect it thoroughly, do you understand? It is my intention to examine the effects of the punishment so far. Then, when I have fully satisfied myself, I will spank you on your bare bottom. On your bare bottom, *mon petit*, very, very hard.'

His gagged curses, protests and pleas were completely ignored, and the thought of him being forced to swallow his anguish brought a grim smile to her expression of determination. Fully exposed, his crimson buttocks dimpled in a reflex of instinctive fear, and lowering her face, she fleetingly kissed each scalded cheek upon its clenched crown.

Then raising her head she ran a fingernail down the length of his dark cleft, and settled herself more comfortably beneath him. To ease the weight across her thighs she adjusted one leg, inching it up a fraction, watching, her eyes narrowing hungrily as his spanked bottom rose and seemed to offer itself for the impending onslaught. The slight movement, to her immense delight, rendered the cheeks more firmly contoured, making them even more invitingly round and temptingly taut. She lifted her hand, and swiped it down again.

Crack! Crack! Crack!

Stripped bare of the stretchy plastic, the cheeks echoed back the three sharp smacks more clearly. As her palm connected directly with his bare bottom, her throat tightened and her nipples ached. She spanked him with savage fervour, swiftly cracking her hot palm down repeatedly across his crimson cheeks; crimson cheeks that glowed as her onslaught escalated. She shuddered as she felt the ripples of an orgasm beginning to crest in her tummy. Spanking a bare-bottomed man lying helpless across her knees and utterly at her mercy brought her to the gates of a splendid delight. Soon, she knew, she would rush through those gates to enter the realm of Sade, where she would glut her senses on the bittersweet perfume emanating from the roses of suffering.

On the floor, her skirt immodestly gathered up around her hips, Andrea caressed her sex with shiny, wet fingertips. The spanking stopped after a final stuttering staccato of seven harsh swipes, and as she masturbated rhythmically, she gazed directly at both the punisher and the punished through the web cam.

The chime of an incoming email surprised them. It was from Cosima in Milan, urging Beatrice to even greater efforts. *Let us see him sob on your naked breasts*, it read, *and you will run the entire London operation for us.*

Spurred on by such an offer and the scent of triumph, Beatrice pulled the cool nappy back up over the smouldering cheeks. She slowly palmed the plastic-sheathed balls of her red bottomed victim, and the web cam's microphone caught the audible squirt as Patrice came again, his seed splattering against the tightly stretched plastic. Andrea almost swooned as she saw his shaft spearing and straining into the opaque sheath. And as he quivered, shuddering in the throes of his orgasm, Beatrice drove her forefinger down between his punished cheeks, deep into his anus, taking the plastic with the sinking digit. Andrea stared open-mouthed, as her normally submissive lover gasped and collapsed over her captive, crushing her naked breasts into his spanked bottom, and a pang of jealousy stabbed her as she watched her naked girlfriend enjoying the body of a submissive man. Then she too succumbed to an orgasm that nearly made her drop the web cam.

Then, gathering herself, Beatrice hauled the shivering Frenchman up and peeled away the blindfold. He was sobbing breathlessly through the gag, and cradling his tear-stained face almost tenderly, she pulled his flushed countenance to her bare breasts. Moments later she turned, her back erect and proud, and offered her tear-soaked breasts to the web cam, and Milan.

Thanks for reading!

If you've not yet read **Correction Squad**, and if you like Sarah Steel's stories, it's also available to order as a paperback from **Amazon**.

Matron was the epitome of stern authority. The note of austerity was sharpened by the seamed nylons, stiff brogues and the faint whiff of carbolic soap. Beetle sensed the Matron's eyes upon her, and quickly glanced down into the glow of the gas fire, grateful that Krystal was doing all the talking. Beetle blushed slightly and her nipples peaked firmly as she succumbed to the thought of being disciplined by Matron...

When a crime has been committed and it is not appropriate to wait for the process of the law, when a swift and painful execution of justice is required, it is time to send for the Correction Squad.

Krystal is Polish. She is also blonde, beautiful, and mean. Pretty Beetle is her assistant, and together they exercise their talents for dispensing justice. And once they've finished with the trembling thief and the impudent cheat, it's time to hone their skills on each other...